THREADS

BRYAN CASSIDAY

Bryan Cassiday
Los Angeles
ISBN 9781737628231
Published in the United States of America
First Edition: March 15, 2022

BOOKS BY BRYAN CASSIDAY

Electric Green Mambas (Scott Brody Thriller 3)
Horde (Zombie Apocalypse: The Chad Halverson Series Book 6)
Ice in the Blood
Crime Blotter USA
Murder LLC (Scott Brody Thriller 2)
Bolt (Scott Brody Thriller 1)
Riptide of Fear
The Payout
Force of Impact (Ethan Carr Thriller 3)
Dying to Breathe (Ethan Carr Thriller 2)
Countdown to Death (Ethan Carr Thriller 1)
The Bus Stops Here—and Other Zombie Tales
Two Moons Rising
Alien Assault
Comes a Chopper
Zombie Apocalypse: The Chad Halverson Series 1–5
Helter Skelter
The Anaconda Complex
The Kill Option
Blood Moon: Thrillers and Tales of Terror
Fete of Death

Chapter 1

Renowned fashion designer Max Reed was strutting around the crime scene directing his models where to stand near the corpse that sprawled in a pool of coagulated blood on Wilshire Boulevard's sun-splashed sidewalk in West LA.

"Don't get too near the corpse," said Lt. George Macready of the LAPD's Robbery-Homicide Division in a brown blazer, his badge fastened to his leather belt, watching a slender blonde model wearing a filmy chiffon dress that fluttered in the breeze strut in her stiletto heels closer to the stiff.

"We have a film permit," said Reed, a muscular guy in his early forties wearing jeans, Nikes, an olive drab wife beater, and a black Windbreaker with the image of a human skull silkscreened on its back.

Known as the crassest designer in the world, Reed was also the richest, worth more than a billion dollars. The tabloids dubbed him "The Vulgarian" for his exploitation of tastelessness. The most beautiful supermodels in the world were standing in line dying to work for him. At five nine, he had a thuggish hatchet face like a muscular version of Jean-Paul Belmondo, green eyes, a Roman nose, sensual satyr's lips, and cropped blonde hair.

His mother was a French model, his father a British barrister. The family immigrated to the United States when Reed was but a child. He grew up in a tough neighborhood in Chicago, where he was bullied because his neighbors considered him an outsider. He lifted weights in self-defense. He wasn't interested in athletics, though. His sole interest was fashion, despite his parents' desire for him to become a doctor.

Encouraged by his parents, Reed moved to LA to attend the prestigious UCLA Medical School. He promptly dropped out, figuring professors focused on teaching students how to become teachers, which was not his goal in life. In any case, he discovered he had no interest in a medical career. He couldn't stand seeing sick people day in, day out. He wanted to see beautiful people wearing beautiful clothing. He wanted to make a splash in the fashion world.

He started small, designing sweaters and booties for pet dogs and cats. The sweaters and booties caught on, and he moved onto fashions for humans. Which did even better than his pet apparel.

And here he was at the top of his game, married and divorced three times, with one of the most profitable lines of fashion in the world, right up there with Gucci, Louis Vuitton, Prada, and Chanel.

Middle-aged, Lt. Macready had short dark hair and a port-wine stain on his wrinkle-creased forehead. He gave Reed a dour stare.

"I'll have you know this is an active crime scene," he said. "We don't want anyone contaminating it. Keep your models away from the corpse."

"I have a permit to film here," said Reed, withdrawing a document from his Windbreaker and waving it in Macready's face. "Signed by the mayor."

"I don't care if the president signed it. Don't get near the corpse," said Macready, brushing the document away from his face.

"The mayor's gonna hear about this," said Reed, face twisted in anger.

"The permit says you can shoot *near* the crime scene, not *in* it."

"We need to get as close as possible to the stiff for verisimilitude."

"I don't give a damn about verisimilitude. I represent the law. It's illegal to contaminate an active crime scene investigation."

Reed searched Macready's face. "You don't look well, Lieutenant. Your face looks wan. Aren't you getting enough?"

"Enough?"

"The wife, you know."

"I'm not married," said Macready, his expression wooden.

"Ah, that explains it. I find that getting laid stimulates my imagination and unclogs my creative juices so I can create masterpieces of art in the fashion world."

"You call filming a porn ad at a murder scene a masterpiece? I call it sick."

"It's not a porn ad, Lieutenant. My ads appear in the most prestigious magazines in the world, including *Vogue*, *Cosmo*, *Harper's Bazaar*, *Paris Match*, and *Elle*, to name a few. Let me clue you in, Lieutenant. Those aren't skin magazines."

"Your ads are torture porn, if you ask me."

"Every time you open your mouth, you show your ignorance of art."

"Look, you jumped-up smut peddler, I'll bust you if you get too close to the murder victim."

"I need that stiff and the blood around it in my shoot. It's essential to my art," said Reed, using his hands to frame a picture with his model and the corpse in it.

"To sell a dress? You gotta be shittin' me."

"A dress?" said Reed, widening his eyes. "It's not just a dress, it's a work of art. All of my creations are works of art. The world's richest people buy them. The nouveau riche adore me. They hang on my every word."

"It just shows money can't buy taste."

Reed flung up his arms in disgust. "How can I discuss high art with a troglodyte?"

Macready eyed Reed suspiciously.

"Caveman," explained Reed.

"Calling me names isn't scoring Brownie points for you."

Fed up with Macready, Reed instructed his cameraman where to put his camera in order to include the corpse and its blood behind his high-cheekboned model, Brigitte Jadot, who was standing in front of the corpse looking bored. Her famous luminous blue eyes could change from translucent to dark depending on her frame of mind.

"I'm losing the mood," she said, and fluffed her full blonde hair, her eyes darkening.

Brigitte, one of the highest paid supermodels in the world at the tender age of twenty-five, had trouble acting glamorous in such an unglamorous setting as a recent murder scene on the mean streets of LA.

"Take a step to your left, Brigitte," said Reed, nudged the photographer out of his way, and peered through the viewfinder of the camera mounted on a tripod. He studied the composition of the layout. "That's better. I can see the corpse's head and some of the blood behind your stilettos." He looked annoyed. "What I'd really like to see is the head right next to your right stiletto. Take two steps backward closer to the stiff."

"Nix that," said Macready.

Brigitte stopped in her tracks, unsure what to do, almost tipping over on her stilettos as she was making up her mind whether to take a second step closer to the corpse.

"You're making my shoot impossible, Lieutenant," said Reed.

"That's nothing," said Macready. "You're making my *job* impossible."

"This film permit cost me good money," said Reed, withdrawing the document from his Windbreaker's pocket and brandishing it in front of Macready.

"Tell it to your buddy, the mayor. I'm not letting you contaminate my murder investigation here."

Balling his fists in suppressed fury, Reed told his photographer, "Shoot Brigitte where she's standing. Ready, Brigitte, dear?"

"Wait a second," she said. "My stiletto almost fell off."

She shifted her foot in her Max Reed stiletto to make the fit more comfortable.

"Now look sexy," said Reed. "You're selling my beautiful dress. Hold your hands behind your head like I told you."

Brigitte struck a pose, clasping her hands behind her head and tilting it off to the right toward the corpse sprawled in its blood on the sidewalk. She hung her crimson lipstick-smeared mouth slightly open.

"Did you ever consider silicone injections, baby?"

Brigitte rolled her eyes.

"Does he treat everybody this bad?" Macready muttered to the uniform near him.

"Keep the pose, baby," said Reed. "Keep the pose."

Brigitte instantly reset her pose, as if she had never changed it.

"Perfect," said Reed. "Stop picking your nose and adjust the scrim on her left," he told the longhaired twentyish grip wearing jeans and a cobalt T. "She's getting too much sunlight on her hair."

The grip adjusted the silk scrim to diffuse the sunlight.

"It's all yours, Johnny," said Reed. "Stop leering at her crotch and start shooting."

Johnny Wikowski, the salt-and-pepper-haired photographer pushing forty, snapped multiple photos of Brigitte, coaxing her to change her pose slightly after taking several shots. He continued snapping groups of photos with each new pose she struck.

Macready looked on with nausea. "Are you trying to get your customers to throw up? Is that the point of these revolting photos? Did you sell your decency for a few bucks?"

Reed waved dismissively at him. "You're a beer-bellied slob with no concept of art."

"Do any of you ghouls care even one iota about the homicide victim?"

Reed ignored him. "Let's get it done, people. What's wrong, Brigitte? Did you find out your boyfriend's gay?"

"A gnat flew in my eye," she said, squinting her right eye, which began to tear, smearing her makeup.

"Break time. Debbie, help Brigitte."

Debbie Hernandez, the thirtyish makeup artist, wearing a loose blouse, jeans, and jogging shoes, hurried to Brigitte's side, inspected Brigitte's watery eye, and wiped the tears away with a handkerchief.

"Your ass looks like a cement mixer," said Reed, watching her jog toward Brigitte.

"How can any of you stand working for this shitheel?" said Macready.

"They know which side their bread's buttered on. Unlike you."

"I wouldn't work for you if you paid me a million bucks."

"You're not worth a million bucks. And you *do* work for me because you work for the mayor, and the mayor said I could shoot here."

"What kind of strings did you pull to get him to cave?"

"At least *he's* worth pulling strings for. You, on the other hand, have the value of a toad."

"I'm not playing nursemaid for you clowns any longer," said Macready, flushing with indignation. "Time for you to pack up and scram. Nobody gives me any lip and gets away with it."

"I'm gonna see to it personally that the mayor fires your sorry ass," said Reed.

Fit to be tied, he stalked off with his film crew toward their vans parked along the side of the street guarded by moonlighting cops.

Chapter 2

That night, Max Reed presided over his fashion show held in a hangar at the Santa Monica Airport. He was showing his new line of fall fashions at one of his typical lurid extravaganzas that spared no expense.

Strobe lights slashed through the dim-lit hangar as rap music blasted the eardrums of wealthy spectators that sat in tiered seats that formed a circle around the runways. In the center of the hangar loomed a thirty-foot-high human skull, an exact replica of the serial killer Ted Bundy's skull with the neon shocking pink letters T-E-D erected on top of it.

Statuesque, blank-faced models sporting Max Reed's latest designs strutted out of the skull's mouth onto runways that crisscrossed the hangar's floor as colored spotlights cut across the ceiling like dueling sabers in rhythm with the pulsating music.

Naturally, Reed had the best seat in the house, lording over the spectacle like a king on his throne sitting above everyone else in a diamond-studded cherry picker where he could watch the action.

Sitting behind him was his righthand man thirty-five-year-old Preston Wells, wearing jeans, skinny as a rock star, looking vaguely like a younger version of the Rolling Stones' Keith Richards, except Wells wore his brown hair cropped. He wore a necklace of silver skulls draped around his neck over his black T that had a silkscreen of a silver skeleton on its front.

"It's all about promotion, Preston," said Reed, gazing down upon his fiefdom of parading models, clad in gold, black, and white outfits designed by him. "Anybody can design clothes. But not everybody can sell them. That's what separates the men from the boys. That's why I rule fashion. My sales. Big sales."

"You got that right, boss," said Wells, and snorted cocaine off the back of his wrist.

"It's all about sex and violence. That's what sells product."

"I'm into it. You're on the mark."

"You better believe it. If it wasn't for me, you'd be strung out in a gutter lying in your own vomit jonesing and staring at the sun like a halfwit with tears in your eyes."

"You're the best."

"I spend millions to promote my fashion, and buyers pay millions more back to me to buy it. Take it from me, you can't make big money without spending big money. I got some of the highest paid models in the business dying to wear my latest outfits."

"We got A-list Hollywood celebs in the audience, too," said Wells, sniffling and surveying the spectators who watched the spectacular show in awe.

"You know it. Can you believe it? I started out selling booties for dogs, and now I'm selling gowns to Hollywood celebs. I made my dream come true—fashion designer to the stars, more famous than Gucci and Christian Dior."

"It's unreal."

"My father wanted me to go to medical school, and I had the grades to get in, but the idea of treating diseased patients every day turned me off. I wanted a job where I could enjoy life and live it to the limit. As far as I'm concerned, there is no limit. And I've proved it. My company Max Reed Enterprises is just getting started. No matter how big it is now, it's gonna get even bigger, as long as I keep putting on shows like this one with all the glam, glitz, and hoopla."

Wearing three diamond necklaces Brigitte Jadot strutted out of Ted Bundy's skull in a silver minidress with a cerise sash tied at the waist. It looked like the minidress was bleeding bright crimson drops of blood. In reality the drops were spangles that gave the illusion of blood. The minidress's hem was lined with grinning human skulls.

"You gotta be fucking bold with fashion," said Reed. "People don't want the same old thing. They want new, outrageous stuff. I dare to give them what they want, and I'm not afraid to break the mold. The other designers are too scared to be daring."

"You got it right, boss."

"I don't blame people for loving me."

"You're the best," said Wells, his eyes watery, looking bored, as though he'd said the same thing a million times before.

Reed sensed Wells's lack of enthusiasm. "You might amount to something if you had any balls. But you're such a sniveling pantywaist, you're going nowhere. Like they say, character is destiny. And, baby, you got none, so guess where you're heading?"

Wells simmered, but didn't fire back in kind.

Instead, he said, "I'm following the master."

"At least you have taste. You know who's the best."

"Max Reed," said Wells.

"Max Reed," said Reed, his eyes gleaming as he took in the pageantry below him watching it like an eagle from his eyrie, watching the spectators doting on the models strutting his stuff down the runways.

How could life be any better? he wondered.

The roar of Harley Davidson motorcycles yanked him out of his thoughts, as two Harleys trundled out of the skull's mouth and down the models' runway. The bearded riders wearing black leather motorcycle jackets decorated with slash zipper pockets on their fronts and the silver image of a human skull stitched on their backs tooled down the runway, revving their nerve-grating engines.

Chapter 3

Not far behind the two Harleys a beat-up vintage tan 1968 VW Bug emerged from the giant skull's mouth, belching grey exhaust fumes. The Bug was an exact replica of the one Ted Bundy had driven to transport the women he had bludgeoned into unconsciousness. He later tortured, killed, and had sex with their bodies.

As in Bundy's Beetle, Reed's VW's passenger seat had been removed. Bundy had removed it so he could hide his coldcocked, kidnaped victims on the floor out of sight of prying eyes. He had also removed the interior passenger's-side door handle on his Bug to prevent his victims from escaping. True to the original, Reed's replica also lacked the same handle.

Following the tan Beetle as it puttered down the runway, statuesque rail-thin models strutted out of the massive Bundy skull's gaping mouth, between its two rows of teeth.

Pushing thirty the first model out, clad in a flimsy black coat, loose white blouse, and flared gold lamé pants had a hatchet buried in her temple. At least, that's what it looked like. In reality the hatchet was a plastic movie prop.

The model behind her, a tall African American in her early thirties with peroxide blonde hair cropped so tight she looked bald with a mantle of frost on her head, marched onto the runway dressed in a long gold lamé dress that stretched from her shoulders to the soles of her scarlet pumps. The head of a hammer appeared to be embedded in her cranium, the wooden handle sticking out at a forty-five-degree angle.

The third model to exit the skull's mouth was a twenty-five-year-old Japanese woman with long straight black hair that reached halfway down her back and with bangs across her forehead. Sheathed in a tight silver dress that looked like chainmail clinging to her figure, she pranced onto the runway in diamond-studded clear stiletto heels, a movie-prop meat cleaver wedged in her cranium.

"A stroke of genius staging it to look like serial-killer Ted Bundy's victims are parading in our fashion show, if I do say so myself," said Reed, watching the extravaganza with eager eyes.

"You're a juggernaut of fashion," said Wells. "Your new TED line of clothes will turn the fashion world on its head. You'll be the toast of the town."

"I already am."

"Of course, boss."

"The fashion world is all about promotion, and nobody can beat me at promotion. Who else would have the audacity and the chutzpah to dream up a fashion line named after one of the most notorious serial killers in history? Can you image Versace, Tom Ford, or Ralph Lauren coming up with an idea like this? Or Nicolas Ghesquière at Louis Vuitton?"

"No way. Not even Philipp Plein."

"They haven't got the imagination or the balls to pull it off. Only I, Max Reed, could do it. I'm the only one who would *dare* do it. Fuck those hidebound clowns. Milquetoast fuddy-duddies with no imagination. Of course, they hate me. Envy breeds hate. I can hear their insults of my brilliant TED fashions now. 'A stomach-churning assault on the senses.' 'A neanderthal lack of taste and refinement.' 'Worthy of a stone-age slob.'"

"They don't understand promotion."

Reed nodded. "Once a fuddy-duddy, always a fuddy-duddy. I'm the vanguard. They're the outmoded rearguard. They're like pubescent kids whose nuts never dropped into their scrotums."

Wells laughed.

"In humor there is truth," said Reed. "Wait till they see the humongous profits I'm gonna reap after my TED line debuts. And they know I'm the only guy that could pull it off. None of them could ever come up with something as brilliant and outstanding as my TED line, nothing even close to it. I can't wait to see their jaws drop when my sales surpass all of theirs combined."

"I bet some of them are in the audience right now kicking themselves for not coming up with your TED line on their own."

The last model to march out of Bundy's immense skull's gaping mouth was a seventyish supermodel dressed as a human skeleton sporting a blonde wig and a silver dress that reached to her bony knees. Her face was made up to look like it had a cadaver's livid parchment skin with carmine lipstick smeared liberally on its lips and silver eyeshade daubed on its eyelids. She represented one of Bundy's necrophilia victims.

Members in the audience gasped with shock and dismay.

Reed heard a grumbling of discontent ripple through the crowd accompanied by boos, as spectators voiced their outrage at Reed's in-your-face, repellant flaunting of tastelessness.

A twentysomething woman wearing jeans, hiking boots, and an apricot T in the audience held up a sign that said Max Reed Is a Misogynist. Shaking her sign up and down, her face twisted with fury, she gazed up at Reed and booed.

"Oh, boo to you, too," said Reed, chiding the audience, "you feckless, overrefined fairies. You're watching the fashion masterpieces of a genius. Behold and enjoy."

"Let them boo all they like," said Wells. "Their boos sell the show. Wait till everyone reads about it in the trades. It'll make the headlines."

"I can see it now. 'Reed Causes Uproar at His Fall Fashion Show.' 'Reed Glorifies Serial Killers.' My creations will fly off the shelves as a result," said Reed, grinning.

"Reed victimizes women," hollered the woman waving the sign.

"What's wrong with that skank? I don't victimize them," Reed told Wells. "I empower them with my exquisite fashions. Why are all geniuses misunderstood?"

"Who let her in here, anyhow?" said Wells. "Did she get evicted from her homeless tent?"

"Tell the Harley drivers to gun their engines to drown out the boos."

"I thought you wanted everybody to hear the boos," said Wells, bemused.

"Nobody gets away with booing me," said Reed through his teeth, the venom in his voice palpable.

Wells called the motorcyclists with his cell phone and relayed Reed's orders to them.

The motorcyclists gunned their engines in response, filling the hangar with cacophonous reverberations that supplanted the scattered boos of disgruntled spectators.

Chapter 4

The next day, Scott Brody PI sat at a small square table on the patio of the Habit, a fast-food chain restaurant in West LA, eating a charbroiled burger with a Coke. The metal chair felt small for his six-two frame.

"What exactly do you want me to do for half a million bucks, Sal?" he said.

"Good question, and I'm glad you asked," said the fiftysomething guy sitting opposite him, working on a cheeseburger and Coke.

His black hair greying at the temples, Sal Andrasi had a large craggy-faced head that thrust out of his broad shoulders like an outcrop on a mountain ridge. The shirttails of his loud button-down black shirt with yellow triangular patterns on it hung out of his baggy charcoal grey trousers.

His prominent nose skewed to the left, the result of a fist to the face when he was a teenager growing up in Brooklyn. The owner of the fist died mysteriously the night of the attack with a screwdriver impaling his temple as he was eating cheese lasagna at his favorite trattoria. Nobody could say how the screwdriver got there.

"You knew I'd ask," said Brody. "And my second question after that is, is it legal?"

Sal chuckled. "Do you think I would hire you to do something illegal?"

"You didn't answer my question."

"Of course, it's legal," said Sal, gesturing with his open hands.

"I can't understand why a simple delivery would be worth half a million bucks."

"Because that's what it's worth to me. A delivery is worth whatever value the sender gives it."

"Why don't you just get FedEx to deliver it? They're much cheaper."

"The delivery has to be made at an exact time. None of the courier services can promise making such a delivery."

"Why does it have to be delivered at an exact time?"

"That's of no importance to you. You're being paid to make the delivery, not anything else."

"It's not narcotics, is it?"

"Absolutely not," said Sal, sitting back in his small chair.

"Then what is it?"

"That's none of your business."

"Because what's in the package is illegal."

"It's not illegal. That's all I can tell you."

"Why so hush-hush about it?"

"You're being paid to deliver a package. That's all you need to know."

Brody thought about it. "It's a good paycheck, I have to admit."

"The best you'll ever see."

"But I'm a private detective. I don't operate a delivery service. I don't get it. Why come to me?"

Sal leaned over the tabletop toward Brody. "It's a valuable package. Under no circumstances are you to let it be stolen. You must guard it with your life."

Brody's interest was piqued. He could use the money. His PI business wasn't exactly booming. But the deal smelled fishy to him.

He had done investigative work for Sal before, but mostly it was checking on wives to make sure they weren't cheating on their mobster husbands, and if they were, Brody was to gather evidence of their philandering.

"Who am I supposed to deliver this package to?" said Brody.

"I'll give you all of the information if you agree to accept the assignment," said Sal, leaning back in his chair and taking a bite of his burger.

"Is there something here I'm missing?"

"It's a simple delivery. The address is not that far away. It's in Beverly Hills."

"It makes no sense. It's too easy."

"Decisions, decisions. I can always get someone else if you're not interested. But I trust you because you've done jobs for me before. With someone else, I'd have to worry about them bugging out with the merchandise and vanishing."

"You're not worried I'd do that?"

"No. You're a stand-up guy." Sal paused. "And you know there's no place you could hide on this earth that would prevent me from finding you . . . and you know the rest of that story."

What Sal meant was that Brody knew Sal was mobbed up and would have no problem hiring a mechanic to whack Brody if he tried to double-cross Sal.

"Why am I getting the feeling you're leaving out something very important in this gig?" said Brody.

"You know all you need to know at this point."

Brody had a feeling this job was going to be trouble. Whatever was in the package must have been valuable. Or why was Sal willing to pay so much to get it delivered? If it *was* valuable, somebody might try to rip it off. Somebody who would be willing to kill for it? And yet it was such a short trip from here to Beverly Hills. What could go wrong for the duration of a couple of miles?

Brody knew he was missing a vital ingredient, but he had no idea what. Yet half a million bucks was too tempting to turn down. He would have to be an idiot to turn it down. Brody was sure Sal knew Brody wouldn't turn it down.

Why couldn't he ever get a simple gig? wondered Brody. And yet this sounded like a simple gig, which was the problem. It sounded too good to be true.

Sal sucked Coke through a plastic straw. "I don't have all day, Brody. Take it or leave it."

"It sounds like a game show. 'Take It or Leave It."

"This ain't no game. I'm not gonna kid you. This gig is harder than it looks."

"It must be for that kind of dough."

Brody couldn't help but feel he was walking into a trap.

"What's your answer?" said Sal. "Are you in?"

Brody felt himself breaking into a sweat. Every fiber in his body told him to reject the offer. The level of difficulty of the job didn't match its price tag. He hated it when things didn't add up. He had to make a decision. He knew he would get only one chance. Sal had made it clear he wasn't going to repeat the offer.

Still, Brody hesitated.

Sal hummed the "Think!" music for *Jeopardy!* The humming grated on Brody's nerves.

Half a million dollars to deliver a package a few miles away, thought Brody, the sweat beading on his forehead. What was in the package? Another half a million bucks? He found the thought amusing and smiled.

"Does that smile on your face mean yes?" said Sal.

"I'm in," said Brody.

And he knew he would come to regret it. But, for the life of him, he could not see how.

Chapter 5

"Good man," said Sal. "I never doubted you."

"So what's the gig?" said Brody, and slipped a golden French fry into his mouth.

"This is very important. As soon as you finish making the delivery, call me on your cell phone."

"No problem. Who am I delivering the package to?"

"Did you ever hear of Max Reed?"

"Can't say that I have."

"You must not be into fashion."

"This is true."

"I could tell by looking at your threads. Jeans, a green polo, and sneakers. All from the Salvation Army."

"What's my taste in fashion got to do with anything?"

"Max Reed is a billionaire fashion designer. He's the most famous designer in the business."

"What about him?" said Brody, and popped another French fry into his mouth.

"He's the one you deliver the package to."

"He lives in Beverly Hills?"

"He has an office there. You deliver the package to his office and—this is very important—make sure he gets it personally. We want to be positive he received it. We don't want him claiming he never got it."

"And what's in the package?"

"That's none of your business."

"You said you'd tell me the details of the job if I accepted it."

"I never said I'd tell you what's in the package."

"Shouldn't I know what I'm delivering? Wouldn't that make me more careful about making sure it got delivered?"

Sal didn't beat around the bush. "No."

"Does it matter which route I take to get there?"

Sal considered it. “No. Going straight down Wilshire is fine.”

“Isn’t that the route everybody would think I’d take?”

“I don’t care what they think.”

“You don’t think anybody’s gonna try to stop me?” said Brody with surprise.

“Why would they?”

“To steal the package.”

“It’s not something you have to worry about.”

“I don’t get it. You hire a PI to deliver a valuable package, and you don’t think anybody’s gonna try and jack it?”

Sal thought about it. “Point taken. You see, that’s why I hired you. Because you know your stuff. You can take any route you want. You don’t even have to tell me what it is. Keep it secret.”

“Does anybody know about this delivery other than you and me?”

“No.”

“Good.”

“I’m glad I hired you. You’re on the ball and then some.”

“When do you want the package delivered?”

“I haven’t decided yet.”

“Is it big? Will I need to rent a van and use a dolly to transport it?”

“Not at all. It’s yay big”—Sal motioned with his hands—"the size of a bowling bag. In fact, it *is* a bowling bag.”

“To make it look like I’m going bowling, so I’m inconspicuous. I get it. And how heavy is it? Will I need a dolly?”

“No. No dolly. I don’t know the exact weight. It can’t be more than ten pounds. Not even that much.”

“So I can carry it into his office with my hand.”

“Absolutely.”

“I’m asking all these questions because I want to know what I’m dealing with.”

“No problem. I have one rule you must follow, however.”

"Which is?"

"Do not, under any circumstances, open the bowling bag to see what's in it."

Which only intensified Brody's desire to know what he was carrying to Reed.

"Understood," said Brody.

"In any case, the package will be locked. Reed will be the only one who has the key."

Brody nodded. "What's Reed's address?"

Sal gave it to him. "He's in the penthouse suite of his office building on Rodeo Drive where it intersects with Wilshire."

"Of course. Only the best for the company boss."

"If only you knew. He owns seven Ferraris. One for each day of the week."

"I'd be happy if I could afford one Porsche."

Sal laughed. "He's enjoying the hell out of the good life."

"How do I get the half a million?"

"We'll wire the first half of it into an account we'll set up for you in the Cayman Islands."

"Won't that take a while?"

"Actually, the account has already been set up for you. I'll give you the number of your account and the password before we leave."

"You knew I'd say yes."

"When the money is wired to your Cayman bank account, we'll notify you via a fictitious e-mail we have set up for you that the money's been deposited. I'll give you the e-mail address when I give you the Cayman account number and your password."

"And when do I get the rest of the dough?"

"After you notify us over your burner cell that you've delivered the package to Reed. Check your Cayman bank account about fifteen minutes later. The money will be there."

"All right."

Sal withdrew his cell phone from his trouser pocket, swiped and tapped its face a couple times, and slid it over the tabletop to Brody.

"Memorize the account number, password, and e-mail that I'm showing you," said Sal, indicating his phone's screen.

Brody followed Sal's instructions. "Done."

Sal returned his cell phone to his trouser pocket. "Check your Cayman account in half an hour. The first payment should be there at that time."

Brody finished the remainder of his burger and washed it down with his Coke.

Sal stood up. "I'll e-mail you when I want you to deliver the package."

"When do I get the package?"

"It's waiting for you at your car."

Brody looked surprised. "Is that wise to leave it near my car?"

"One of my men is waiting there with it."

Chapter 6

Brody drove his Mini back to his apartment, awoke his laptop from Sleep mode, and checked on the account Sal had set up for him in the Cayman Islands. The account showed only five hundred dollars. Brody figured that was the amount needed to set up the account.

Next, he checked his fictitious e-mail. No word from Sal.

Brody glanced at his wristwatch. Not quite a half hour had passed since he had eaten lunch with Sal.

Brody looked at the bowling bag he had brought with him from his car and set near the door. The bag was constructed of brown leather and looked like a carryon. It had a lock on the zipper. He couldn't help but wonder what was inside. He wasn't going to rack his brains thinking about it. It could be anything.

He felt his cell phone vibrate in his trouser pocket, withdrew it, and saw he had an e-mail at his fictitious address from Sal.

Now, was all it said.

Brody logged into his Cayman bank account.

A quarter of a million dollars had been deposited in it.

Time to deliver the package, he decided.

He retrieved the bowling bag, exited his apartment, locked the door, and made for his Mini, which he had parked on the side of the street. He stashed the bowling bag in the passenger's-side foot well.

Sitting in the driver's seat he wondered which route to take to Reed's office building. The most direct was to drive east on Wilshire Boulevard straight into Beverly Hills. The question was, was somebody following him in order to prevent him from accomplishing his mission? Sal hadn't said anyone would try to thwart his delivery.

And yet the package must have had valuable merchandise inside it, or why was the simple and short delivery of a mere six miles worth half a million bucks?

When he pulled onto the street, he checked his rearview mirror to make sure no vehicle pulled out at the same time behind him. He didn't see anyone.

He drove down to Wilshire and hung a left heading eastward. The traffic was heavy as usual. He checked his rearview mirror and side-view mirrors frequently, but didn't pick up on anyone hanging a tail on him.

He decided to pull off Wilshire and use side streets, continuing to bear toward Beverly Hills. He was familiar with the area, since he lived in West LA, and knew many side streets that had less traffic than the congestion on Wilshire.

He wondered why Sal hadn't been concerned that somebody might be following the package on its way to Reed's. This job was too damn easy, decided Brody. What was he missing?

Call it instinct or a sixth sense or intuition, but he knew this job was going to go haywire. If only he could figure out how—before it was too late.

He drove back onto Wilshire. Nothing untoward in his surroundings. No ominous-looking cars closing in on him.

"You've done jobs for me before," he could hear Sal saying in his memory.

It made sense Sal would pick him for another job, decided Brody. But those jobs paid pin money compared to this one.

Brody drove his Mini onto Rodeo Drive and pulled into the underground parking garage in Reed's office building. He slotted his car in a parking space next to a fluorescent lime Lamborghini Huracan that looked like new.

He killed his engine, set the emergency brake, got out of his car, retrieved the bowling bag, and locked his car electronically with his key fob.

His cell phone vibrated in his pocket.

He's waiting for you, said Sal's e-mail.

Brody rode the elevator to the lobby that had a green marble floor that glittered like an emerald. He felt like running and sliding on it like a kid. But he was wearing sneakers. The rubber soles wouldn't slide. They were making squeaky sounds as he strode toward the guard manning the front desk, sounding like basketball players' sneakers running on a parquet gym floor.

"I need to see Max Reed," said Brody.

The uniformed thirtyish guard had brown eyes, black bushy hair, and broad shoulders. His brown eyes stared at Brody like Brody with his imposing build was going to make trouble.

"Nature of your business?" said the guard.

"I have a delivery for Max Reed."

"Is Mr. Reed expecting it?"

"He is."

"What is your name?"

Brody told him, wishing this would go faster.

The guard didn't look any more agreeable.

Sal had told Brody he was expected. Brody figured his name should be opening doors.

"Max Reed is expecting me," said Brody.

"Hold on," said the guard.

He put through a call to Reed's office in the penthouse and waited for the receptionist to pick up.

"Mr. Reed doesn't bowl," the guard told Brody, noticing the bowling bag in Brody's hand.

"I wouldn't know."

"If he doesn't bowl, why are you delivering a bowling ball to him?"

"My instructions are to deliver the bag to him. That's all I know."

Brody started getting nervous. Was this where the guard prevented him from seeing Reed? Was this why the delivery was worth half a million bucks? Because he would have to fight his way to the penthouse?

"Mr. Reed will see you," said the guard, cradling his handset. "Take the elevator on your left to the penthouse."

Chapter 7

"I know I have enemies," said Max Reed, standing behind his massive teak desk, wearing a wife beater and grey sweatpants, both designed by him. "Only the best have the most enemies. It's called jealousy."

"Maybe you should take precautions," said Preston Wells, clad in tight jeans and a body-hugging black T sporting a silkscreen of a white human skeleton on his chest.

"Precautions? What kind of precautions? Are you talking about a bulletproof vest?"

"Maybe you shouldn't make so many public appearances."

"I have to promote my brand. How else can I do promotions without public appearances?"

Wells scratched his ear. "I'm just throwing out suggestions."

"You're making me paranoid with your suggestions. Maybe if you showed more balls, you could rise to the top like me, Preston."

Wells simmered with resentment. Working for Reed, Wells was used to suppressing his emotions. To do otherwise could be hazardous to his employment status.

"I'm only thinking of your well-being, sir," said Wells.

"Let me tell you, cowards don't get anywhere in the world of big business, especially the fashion business. And don't tell me half of them are gay. They still need big balls to make it in such a cutthroat jungle."

"I'm just saying maybe you should consider hiring a twenty-four-hour bodyguard service."

"I already have bodyguards."

"But they're not with you all the time."

"What do you want me to do? Take them to the head with me? Share a stall? Give me a break."

"I'm thinking of your well-being, is all."

"The price of fame is enemies. Get used to it. Fame isn't for pantywaists. Not that you would know anything about pantywaists, Preston."

Wells smoldered. He knew it was a backhanded compliment aimed at him. He knew irony when he heard it, and he heard it all the time from Reed.

You prick, thought Wells, but said nothing, his face a mask. He wondered how he could stand working for this louse. Money was the answer, of course. Reed paid well. He treated his employees like dirt and paid for the pleasure.

The receptionist buzzed Reed's speakerphone that sat on his desktop.

Reed acknowledged it.

"There's a delivery out here for you, Mr. Reed," said the receptionist's voice over the speakerphone.

"So why interrupt me? I'm thinking great thoughts in here. Tell the carrier to leave it and go."

"He says he needs to hand it to you personally."

"Do I look like someone who has time to waste?"

"I'm just repeating what he told me."

"Who's the delivery from?"

"Sal, he says."

Reed turned around to look out his window that showed the whole of LA spread at his feet, a big rambling city with millions of potential buyers of his fashions. Like his own private kingdom, he decided.

"OK," he said. "Let him in."

Wells took the opportunity to leave the office, as Brody entered, bowling bag in hand.

Reed turned around to face the door as he heard it open.

"You can put it down there," he said.

Brody nodded.

"Do I need to sign?" asked Reed.

"No. I'm just supposed to deliver it to you in person."

"Do you think I care about your instructions?"

Brody glared at Reed. "I'm doing a job. That's all."

"Pretty tough job you got there. What do you get? Six bucks an hour?"

If only you knew, thought Brody.

"My job is done," said Brody, refusing to be baited.

"Then get out of here. Who asked you to stay?"

Brody restrained the urge to pounce on Reed and deck him.

"Do you think my job is as easy as the one you got?" said Reed.

Brody wanted to get out of there, but the guy was annoying him.

"You mean, you gotta look out your window all day at the view?" said Brody.

"You got all the answers, huh? You deliver a package, and that makes you an expert on everything. I rake in millions of dollars a year. What about you? Millions of pennies?"

"I'll leave you alone to your great thoughts," said Brody, and left, slamming the door behind him.

Chapter 8

Still steaming, Brody took the elevator down to the lobby.

It wasn't until he walked into the lobby that he remembered he was supposed to call Sal as soon as he had delivered the package to Reed. Brody halted in the lobby, produced his cell phone, and called Sal.

The call went direct to voicemail.

Odd, decided Brody. Sal must have been expecting the call. Why didn't he pick up?

Brody terminated the call. He would call back later.

He angled toward the plate-glass doors that led to the busy Wilshire Boulevard that intersected Rodeo Drive.

He all but jumped out of his skin when a deafening explosion rocked the building. He looked upward. The source of the blast had come from a higher floor.

What the hell happened?

He had been walking across the lobby, and out of nowhere the whole building had shaken as if struck by an earthquake. He had completed a simple job, and chaos had been unleashed. Had he been in the wrong place at the wrong time, or was it more complicated? Was his luck incredibly bad, or was he somehow connected to the unfolding disaster? Even more disturbing, had he somehow precipitated the cataclysm?

He saw the security guard at the front desk scoff up his handset and stare at the ceiling as if worried it might collapse. Indeed, small chunks of plaster dislodged from the ceiling fell to the floor. He began talking in earnest on the phone.

Brody approached him, picking his way through frantic people headed in the opposite direction scurrying out of the lobby, cramming through the plate-glass front doors, and swarming onto the sidewalk in packed knots.

"It's burning," cried a woman in a green pencil skirt standing on the sidewalk and gazing at the top of Reed's office building being consumed by leaping flames tonguing the sky.

The din of panicked office workers fleeing through the lobby made it difficult for the guard to hear the person he was talking to on the phone. The guard yelled into his handset.

"What the fuck happened?" he said, his knuckles turning white as he clenched the handset. "I heard an explosion. All hell's breaking loose down here."

Straining to listen to the receiver he widened his eyes. "The whole office? . . . And Mr. Reed? Is Mr. Reed OK? . . . I can't hear you. There's too much noise down here. Everybody's screaming and running for their lives out the doors."

The guard put the call on speakerphone.

"Mr. Reed's office was totaled," said the fraught female voice over the line.

"These things don't happen in Beverly Hills."

"Shit can happen anywhere."

"This is Beverly Hills, god damn it. The home of the rich and famous."

"Tell that to the fire burning this building," yelled the woman.

"And Mr. Reed?" said the guard, lowering his voice with concern.

"We don't know. We can't get in there. Flames are burning out of control. Half of the penthouse floor is on fire."

"Did you notify the fire department?"

"We called it in. What's taking them so long to get here?"

"Rubberneckers are thronging the street outside watching the building go up in flames," said the guard, eyeballing the scene from a Hollywood disaster movie.

"The elevators are out of order. The only way up and down is the stairwell."

"Is anyone else with you? Are you safe?"

"There are three of us here," said the woman's voice becoming more strained. She coughed. "The smoke is getting thicker. The fire door to the stairs is jammed. The janitor said the fire must have welded the latch shut so we can't budge the door. Where are the firemen?"

"What good's a fire door that melts?"

Brody heard a fire siren knifing through the cries of the raucous crowd blocking Wilshire Boulevard beyond the plate-glass doors.

"They're coming," said the guard.

"We can't last much longer up here," said the woman, suffering a coughing fit. "Help us for Christ's sake."

"You need to hold on. The fire department will be here any minute. They have axes that can cut through the fire door."

"How are we supposed to breathe?"

Preston Wells's voice came on the line. "What the fuck are you doing in the lobby? People are dying up here. The boss's office is an inferno." He gagged and coughed. "Help us."

"The fire department can break down the door."

"Where are they?"

"I don't understand what exploded," said the guard.

"Something in the boss's office."

To enter the lobby, firefighters in bulky yellow Nomex suits plowed their way through the plate-glass doors, thrusting back the outgoing tide of panic-stricken workers of Max Reed Enterprises.

"People are trapped on the penthouse floor," the guard hollered. "The fire door's stuck."

The firefighters clambered into the stairwell and lugged their heavy gear up the steps.

Outside, amid the chaos of terrified onlookers, the firemen raised ladders from their trucks to the top of the building so they could douse water from their hoses on the flames that were devouring the penthouse floor.

The guard riveted his eyes on Brody's face. "You're the guy that made the last delivery to Mr. Reed's office."

"So?"

"What was in that package?"

"How do I know? I was just the deliverer. I didn't send it," said Brody, backing away from the guard toward the exit.

"I think you better hang around here till the cops come."

Brody decided it was time to leave. The more he thought about it, the more he realized how suspicious he looked.

Was the bowling bag what had exploded? he wondered, elbowing his way through the crowd to the doors. If so, he was the prime suspect. After all, the blast had occurred shortly after he had delivered Sal's package. Had Sal set him up? Wait a minute. If Brody had called Sal like Sal wanted him to do as soon as he had delivered the package to Reed, Brody would have been blown to bits in the explosion. *Sal wanted him dead along with Reed.*

Or, could it be possible Sal didn't know what was in the package, had no idea a bomb was inside it? Brody doubted it.

He had no time to think about it. He had to beat it.

The guard had leapt from his seat and was giving chase.

Brody saw cops trying to control the crowd on the sidewalks and in the street, keeping them away from the firetrucks. He had to get out of here before the guard alerted the cops to bust him.

The guard screamed at the cops to stop Brody. The cops couldn't hear him thanks to the din of the milling, agitated mob outside.

Brody slammed into a wall of people on the sidewalk and jostled through them, eliciting angry rebukes from the mob trying to watch the flaming penthouse that was filling the sky with a plume of smoke.

Brody kept going.

"Stop that man," bellowed the guard, who emerged onto the sidewalk pointing out Brody.

Nobody laid hands on Brody. First, nobody knew it was Brody the guard was pointing at because of the confused mass of rubberneckers jamming the street. Second, nobody wanted to get involved.

The guard yelled at the cops to help, but his voice was lost in the ruckus.

Brody ducked down a side street, clear of pedestrians, where traffic was snarled because of the cops' closing of Wilshire. Irate drivers leaned on their horns.

He climbed the metal steps of a bus parked at the side of the street and rode the bus back to West LA.

He wondered how long it would take the cops to put out a BOLO for him as a suspect in the suspicious explosion at Max Reed Enterprises. He would have to go to ground.

Chapter 9

Wearing his Nomex uniform in the stairwell, the six-five fireman wielding his ax against the jammed steel penthouse fire door looked even more imposing than usual, like some kind of giant from another planet bent on destruction. The ax blade thwacked against the door latch repeatedly.

The door finally shivered open, smoke from the penthouse hallway billowing into the stairwell.

"Let's go in," said Lt. Meechum, a five-eight guy with the build of a bull, wearing a Nomex hood with a dark tinted face mask along with his uniform. "Watch out for the smoke. Don't stay in there any longer than you have to. Just until you find all the survivors."

A skinny guy with a haggard, sooty face and singed hair staggered out of the hallway toward the fire door.

"Are you Max Reed?" said Meechum in a voice muffled by his mask.

Wells bowed his head and coughed. "I'm his assistant Preston Wells."

Two women stumbled out of the hall into the stairwell, reeking of smoke.

"The guard said Reed is up here," said Meechum.

"He was in his office when it exploded," gasped Wells, collapsing and passing out.

"Get him to an EMT," Meechum told his men.

Two of them dragged Wells to his feet, draped his arms over their shoulders, and hauled him down the stairs

"I feel sick," said one of the women, a slender thirtyish Korean American with large brown eyes and a disheveled blue-tinted perm, her lilac lipstick smeared, her yellow minidress smudged with soot.

"Where's Max Reed?" said Meechum.

"I have no idea."

"Is anyone else alive on this floor?"

Succumbing to a coughing jag, her face flushing, the woman shook her head, indicating she didn't know.

"Get her downstairs," Meechum told his men.

Two of his men helped her down the steps, as two more burst into the smoke-filled hallway searching for more survivors.

An ashen-faced twentysomething blonde with a buxom figure clad in skintight jeans and a lavender tank top staggered out of the smoke past the two firefighters, reached Meechum, and stared at him with dazed, bloodshot blue eyes.

"Where's Max Reed?" said Meechum.

Befuddled, the blonde kept staring at his face mask like he was an unidentified creature.

"Reed," said Meechum. "Where is he?"

She doubled over, vomiting onto the floor and coughing.

One of the firemen grabbed her before she collapsed and escorted her down the stairway.

Meechum tried to peer into the smoky hallway, but couldn't make out anything in the rolling clouds of smoke. He could tell from the sunlight filtering through the grey haze that portions of the penthouse roof had been blown off in the explosion. Farther down the hall he could barely make out lurid flames, advancing toward the stairwell in a threatening danse macabre. His men were attempting to douse those flames with the hose located on the floor, while additional firefighters standing on ladders outside were hosing down the penthouse struggling to quell the fire.

He assessed the situation and decided the fire was contained. He doubted it would spread to the next floor, as long as his men kept bombarding it with water.

Despite the protection offered by his mask, his eyes and throat burned from the smoke. He thought he could discern Reed's office through the smoke enshrouding the entire floor. The charred, disintegrated room looked like the remains of a Berlin building bombed by the Allies in World War II. The ceiling had been sheared off, and one wall had been obliterated, allowing the firefighters outside to deluge the office with water.

If Max Reed had been in his office at the time of the blast, Meechum didn't like the guy's chances. The guy's body had probably been catapulted to West Hollywood. And the same was true for anyone else who had been in his office with him.

Meechum lumbered in his bulky uniform through the office doorway, whose door had been blown off its hinges into the hallway, and cast around the premises. He saw no signs of life, only the queasy sight of globs of torn flesh and gouts of blood splattered against one of the remaining walls.

A high explosive like TNT or C-4 must have been used, he decided, taking in the thorough devastation of the room. He didn't smell gas. He didn't see any remnants of a stove or other gas-powered appliance that might have blown up accidentally. He felt confident the explosion had been deliberate.

Were they dealing with terrorists? he wondered. Terrorists liked to use bombs. The ATF would have to figure it out. They had the equipment to analyze residue at the scene of a bombing. They could come up with the type of high explosive used.

Why would terrorists go after a fashion designer? he wondered. The FBI and the LAPD would come up with the motive. Meechum was a firefighter, not a cop.

If Max Reed had been in his office at the time of the explosion, he was dead. No question about it. The DNA experts would have to determine if the flesh and gore on the walls belonged to Reed.

Feeling overcome by the heat and smoke, Meechum retreated to the stairwell. Ghastly visions of Reed's office would visit him in his nightmares tonight, he decided.

Chapter 10

On the run again, decided Brody. So what else was new?

He had returned to Beverly Hills an hour after the explosion to collect his Mini from the parking garage and had headed west.

He parked his Mini in the lot of a powder blue stucco budget motel with a red-tiled roof in Culver City, not far from Sony Pictures Studios, which used to be Lorimar-Telepictures Studios, and, originally, Metro-Goldwyn-Mayer.

He had come to the conclusion it wasn't a good idea to return to his apartment. If the cops were searching for him, his apartment would be the first place they would look.

The guard at the front desk of Max Reed Enterprises must have told the cops by now that Brody had delivered a package to Reed's office just before the explosion ripped the roof off the penthouse floor.

Brody checked into the motel using a credit card for a shell company he had set up in Delaware with no list of its owners available for public viewing. He had to stay somewhere while he planned his next move.

Wearing a half-buttoned red cardigan the round-faced, bespectacled, middle-aged motel manager sitting behind his desk handed Brody a key card.

"You're in number six," said the manager. "Have a nice day."

"Thanks," said Brody, accepting the key card.

"Like the sign says outside, we got Wi-Fi."

"Good," said Brody, not caring, making for the door.

"Is that why you checked in here? I do an informal survey as people check in."

"No."

"Then why, may I ask?"

"Uh, I—uh—liked the color of your motel paint."

"You don't say. My wife picked it out. She'll be glad to hear that."

"It looks like the sky."

"Did you hear the news?"

Brody froze in his tracks as he reached the door. "What?"

"Max Reed Enterprises in Beverly Hills was hit by a bomb."

"Oh?" said Brody, hunching over and trying to conceal his face. "Do they know who did it?"

"The cops have a suspect, but they haven't broadcast his name yet."

"What was the motive?"

"The cops aren't talking."

"How's Reed?"

The manager shrugged. "What's left of him can be scraped off the walls, is all I heard."

Exiting the manager's office Brody made a beeline for his room. He used the key card on the door lock and entered the room after the light on the lock flashed green.

Brody locked the door behind him, flopped down on his back on the bed, and contemplated his next move, staring at the patterns in the white stucco ceiling.

He would have to get rid of his Mini and rent a car, he decided. The cops would put out a BOLO on his Mini as well as on him.

Next, he had to find Sal.

Sal had set him up. Brody was supposed to die in the blast along with Max Reed. That was why Sal wanted Brody to call him as soon as Brody had delivered Reed the package. As luck would have it, Brody had forgot to call Sal the minute he had delivered the package to Reed. Brody didn't remember to place the call until he was down in the lobby, far away from Reed's office.

He ought to kill Sal for setting him up.

But he wasn't going to kill anyone till he knew why Sal had suckered him.

What did Sal have against Max Reed? wondered Brody. Did Reed's business have financial problems that nobody knew about? Had Sal acted as a loan shark for Reed and Reed had failed to pay Sal back? Instead of breaking Reed's legs, had Sal blown the guy up?

Brody could speculate about it all day. The only way he was going to find the truth was to find Sal and get it out of him.

Brody hated being suckered. Why had Sal done this to him? Brody knew the guy worked for the mob, but Sal had always been on the level when dealing with him. Sal had always paid him after hiring him to do jobs. No problem.

Brody snagged the TV remote from the nightstand near his bed and switched on the TV.

The Reed bombing was all over the network TV channels, interrupting regularly scheduled programing. It was big news. Reed was the richest fashion designer in the business. His murder was front-page news.

A happy-faced, immaculately coiffed brunette newscaster was announcing the explosion in her air-conditioned TV newsroom as a video shot from a private surveillance camera near the Reed building played behind her showing the Reed building's penthouse blowing up. Smiling and calm, she related that the cops suspected Reed had died in the explosion, but they had not made any positive identification yet. It was like she was in another universe drinking iced tea beside her pool smiling and enjoying the sun as she broadcast the horrific news.

Brody supposed the only way people could tolerate the news was by having it spoon-fed to them by genial newscasters who pretended to be their friends.

The newscaster added that two other people in Reed's office were confirmed killed in the explosion.

Brody didn't hear on the news that the cops were looking for him. Which meant nothing. The cops could have put out a BOLO on him without notifying the media. It wouldn't be the first time they had held back their actions from the media.

The good-looking brunette announcer, but not too good-looking, said the ATF and the FBI had been called in to determine whether terrorists had bombed Reed, though he had no known connection to any terrorist group.

Brody wondered if he should give Sal Andrasi's name anonymously to the cops as the guy that had sent the bomb to Reed. The problem was, if the cops questioned Sal, he might give them Brody's name to get the heat off himself. Even now, Sal might be calling them and ratting out Brody.

What really stuck in Brody's craw was not the fact Sal had used him as a cat's paw. It was the fact that he was supposed to die in the blast along with Reed. There was no getting around it. Sal had told him to call him as soon as he had delivered the package to Reed. If Brody had followed Sal's instructions to the T, the cops would be scraping him off the walls along with Reed.

The Beverly Hills Police Department would be in charge of the investigation since the explosion had occurred on their turf, but Brody was sure they would be in touch with the LAPD, which was a much larger force and had more, and better, state-of-the-art equipment. Brody wouldn't be surprised if the LAPD took over the investigation, especially considering the involvement of a victim with the notoriety of Max Reed.

No expense would be spared by the government to find Reed's murderer. As well, the multibillion-dollar House of Max Reed would be turning up the heat on the cops to find their boss's killer.

The TV newscaster started reading tweets coming in from Hollywood A-list celebs expressing their condolences for Max Reed, even though he hadn't been officially pronounced dead yet. The tweets appeared as chyrons on her left as she read them from her teleprompter.

"Max Reed made me, tweeted the international movie star Shenandoah Little. Without his fashion I'd still be a ghetto girl.

"My condolences to Max Reed, an inspiration to us all, tweeted the next James Bond, Johnny Poldark.

"Max was a god, tweeted the supermodel Jennifer Marie Ashley. He will be sorely missed.

"I can't believe Max is gone. Tell me this is a nightmare, tweeted Reed's favorite supermodel Brigitte Jadot.

"Max was a mensch, tweeted his lawyer Burton T. Hall. The world won't be the same without him.

"And the list goes on," said the newscaster.

Anything for publicity, decided Brody, listening to the tweets from the rich and famous.

He rose up in bed as he caught sight of a squad car cruising along the boulevard in front of the motel. Had the cop spotted his Mini? wondered Brody, his heartbeat accelerating. Or was there even a BOLO out on him yet?

Brody bolted out of bed, darted to the window, and, hiding behind the vertical blinds, watched the black-and-white pass the motel and disappear into traffic. He couldn't take the chance that the cops weren't searching for him. He had to assume they were.

Brody left his room, retrieved his Mini, fired the engine, backed out of his space, and drove out of the parking lot.

He parked in a remote area of a public parking garage, slid out of his Mini, retrieved fake license tags and a screwdriver from the trunk, made sure no one was watching him and there were no surveillance cameras in the vicinity, and replaced the Mini's tags with the fakes.

He took the bus to a rental car agency and rented a black Toyota Prius, a ubiquitous car in West LA and its environs, using his shell-company credit card to pay for it.

The casually dressed twentysomething rental agent told him to drive safely and handed over the keys to Brody.

The next thing Brody had to do was find Sal. Sal had a lot of explaining to do.

Brody wondered if Sal even knew he was alive. Brody figured the guy thought he was dead, in which case Sal wouldn't be trying to hide from him, making Brody's job of finding him that much easier.

Chapter 11

The Beverly Hills Robbery-Homicide Division sent Lt. Ben Chowder to investigate the bombing of Reed's penthouse office.

In his early forties with a thick black walrus mustache, standing at five nine, Chowder had even features and piercing blue eyes. He wore a tan blazer, a turquoise necktie, and black trousers with knife-edge creases.

He entered Max Reed's lobby with three of his uniforms flanking him.

"Tell me when Macready of LAPD gets here," he told one of his men.

"I'm already here," said Macready, approaching Chowder from the guard's desk in black slacks and an unbuttoned brown blazer sans tie.

"You said you had information about the bombing here," said Chowder.

"I had a run-in with Reed at a photo shoot he was taking in LA."

"You think it has something to do with the explosion here?"

"I couldn't say, but he was a pain in the neck, and I could see how he might have a lot of enemies."

"Guys that would like to see him dead?"

"Including me."

Chowder did a double take. "He must've been a real prick to make you want to hate him at first sight."

Macready nodded yes.

The truth was, Macready didn't like Chowder and he didn't want Chowder getting the credit for solving the Reed case, which was an explosive case (in more ways than one) that was going to garner massive worldwide media interest. A case like this could make or break a cop's career. The name of the cop that solved the Reed murder would be forever on everybody's tongue. Macready wanted that cop's name to be his. He could write a book about it and make millions.

"Our initial investigations bear you out that it was murder," said Chowder. "Our explosives expert thinks C-4 was used on Reed's penthouse. In any case, it was a high explosive."

"No accident then."

"It was deliberate."

"I bet it was that Brody guy who delivered a package to Mr. Reed's office right before the explosion," said the guard, as Chowder and Macready approached his desk.

"You think he was carrying a bomb in the package?" Macready asked the guard.

"I wouldn't bet against it," answered the guard. "And he was acting suspicious."

"How so?"

"I told him to stay here and talk to the police. As soon as he heard me, he ran for his life. I couldn't catch up to him. There were too many people jamming the street and the sidewalks."

"Do you know his first name?"

The guard consulted his registration book. "Scott Brody."

"The name sounds familiar," said Macready. "Isn't he a PI in LA?"

"Never heard of him," said Chowder.

"Are you sure plastic explosives were used?"

"No. We'll probably have to call in the FBI's TEDAC, since this could be the work of terrorists. They like to use explosives."

TEDAC, Terrorist Explosive Device Analytical Center, decided Macready. They were world-renowned for their chops in their field.

"You really think it was terrorists that did this?" said Macready.

"I don't know what to think," said Chowder. "Maybe they were making some kind of left-wing political statement against capitalism when they blew up the richest fashion designer in the world. Workers of the world unite. You have nothing to lose but your chains. That kind of thing."

"Why not right-wing terrorists that don't like Reed's political views?"

"Was Reed a socialist?"

"I don't know anything about his political views. I don't follow the fashion world."

"All I know is, bombs are the weapon of choice for terrorists. You don't often hear of spouses killing each other with bombs."

"We could still be dealing with a maniac."

"Yeah. LA's loaded with them."

"Have any terrorists claimed credit for the bombing?"

"Not so far as I know."

"It wasn't terrorists," said the guard. "It was this Brody character. I'm telling you, this guy is hinky. I knew right away something was off with him. He's bad news."

Macready nodded yes. "We've had problems with him before. He thinks you spell law B-R-O-D-Y."

"Does he have any connections to terrorist organizations?" said Chowder.

"I don't know of any. That doesn't mean he didn't blow up Reed, though."

"Agreed. He could have done it on his own. But what's his motive?"

"He was carrying the bomb in a bowling bag," said the guard. "I remember it as clear as day."

"You saw the bomb in the bag?" said Macready.

"Uh—why no, I didn't actually see it. But it's obvious he had a bomb inside it."

"That's it, then," said Chowder. "I'll tell my men to look for traces of a bowling bag and test them for the presence of C-4 or any other high explosive that could have been used."

"They do that, we can nail Brody's ass," said Macready.

"We're still lacking motive."

"This is how I see it," said the guard, putting in his two cents. "Brody delivers the bomb to Reed, comes back downstairs where he knows he won't get blown up, and detonates the bomb with a signal from his cell phone."

"You seem to know a lot about police work," said Macready.

"I used to be on the force in San Diego," said the guard, smiling proudly.

"Did you see him use his cell phone right before the explosion took place?"

"Uh, no. I wasn't looking in his direction. But five will get you ten, that's how he did it."

"He's probably in LA by now. I'll put out a BOLO on him."

"Let's put a lid on it," said Chowder. "The media doesn't need to know about this yet. We don't want Brody to know he's a person of interest."

"He's more like a suspect, if you ask me."

"Again, what's his motive? Did he even know Reed?"

Macready shrugged, said nothing.

"We need to find out more about Mr. Max Reed," said Chowder.

"I'm telling you, it was Brody that killed him," said the guard. "The CCTV will bear me out. Watch the tape, and you'll see."

"I intend to do just that."

Chapter 12

Brody took the 10 eastbound and drove his rental to Sal's office on Spring Street in downtown LA. Sal was in for the surprise of his life, decided Brody. He couldn't wait to see the expression on Sal's face when he strolled into the guy's office all in one piece.

Brody parked his rental in an overpriced multilevel public parking garage.

Sal's office was in the back of a trattoria that he owned.

The tables in the restaurant had red and white checked tablecloths. The dining room was half full. The same could be said for the bar. Frank Sinatra was singing "My Way" over the speakers.

Brody approached the bartender, a beefy thirtysomething guy with a gleaming bald head and a lot of steel rings on his fingers that could double as brass knuckles when he had to assume the role of bouncer.

"Where's Sal?" said Brody.

"Who wants to know?"

"Is that any of your business?"

Brody didn't want to spoil the surprise of his visit to Sal by having the bartender announce his presence.

"Get lost," said the bartender, and commenced drying off a beer mug with a dishcloth.

"I have business with Sal. He's not gonna like it if you turn me away."

"Tough."

"I wish you had hair," said Brody, eyeballing the bartender's bald head.

"What?" said the bartender, puzzled, and scowling.

"If you had hair, I'd grab it right now and smash your face against the countertop."

"Oh, yeah?" said the bartender, jutting his square jaw at Brody.

Brody grabbed a beer bottle on the mahogany bar, smashed it against the bar, and thrust what was remaining in his hand toward the bartender's throat. The bartender's eyes widened as they took in the jagged glass poised inches away from his Adam's apple.

"Take me to Sal," said Brody. "Or . . ."

"Or what?"

"Or you don't want to know what I'm gonna do to your throat," said Brody, thrusting the broken beer bottle closer to the bartender's Adam's apple.

The bartender's face broke into a sweat.

"Take me to Sal," said Brody. "You won't get in trouble. Believe me, he wants to see me. He wants to know the truth."

The bartender had no idea what Brody was talking about. He didn't want a hole in his throat so he led Brody to the end of the bar. Brody continued to brandish the bottle near the bartender's throat as he walked along the front of the bar and the bartender walked along the back of it. They met at the end of the bar and headed to a door that led to a backroom.

The bartender knocked three times on the door, slow.

A signal, decided Brody. *Sal, you son of a bitch.*

"Come in," said a gravelly voice behind the door.

"You're a dead man when you come out of there," said the bartender under his breath, letting Brody into Sal's office.

"This guy wants to see you," the bartender told Sal, who was sitting behind his cluttered desk, a smoking cigar in his hand.

Sal's eyes bugged out of his head at the sight of Brody. The saliva-coated cigar fell out of Sal's hand onto the desktop.

"Want me to throw the jerk out?" said the bartender.

"Uh, no," said Sal, trying to recover from the shock of seeing Brody alive.

"All I want to do is talk," Brody told Sal.

"Sure, sure, come on in, Brody."

"I got questions for you, is all."

Brody removed the jagged bottle from the bartender's throat and strode toward Sal's desk, where he set down his punched glass admission ticket.

"You can go," Sal told the bartender.

"I'll be right outside, boss, with a .38 in my hand."

The bartender left and closed the door behind him.

Sal bolted to his feet, kicking his chair back behind him so hard it slammed against the wall.

"Why didn't you do what I told you to do?" he demanded, apoplectic.

"I'd be dead if I did. And you know it."

"You didn't follow my orders, so I'm not paying you the balance of the money I promised you."

"The cops are coming after me because you set me up. Are you happy with that?"

"This wouldn't have happened if you did what you were told."

"I'd be dead if I did what you told me and called you as soon as I delivered the package to Reed. You sent a signal via your cell phone probably and detonated the explosive in the bowling bag."

"I have no idea what you're talking about."

"Are you denying you blew up Max Reed?"

"I sure as hell am."

"Then how do you know I didn't call you as soon as I delivered the package to Reed? And why do you even care?"

"You didn't follow my orders. So I'm not paying you the balance of the money I promised you on completion of your assignment."

"I repeat," said Brody, exasperated. "How do you know I didn't call you as soon as I delivered the package?"

"Because I had a mole in Reed's office watching you."

Brody stood at a loss for words.

"I don't believe you," he said at last.

"I don't care what you believe. Just don't come here begging for more money."

"I didn't come here to do that," said Brody, calmly. "I came here to kill you for setting me up."

Chapter 13

Brody withdrew his SIG Sauer P365 from his ankle holster and trained the muzzle on Sal's face, which rearranged itself into a mask of fear.

"Put that down," said Sal. "You'll never get away with it. My boys'll blow you away the instant they hear a gunshot in here."

"Maybe I don't care what happens to me after you're dead."

"Oh, you care all right. Nobody wants to die."

Brody knew what Sal said about his men was true. If they heard a gunshot, he would never get out of here alive.

"I might let you live on one condition," said Brody, bluffing.

Sal retrieved his chair from the wall, plumped down on the cushion, feeling relaxed now, certain Brody wouldn't pull the trigger, blow him away, and commit suicide as a result. Sal went so far as to retrieve his smoking cigar from the desktop, raise the cigar to his mouth, and blow a smoke ring across his desktop, looking as contented and smug as the proverbial cat that ate the canary.

"Go ahead," said Sal. "Name your condition, if that'll make you feel better. I know it's bullshit. You're not gonna pull that trigger."

"Why did you send me to blow up Max Reed?"

"I didn't," said Sal, and took another enjoyable pull on his Havana Montecristo, sitting back in his chair.

Brody's eyes bugged out, his gun hand shaking. "Stop lying to me."

Sal looked concerned. "Don't blow a gasket, man. Get a grip. You don't want that piece going off."

"I've had it with your lies," said Brody, his face flushing. "Why did you have me kill Max Reed."

Sal felt the icy grip of fear clench his heart. Brody looked like he was capable of anything at this point.

Sal sat up straight in his chair, his expression serious, leveling with Brody.

"It wasn't me," said Sal.

"You're the one that hired me," spat Brody. "How could it not be you? Stop lying."

"Somebody hired me to hire you. I don't give a flying fuck about Max Reed. Some faggot fashion designer. You think I give a shit? I don't even have a tailor. Do I look like the Dapper Don?"

Brody decided Sal could be telling the truth. After all, the guy's life was on the line. He was staring down the barrel of a gun.

"Who hired you?" said Brody.

"I can't tell you," said Sal, and bit his cigar, grinding it, his jaw tense.

"Tell me or I'll kill you," said Brody, and pressed his SIG's muzzle against Sal's sweat-slick forehead.

"He'll kill me if I tell you."

"He'll never know you told me. What you tell me stays in this room."

Conflicted, Sal couldn't make up his mind what to do. "Promise?"

"You have my word I won't tell him you fingered him."

Mulling it over, Sal chewed the Montecristo between his teeth, his nerves taut.

"Rafe Calabrese," he said, barely audible.

"Who?"

"Rafe 'The Saint' Calabrese," said Sal, his face grim.

"The Mafia capo?"

Sal nodded, white-faced.

"Why did he hire you to kill Reed?" said Brody.

"He hired me to hire you to deliver the package to Reed. He didn't say anything about whacking anyone."

"Why did he want *me* to deliver the package?"

“It was my idea. I said you were dependable, because I’d hired you for other jobs.”

“Level with me.”

“I am.”

“I’m waiting.”

“You can wag that piece in my face all day. My answer’s the same. I knew you were dependable.”

Brody thought about it. “Not everything you say adds up.”

“Am I supposed to care what you think?”

“You said you didn’t know what was in the package.”

“So?”

“Then why were you so surprised to see me walk into your office a moment ago?”

Sal shifted uncomfortably in his seat. “I’m surprised whenever I see anyone not in the family in my office.”

“You looked like you saw a ghost when you saw me.”

“You’re exaggerating. You’re a bottom-feeding rent-a-cop. Why would I be scared of you?”

“Because you thought I’d been blown to smithereens with Reed.”

“Bullshit. You can’t read minds. You don’t know what I’m thinking or anyone else is thinking.”

Brody thought Sal was lying. Sal had wanted him to die in the explosion. So there would be no living link to incriminate him in Reed’s murder.

“Why did Calabrese hate Reed?” said Brody.

“Ask him.”

“I intend to. Where can I find him?”

“You’re out of luck. He’s in Vegas.”

None of it made any sense to Brody. He had never met Calabrese. Why did a Vegas capo want him dead? For that matter, why did the guy want Max Reed dead?

“Do you have a back door?” said Brody, scoping out Sal’s office, determined to avoid a confrontation with the bartender, who was armed with a .38.

"It's over there," said Sal, pointing with his thumb. "Not that it will do you any good."

"What do you mean?"

"I mean, you're dead, no matter what door you go out. Nobody pulls a gun on me and lives to tell about it."

"I never thought you'd double-cross me, Sal."

"Never trust anyone. You'll live longer." Sal paused. "Except in your case, it's too late. You pulled a piece on me. Nobody gets away with that. A brief, violent future awaits you."

"The same could be said for Rafe Calabrese."

"You don't want to tangle with Calabrese. That's the last guy you want to pick a fight with. If you live long enough to make it to Vegas. And that's debatable."

Brody cut across the office to the back door.

"I'm gonna check out your story with Calabrese," he said, drawing up at the door and turning to face Sal. "If he says you're lying about his involvement, I'll be back for you."

Sal snickered. "His enforcers will cut you down before you get within two feet of him."

"Like your bartender did for you?"

Sal glared at Brody.

Brody slipped through the doorway and barreled into the alley, SIG in hand in case one of Sal's goons gave chase. He pelted down the alley and emerged onto the sun-washed sidewalk that skirted the street where an MTA bus ground past him, belching black diesel fumes and emitting a deafening groan.

He saw sparks shoot off the concrete sidewalk two feet in front of him.

It was a bullet.

Somebody had fired a gun at him, though he hadn't heart the gunshot, which had been drowned out by the rackety bus. One of Sal's mechanics, figured Brody. Without the help of the noise of the gun report to locate the shooter, Brody couldn't tell which direction the bullet had come from. He couldn't tell from which angle the slug had struck the sidewalk. It had all happened too quickly.

Brody figured the shooter must be above him, since the bus was in front of him shielding him from the view of people on the other side of the street. Glancing upward, Brody couldn't make out any gun barrels aimed in his direction.

He couldn't stay here.

SIG in hand, he ducked into a nearby alley, hoping he was out of sight of the shooter.

He didn't hear a gunshot.

Approaching the road that skirted the alley he peered out at his surroundings. Office buildings, hair stylists, nail salons, and laundromats. Sandwiched between two beige office buildings was a bail bondsman's establishment with a yellow sign along the façade of the building that advertised he was open twenty-four hours.

Brody doubted the shooter was on the other side of the street. The guy must be firing from Sal's chophouse.

Brody had to retrieve his rental and beat it.

He holstered his SIG, took a couple of deep breaths, and belted out of the alley toward the parking garage that housed his rental. Bullets shattered windshields of cars parked along the side of the street as he hightailed it.

He jinked down the sidewalk, giving the shooter a more difficult target, bumping into pedestrians, knocking them over.

A stray bullet found the forehead of a roly-poly middle-aged woman waddling with thick varicose legs, her nylon stockings rolled down below her knees, who dropped dead in her tracks. Another woman screamed.

Brody dashed into the parking structure, clambered into his rental, reversed out of his space, sped to the exit, paid cash to the cashier, and peeled out of the structure.

Chapter 14

Megan Reed had just touched down in her British Airways flight from London Heathrow Airport when police contacted her. Max's twenty-year-old daughter Megan had slept during most of the eleven-hour flight, downing a Halcion to help her sleep when she had begun the trip to Los Angeles, even though she was exhausted to begin with from preparing the fall fashion line at Max Reed Enterprises' London branch.

She was still groggy from the pill as she was sitting in her first-class seat, a pillow behind her head, as her jet taxied down the tarmac to approach its disembarkation terminal when her cell phone chimed in her purse. Yawning, she blinked, produced her cell, and took the call.

"This is Lt. Ben Chowder of the Beverly Hills Police Department. Could I speak to Ms. Megan Reed?"

"Speaking," said Megan.

"I'm sorry to have to inform you that your father Max died in an explosion in his penthouse suite."

"Ohmigod," said Megan, becoming alert. "Can this be real? Who is this?"

"Lt. Ben Chowder."

"There must be some mistake," said Megan, straightening in her seat.

"No mistake. We confirmed his identity with his DNA we found at the bomb site."

"Bomb site?"

"Yes. An explosion killed him."

Megan sobbed. "I don't—I don't . . . This can't be true."

"I'm sorry for your loss."

"Don't I have to identify the body? I'm sure there's a mistake."

Chowder cleared his throat. "There's not really much left of him to identify. High explosives were used. The only way we can ID him is with his DNA we found at the scene of the blast."

"It must be someone else's DNA. You've obviously made a mistake."

"No mistake, ma'am. I'm sorry. We thought you should be the first to know as you are his only daughter. We haven't notified the media yet."

"He can't be dead," muttered Megan, at a loss. "He can't be dead."

A beautiful, svelte woman in her own right with her long white legs, her height of five nine, her striking blue eyes, and her chiseled cheekbones, Megan had done some catwalk modeling for her father, but had decided she was more interested in business management. It turned out she had a head for figures. And she liked being involved in management decisions.

"Did you say a bomb blew him up?" she said, as Chowder's words were sinking in.

"Yes. It was deliberate. It wasn't an accidental explosion."

"Who would do such a thing?"

"We'd like you to come down to the station and talk to us about that. Or we could meet you at your office or residence."

"I guess. But I don't see how I can help."

"Where are you?"

"I'm on a jet from London. We just landed."

"We need to know if your father had any enemies who might do something like this."

"I need time to gather myself. I'm not used to . . . to . . . ," she said, sobbing.

"I understand. When I lost my mother, it was the end of the world for me. But I recovered. The old adage is true—time heals all wounds."

"My father is—was—divorced."

"Did he have any enemies?"

Megan laughed despite herself. "Virtually every fashion designer in the business hated him."

"Really? Why?"

"He was too successful. Too good. Success breeds envy."

"What about your mother? Was it a messy divorce? How does she feel about your father?"

"I should tell you, my father's been married three times. I'm the product of his second marriage to Brittany Skarsgaard, one of his most famous fashion models. His messiest breakup was with his most recent wife. I don't blame him for breaking with her. Even I hated her."

"A lot of animosity there?"

"Definitely."

"What is her name?"

"Rachel Bean."

"As in LL Bean?"

"The spelling's the same, if that's what you're asking—"

Megan broke down, as if the full realization of her father's death had finally struck her like a Mac truck at full throttle. She dropped her cell phone and couldn't continue.

"Ms. Reed?" said Chowder, concerned he might have overdone it with his interrogation. "Are you all right?"

No answer.

"I'll be in touch later," said Chowder, and hung up.

Megan stared at the jet's bulkhead in front of her seeing nothing.

Chapter 15

Brody heard on his car radio that Megan Reed had just landed in LA and was heading for the scene of her father's murder in Beverly Hills.

Brody wanted to talk to her. He wanted to find out if she knew why the Mafia capo Rafe Calabrese would want to murder her father.

Brody knew it was a dangerous move to return to the scene of the crime, especially since he was a suspect in the case, though he didn't hear on the radio whether the cops had put a BOLO out on him yet. It was only a matter of time before they did, he decided. It was even possible they had already issued a BOLO without informing the media, who the cops feared might spook him into going into hiding.

Brody had to keep a low profile as he drove to Reed's office in Beverly Hills. Cops were still milling around the crime scene, but the teeming crowds of rubberneckers had for the most part dispersed now that the fire had been put out in the building.

Max Reed Enterprises was still open for business, and its employees had returned to the building after the Beverly Hills Fire Department had declared the fire a hundred percent contained and had determined there was no severe structural damage beneath the penthouse floor, which was the only floor that was now closed to the public because it was the scene of an active crime investigation.

Brody parked in a public parking garage several blocks from Max Reed Enterprises, got out of his rental, and walked to the office building. He hoped he had arrived here before Megan Reed, though it wasn't a very long drive from LAX to Beverly Hills. She could be in the building already.

Sporting sunglasses and a ball cap as he stood at a magazine kiosk flipping through *GQ*, he caught sight of a late-model black Porsche Cayenne GTS tooling down Wilshire and pulling up in front of Max Reed Enterprises beside a line of patrol cars that were parked along the curb.

Brody didn't see any cops nearby, so they must have been in the penthouse combing through the evidence left behind by the explosion.

Two burly, cropped bodyguards clad in black suits piled out of the Cayenne onto the sidewalk. One of them opened the back door for Megan Reed, who climbed out onto the sidewalk. Her jeans and her pair of running shoes both cost over five hundred dollars and were designed by her father's company.

Trying to hide her identity with oversized black designer shades that cloaked her eyes, she made for the plate-glass doors, two bodyguards in tow.

Brody replaced his magazine in the kiosk rack and approached Max Reed Enterprises.

As nobody attempted to stop him, he entered the building's lobby.

Megan Reed and her bodyguards were standing at the guard's station talking to the security guard.

Brody glanced apprehensively at the guard and relaxed when he realized it was a different guard than the one that had permitted him to deliver the bowling bag to Max Reed and had chased him down Wilshire. The current guard was a ponytailed blonde pushing thirty with stern features and a dimpled chin.

Brody produced his cell phone and, studying its screen, edged closer to Megan Reed.

"Ms. Reed, could I speak to you about your father?" he said, studying his cell.

The two bodyguards hastened to converge on Brody, their faces clouding with menace.

"Who are you?" said Megan, eyeballing Brody and gesturing to her bodyguards to stand down for a moment.

"I'm a private detective," said Brody. "Do you know who killed your father?"

"He had a lot of enemies."

"Could you make an educated guess?"

"Anyone of them could've done this."

"What about Rafe Calabrese?"

"Who?"

"The mobster Rafe Calabrese."

"Oh no. My father didn't deal with mobsters. He made his money the hard way. He worked for it."

"He didn't ever have to borrow money, say from Calabrese?"

"If he borrowed money, it would be from a bank. He wouldn't go to a mobster. Are you trying to insinuate something?" she said, cocking her eyebrow with suspicion.

"My client wants to find out who killed your father. It's very important to him."

"It's very important to me, too. More so, I believe."

"Calabrese is a loan shark. Sending a bomb to someone who defaulted on a payment is right up his alley. This has all the earmarks of a mob hit."

"I never heard of him. And I doubt my father ever did either. Our company is raking in billions of dollars a year. I resent your insinuations that we would be in such a poor position financially that he would need to seek money from a mafioso."

"Could Calabrese have some other motive for wanting your father dead?"

"I have no idea," said Megan, losing her patience. "I'm busy now. I need to inspect my father's office." She turned to the lobby guard sitting behind his desk, ensconced behind an array of video screens. "I need to see my father's office. Which elevator do I take?"

"None of the elevators are going to the penthouse anymore," said the guard. "The blast took out the penthouse elevators."

"Then how do I get there? This is an emergency. I'm Megan Reed. My father's Max Reed. I need to examine documents in his office."

"I know who you are, Ms. Reed, and I'm sorry for your loss."

"Thank you."

"You can take the elevator to the floor beneath the penthouse, Ms. Reed. Then you'll have to take the stairwell to reach the penthouse. There are police on the penthouse floor. You'll have to get their permission to use the stairs to reach the office."

"Fine."

"One more question," said Brody.

"No more questions," said Megan.

Her two bodyguards glowered at Brody and formed a wall between him and Megan.

"Does Rafe Calabrese own stock in Max Reed Enterprises?" said Brody.

Megan ignored him and angled across the lobby to the bank of elevators.

Brody retreated. He didn't come here to cause a commotion and attract the attention of the cops.

He saw a tall, swarthy cop strut into the lobby from the street.

Brody studied his cell phone and turned away to avoid the cop's gaze.

Megan's answers hadn't been much help. He needed a motive for Rafe Calabrese to murder Max Reed.

Maybe one of Max's employees could be more helpful in that regard. Could there be a dirty side to Reed's business that he kept shielded from his daughter?

Chapter 16

In his office at LAPD headquarters in downtown LA, Macready was studying preliminary forensic reports of the blast at Max Reed Enterprises. All of the reports agreed that the explosion was no accident.

The LAPD's crack bomb unit had used an ion mobility spectrometer, a handheld chemical detection device, to identify residues left in Reed's office.

Suspecting a terrorist bombing, the FBI's TEDAC got involved in the bomb analysis, despite the fact that no terrorist organization had as yet claimed credit for the explosion.

Macready was expecting a call from TEDAC any minute, which was why he was skimming through a preliminary report, stuffed with incomprehensible technobabble that they had already sent him via an encrypted e-mail. He hoped their phone call would clear everything up.

His cell phone lying on his desktop blotter chimed.

Relieved at being freed from reading any more mind-numbing techno jargon, he snatched up his cell phone and took the call.

"Lt. Macready here."

"This is Special Agent Rieber at TEDAC. I understand you're handling the investigation of Max Reed's murder."

"That's right. We have more manpower and better equipment. Our mayor pulled some strings, and we've taken over the investigation from the Beverly Hills PD. The media are all over this, and we can't afford to make any mistakes."

"We have preliminary analyses ready for you, Lieutenant, as to what type of bomb was used at Reed's penthouse office."

"Shoot," said Macready, champing at the bit.

"By way of explanation, let me say blast residues can be analyzed by infrared spectroscopy, gas chromatography/mass spectrometry, energy dispersive X-ray analysis, and Raman spectroscopy—"

Macready cleared his throat. He shook his head in confusion. Rieber sounded more confusing than the e-mail TEDAC had sent him.

"In layman's terms, if you don't mind," said Macready. "I don't have a degree in physics."

"As I was saying, to ID C-4 we can use thin-layer chromatography, infrared spectroscopy, and X-ray crystallography—"

"Does it matter I have no idea what you're talking about?"

"If you'd stop interrupting me, Lieutenant," said Rieber with not a little hostility. "Thank you. Small particles of C-4 can be ID'd by mixing them with thymol crystals and drops of sulfuric acid. This is what we did with some of the particles gathered at the blast scene."

"You're welcome."

"Let me remind you, this is a federal investigation because of a suspected terrorist attack, Lieutenant. You do not have jurisdiction at the blast scene."

"What the hell did you find out?"

Rieber sniffed. "I'm not required to tell you anything."

Macready rolled his eyes. "What explosive was used?"

"We concocted the aforesaid mixture and it turned red when we added drops of ethyl alcohol to it."

"And?"

"It means the particles we recovered from the blast scene were C-4."

"The C-4 was in the bowling bag," said Macready with earnest.

"Correct."

"Do you know how it was detonated?"

"A thyristor, or semiconductor."

"How was it triggered? A timer? Do you know?"

"We believe the IED was triggered by radio waves transmitted via a cell phone to another cell phone attached to the IED."

Macready nodded. "Do you think terrorists were involved?"

"The bomb doesn't have the trademarks of any terrorist faction we know of. Of course, it could be a new faction. I should note, it wasn't just C-4 that did the damage."

"Huh?"

"The bomber packed ball bearings into the plastic explosive to achieve maximum damage to the office."

Macready grimaced. "I suspected as much, unfortunately."

"The bomber didn't want the victim to survive the attack."

"He got his wish. We're dealing with a sick individual."

"We can't rule out a terrorist attack."

"From what I've found out about Reed, he wasn't politically motivated. He was financially motivated. He wanted to succeed at all costs."

"People have been known to profit off of their political ties. It happens all the time. Money and politics go hand in hand. Look at all the lobbyists in Washington."

"This is a tough case, because so many people hated the guy—business associates and rivals alike. He seemed to feed off others' animosity."

"How do you know the bomber's not someone from PETA who hated him because he used real leather in his fashions?" said Rieber.

"I don't know anything about what materials he used in his fashions. But I'm not ruling out anyone as a suspect."

"Reed might even have been working for the CIA. The guy traveled all over the world to flog his threads. The agency would love to get their hooks into someone like that."

"CIA? You're kidding," said Macready.

"Not at all."

"Have you found out where the C-4 was purchased? Was it military-grade explosives? Could it be from the CIA?"

"We're working on it."

"Keep me posted."

Macready terminated the call.

Chapter 17

Brody drove his rental back to his motel room and got on his laptop to find out everything he could about Max Reed Enterprises.

Dubbed "The Vulgarian" by the tabloids, Max Reed would go to any length to sell his fashion, no matter how tasteless and exploitative his designs. Other designers hated him for his dearth of artistic talent. They claimed he not only debased their profession by monetizing it in such a blatant skeevy manner but stole designs from rival designers, and instead of improving on them, made them worse with his execrable fashion sense.

Reading Reed's Wikipedia biography, Brody couldn't find anybody in the article who had anything good to say about Reed. The guy was known for belittling everyone, not only his rivals, but his employees as well, and to belittle them in public. His browbeaten employees catered to his every whim to avoid being disparaged in front of their fellow workers.

Brody saw no mention of Rafe Calabrese in Max Reed's bio. Whatever relationship the two had, if any, was private.

Brody searched the Max Reed Enterprises website and found a list of employees and their contact numbers.

He called Reed's photographer Johnny Wikowski, who was famous in his own right.

"This is Scott Brody PI. Do you know who might have killed Max Reed?"

"Is that any of your business?"

"I thought you might like to talk about him, get things off your chest."

"Don't get me started."

"I'm getting the impression you know who had motive to kill Reed."

"A couple thousand people," said Wikowski.

Brody let it sink in. "Which one of them do you think killed him?"

"It wasn't me. I did hate him, like everybody else, but I was planning to quit. I don't get rid of my enemies by blowing them up. My motto is, Stay Away from Assholes. Life's too short. Reed was an asshole, and I was getting ready to walk."

"But you didn't walk. You continued working for him."

"I got bills to pay. What I'm saying is, it was only a matter of time before I walked."

"Do you have any leading suspects?"

"Somebody with knowledge of high explosives, I guess. Somebody knew what they were doing. Did you see the wreck that bomb made of his penthouse office?" Wikowski whistled.

"The killer must've really hated Reed."

"You're darn tootin' they did. 'Bomb voyage, Max Reed,'" said Wikowski, chuckling.

"You sound glad to see him gone."

"He might've been a fashion genius—and that's debatable. What isn't debatable is, he made a ton of dough at it. He was a genius at coining money. But if anyone deserved to be murdered, he did."

"Where were you when the bomb blew up?"

"No way are you gonna pin that on me. I was on the penthouse floor when it happened. I'm lucky I wasn't in his office, or I'd be splattered all over his walls like him."

"Do you know if Rafe Calabrese had anything to do with Reed?"

"Never heard of him. He sounds like the second baseman for the Dodgers."

"He's a Vegas mobster."

"You don't say. Well, Max *did* spend a lot of time in Vegas promoting his fashion lines. Mobsters always want the best of everything for their mistresses, and everybody knows Vegas is a great place to promote fashion."

"Thanks for your help."

"Did you hear the latest? And this could only happen to someone like Max Reed."

"What are you talking about?"

"Someone on eBay is auctioning the tattered shirt worn by Max when he got blown up. The shirt is splattered with his blood and DNA, according to the description on eBay."

"Are you kidding?" said Brody, repelled by the idea.

"Nope. And it's getting bids. Up to a thousand dollars the last I heard. They're showing a picture of the shirt on eBay and everything. Can you believe it?"

"It doesn't sound legal. Isn't that evidence in Reed's murder investigation?"

Wikowski changed the subject. "Look, don't tell anyone what I told you. I'll deny every word of it. I might never work again in this business if people found out what I really thought of Max."

"No problem."

"You're good at getting people to talk, aren't you?"

"I found out a long time ago people love talking about two things: themselves and their relationships with famous people."

To keep himself from spilling any more secrets Wikowski hung up before Brody finished his sentence.

Brody returned to researching Max Reed on the Internet.

He checked out eBay and saw the shirt Wikowski had mentioned. The bidding had gone up to seven thousand dollars and was climbing every second. A photo of a ragged, blood-splattered white button-down shirt appeared to the left of the bidding results.

Whose bright idea had that been? Brody wondered. Max Reed would probably have done the same thing with his shirt if he was still alive. Was he still alive? Was this all an over-the-top, outrageous publicity stunt dreamed up by Reed for promotion of his brand to ramp up sales?

But the cops had ID'd Reed's DNA in his penthouse office. Or so the news said. And he himself had delivered the bomb to Reed.

Brody could see Max Reed Enterprises' sales going through the roof as the result of his murder. Murders grabbed front-page headlines. What better publicity could you get than headlines in the major newspapers, as well as 24/7 news coverage on TV?

And now Reed's DNA-stained shirt being auctioned on eBay ginned up even more publicity. The sales of Max Reed fashions should skyrocket.

Bidding for the shirt was already up to eight thousand dollars.

Everything that was happening now in regards to his savvy business sense just went to prove Max Reed was right in his belief that tawdry, outrageous hype racked up huge sales.

If Reed was alive today, he would be sporting a grin as wide as a Cheshire cat's.

Brody received news update pushes from the *Los Angeles Times* on his cell phone, which was lying next to his laptop on his motel desk. The latest update flashed on his screen.

Scott Brody Wanted for Max Reed's Murder.

Chapter 18

Brody knew it was bound to happen sooner or later. He was the only suspect in Max Reed's murder. After all, Brody had delivered the bomb to Reed, which the lobby guard had brought to the attention of the cops, and, no doubt, CCTV footage taken in the building confirmed the guard's accusations.

Brody racked his brains trying to figure out his next move.

He debated whether to turn himself in to the cops and tell them the truth—that he had delivered the bowling bag to Reed, but had no idea of its contents. He had to clear his name.

He had read the *Times* article following the push update on his cell phone. The article said Lt. Macready of the LAPD had taken over the investigation of the bombing.

Standing up and pacing around the motel room, Brody used a burner app on his cell phone to call Macready.

The LAPD receptionist put him through to Macready.

"Macready here."

"This is Scott Brody."

Macready didn't answer right away, trying to figure out if it was a prank call.

"Lieutenant?" said Brody. "Are you there?"

"Is this on the level?"

"It is."

"Do you want to turn yourself in for the murder of Max Reed? The DA might cut you slack if you come in of your own accord and come clean."

"I didn't do it."

"That won't fly, Brody. We have videotape and a guard's testimony putting you at the scene of the crime when the explosion went off."

"I admit I was there and I delivered the package to Reed—"

"That's as good as a confession for me. Come down to the station."

"Let me finish. I delivered the bowling bag, but I had no idea what was inside it."

"You expect me to believe that cock-and-bull story?"

"It's the truth."

"Do you take me for a fool? Why would you deliver a package to someone without knowing what's in it?"

"Somebody paid me to deliver it. He didn't tell me what was inside."

Macready laughed coarsely. "Oh, sure. And you didn't even ask him what's inside?"

"Why should I? It was just a job. He paid me to do it. I did it."

"Then you're a fucking idiot, and you deserve to be convicted of murder. Pleading ignorance won't get you off."

"How was I supposed to know there was a bomb in the package?"

"Tell it to the judge." Macready paused. "Just for the sake of argument, suppose I believe you. Who hired you?"

Brody hemmed and hawed. "I'll tell you if you promise not to arrest me."

"No deal. I don't cut deals with murderers."

"He said he didn't know a bomb was in the package either."

Macready unleashed a caustic laugh. "Of course. Even the guy that hires you to deliver the package has no idea what's in it. That makes sense. In a pig's eye."

"That's what he told me. He said somebody else hired him to hire me."

"You're jerking my chain. The warrant for your arrest stands. Turn yourself in and you'll get a better deal."

"No can do."

"You'll never get away with it. You haven't got a prayer. We'll nail you sooner or later. Do yourself a favor and turn yourself in."

Brody terminated the call.

He couldn't say he was surprised Macready had turned down his offer. The only way Brody could clear his name was by finding the murderer. He had to get Calabrese to talk. The problem was, Brody couldn't find any motive for Calabrese to want to whack Max Reed. Brody couldn't find any connection between the two. He would have to get the info, the missing piece of the puzzle, out of Calabrese in person. To beard the lion in his den in Vegas.

Chapter 19

Her hair in a platinum blonde perm, Bambi Patterson, Max Reed's twenty-eight-year-old mistress, lay on her bed in a filmy black negligee in her fifty-thousand-dollar-a-month penthouse apartment in West Hollywood.

She was sobbing as she inspected her collection of dildos that lay in front of her on her bed. Every time she saw them with her limpid grey eyes she thought of Max. He had bought them for her. She liked the pink one with rabbit ears on it because of the sensation it gave her, but her favorite was the flesh-colored Wi-Fi one. Max had given it to her as a present and had said she could use it when he was out of town. When she called him and told him she had it inside her, he could activate its switch on an app on his cell phone and start it vibrating.

Those days were gone.

Nobody would ever activate that switch again, she decided with regret. Max was dead.

Tears rolled down her cheeks.

Sure, there was a big age difference between them, but what did that matter? What was wrong with May-December relationships? Nothing that she could see.

Preoccupied with the memories stirred by her looking at the Wi-Fi dildo, she didn't notice a figure in a black trench coat and fedora descend on a rope from the roof, release the rope, and land in the dark on the balcony floor with a soft thud outside her room.

There was no question that Max could be a condescending creep, she decided. He treated everyone like dirt, even her once in a while, but he had the right, as she saw it, because he was better than everyone else. He had made more money than just about everyone in a cutthroat business and owned an empire that spanned the globe. How many others could say the same?

Very few, was the answer.

Wearing a black balaclava, gripping a purple plastic batonlike object, the figure in the trench coat slid open the French window and stole into Bambi's apartment, the lights of Los Angeles blinking in the sable velour of night beyond the balcony.

Bambi was still lost in her thoughts and didn't notice.

Trench Coat whistled toward her. Two notes.

Bambi looked up. Her eyes widened in fear.

Trench Coat tossed a purple, foot-long dildo at her and dove behind a sofa in front of the window.

Startled, Bambi caught the dildo in a reflex motion preventing it from striking her face.

It blew up on contact with her hand, tore her face off, and made mincemeat of her carotid artery, which spouted bright, oxygen-rich blood to the ceiling painting it with vermilion splotches that would rival any artwork by Jackson Pollock.

Trench Coat jumped up from behind the sofa and, knowing security guards would be descending on Bambi's room lickety-split, belted to the balcony, snagged the rope dangling from the roof, shimmied up the rope, mounted the roof, pulled up the rope, dashed across the roof's tar paper and gravel to the stairwell, and raced down the steps, ears ringing from the ferocity of the blast.

Chapter 20

Early the next day, a hot cup of coffee on his desk in front of him, Chowder sat in his Beverly Hills PD office and called Macready.

"We had another one," said Chowder.

"Another what?" said Macready.

"Another bombing. And it has to do with Max Reed."

"I'm listening."

"Actually it didn't take place on my turf. It happened in West Hollywood. Their police chief knows about Max Reed's murder in Beverly Hills, so he contacted me."

"Why didn't he contact me?"

"I know him. Maybe that's why," said Chowder, and took a pull on his coffee.

"What's the deal?"

"Somebody blew up Bambi Patterson."

"Bambi Patterson? Am I supposed to know who that is?"

"Apparently it's an open secret in the fashion world that she was Max Reed's mistress, or one of them, anyway."

"I see. You think it's the same murderer?"

"The same MO. How many perps use bombs to whack people? And then there's the fact Reed and Patterson were lovers. You gotta figure it's the same murderer."

"Do you know the kind of explosive used? Was it C-4?"

"I informed TEDAC of the bombing. They're investigating it now. When they tell me, I'll tell you."

"What do your forensic people say?"

"They know this much. It was no accident. She didn't have anything in her penthouse suite that would go off accidentally. No gas range or anything. Everything was electric." Chowder took another pull on his coffee and screwed up his face. "Do you know where I can get a decent cup of java?"

"That's all they know?" said Macready, impatiently.

"They say—but they're not a hundred per cent sure—it was an exploding dildo that did her in."

There was a pause on the line.

"Did I hear you right?" said Macready.

"They found pieces of a dildo all over Patterson's bedroom."

"Jesus."

"Her room was filled with dildos, actually. They were all over the place."

"Dildos?"

"Yeah."

"Could this be a sex crime?"

"The ME said she wasn't raped."

"Maybe the bomber was sending some kind of message to Patterson by using a sex toy as a murder weapon."

"Max Reed's jealous lover?" said Chowder, sniffing his coffee as if something had crawled into it and died.

"But it's not a crime of passion. The perp went to the trouble of constructing a bomb and hiding it inside a dildo. That's premeditation."

"Still, using a dildo as a weapon suggests some kind of sexual messaging."

"I'm doing research on the guy," said Macready. "Rumors have it that he had more than one lover. We have to figure it could be the same perp that blew Reed up. Similar MO, and all that."

"Great minds think alike. That's why I got in touch with you about it first thing."

"But then how does Brody fit in?"

"Brody?"

"The guy that delivered the bomb to Max Reed."

"Oh, yeah. How do we know he didn't take out Patterson, too?"

"He remains our prime suspect in Reed's murder. Let's put him at the top of the list of suspects in Patterson's murder."

"What kind of motive are we talking about with Brody?"

"He called me—"

"Called you?" said Chowder in surprise. "Doesn't he know he's a suspect in Reed's murder?"

"He knows. He told me somebody hired him to deliver the bomb to Reed."

"SOP—criminals saying they were set up," said Chowder, downplaying the significance of Brody's words.

"I'll send some men over to West Hollywood to help with the Patterson investigation. I'm with you. I figure these two bombings are related. Did you give this to the media yet?"

"I couldn't keep them away," said Chowder, drinking his coffee and staring at the rest of it with distaste. "They know something's up. I didn't give them the name of the victim, though, because West Hollywood hasn't contacted her next of kin yet."

"Another high-profile bombing having to do with Max Reed isn't gonna escape media attention. It's gonna be a three-ring circus for those jackals."

"Thank God, it'll be in West Hollywood, not here."

"I can hear the tabloids howling now. 'Fashion Icon's Mistress Murdered by Exploding Dildo.'"

Chapter 21

In his motel room Brody saw the TV news about Bambi Patterson's murder.

Her death by high explosive had to be connected to Max Reed's, decided Brody. He wondered if Calabrese had anything to do with Patterson's death. Was somebody else related to Max Reed going to die in an explosion? What was Calabrese's motive? Maybe Patterson's death had nothing to do with Calabrese. Maybe a jealous lover was wreaking revenge on the House of Max Reed, doing away with Reed and his many lovers.

Brody decided it was time to question Calabrese. Brody had to get to him in person. He might even have to put a gun to Calabrese's head to get the capo to talk.

Brody decided to drive to Vegas. The cops would have the airports staked out, searching for him since a warrant had been issued for his arrest.

He took his laptop with him, climbed into his rental, backed out of the motel parking lot, got on the I-10 eastbound, and took the I-15 north straight through the desert toward Vegas. When he hit Palm Springs, he pulled over at a diner to stretch and grab a bite to eat.

Sitting at a stool at the counter, he ordered a charbroiled burger, fries, and a Coke. The diner smelled of burning grease. It was a good burger, had good flavor, but the fries were too greasy.

An hour out of Palm Springs, riding the I-15, he hit trouble.

The passenger inside a black Mercedes G-Wagen opened fire on him with a pistol from behind.

Brody flinched in the driver's seat when a bullet spiderwebbed his rear window.

Sal Andrasi's men must have tracked him somehow, decided Brody.

He scoped the rearview mirror.

The G-Wagen was gaining ground on him. The passenger was sticking his head out his open window and drawing a bead on Brody.

Brody pulled off the road onto the shoulder and kept driving onto the desert, kicking up a rooster tail of dust behind him. The G-Wagen gave chase. Slugs continued to fly in Brody's direction, despite the cloud of dirt swirling around Brody's rental.

He must have slipped up somewhere and revealed his whereabouts to Andrasi's soldiers, decided Brody. Too late to do anything about it now. All he could hope to do was to avoid capture or a violent death at the hands of the pursuing triggermen.

He figured the G-Wagen could handle the uneven dirt terrain better than his rental.

He decided to give them something to think about. He swung into a U-turn, fishtailing in the dirt, withdrew his SIG P365 from his ankle holster, aimed out his open window, and fired at the approaching G-Wagen's driver's-side window, hoping to hit the driver and bring the G-Wagen to a halt.

The G-Wagen kept coming.

Its passenger returned fire.

Brody saw the hit man with a man bun sticking his head out the window to fire at Brody, who also had his head outside his window and was firing back. Man Bun's shot struck Brody's driver's-side mirror, shattering it. Brody's shot hit its target. A pink mist spurted out of the back of Man Bun's head along with a shard from his occipital bone. Man Bun slumped, hanging his head out the window down the side of his door.

The G-Wagen kept coming at Brody.

Brody fired at the driver's-side windshield. His bullet didn't penetrate the glass. The G-Wagen's windshield must be bulletproof, he decided. He couldn't whack the driver unless the guy stuck his head outside the window. He looked like he had other ideas—like ramming Brody's rental. If the entire G-

Wagen was bulletproof, it could do some serious damage to Brody's vehicle in a head-on collision.

Instead of discharging a shot, Brody floored the gas pedal. His rental lurched out of the way of the fast-closing G-Wagen, spinning its wheels furiously, spewing out dirt at the G-Wagen.

The G-Wagen clipped the rental's left rear fender as it blew past Brody. Brody felt the jolt to his car, but kept on driving in the opposite direction. The G-Wagen's driver slammed on his brakes, executed a U-turn, and sped after Brody.

Brody wondered if the G-Wagen was equipped with run-flat tires. There was only one way to find out. He veered to his left and fired out his window at the G-Wagen's driver's-side front tire. The G-Wagen kept coming. Brody loosed three shots then stepped on the gas to get out of the way of the thundering, hard-charging, G-Wagen.

The G-Wagen swerved around, fishtailing, kicking up an arching sheet of dirt. The right rear wheel crashed into a dirt hummock, which rocked the G-Wagen with its high center of gravity and precipitated a rollover.

Wearing a black wife beater the incensed driver clambered out of the upended vehicle, stuck his torso out of his open window, raised his meaty tattooed arms, and, face sweaty, emptied a MAC-10 machine pistol's magazine of full metal jacket .45 ACP rounds at Brody's retreating rental.

Brody pushed his rental to its limit, considering himself lucky the G-Wagen had rolled over, and made a beeline for the interstate.

Maybe he should have whacked out Sal Andrasi in the wiseguy's downtown office when he had the chance, decided Brody. As long as Sal was alive he would keep sending enforcers after him. He could still take Sal out after he dealt with Calabrese. Calabrese was the brains of the outfit. Sal was just carrying out orders when he had hired Brody—according to Sal, anyway. And Calabrese, being the boss, was the one that owed Brody the rest of his money for delivering the bomb to Max Reed.

Brody didn't like the idea of collecting money for killing someone, but that wasn't why he was collecting it. He was collecting it because he had delivered the package as he had been hired to do.

Chapter 22

Vegas was over a hundred degrees when he drove onto the strip a little before six p.m. toward Caesar's Palace near the center, where most of the action was.

He parked in Caesar's parking lot and walked to the sprawling casino. He had heard on the street that Calabrese spent most of his time at Caesar's and owned a penthouse suite there.

His back sore from the long drive, he was stunned to see a large ad in the capacious casino hallway for a Max Reed fashion show at Caesar's Palace. The show was taking place in the convention center even now featuring Reed's new TED fall line of clothing, accessories, and furniture.

He couldn't escape Reed, decided Brody. The guy's fashion was everywhere, as well as his name.

Brody wandered through the palatial hotel/casino complex, not certain how he would go about tracking down Calabrese.

He eventually made his way to the sportsbook, where hundreds of TVs mounted on the wall were showing live sports events so gamblers could place their wagers on the games. He approached a tall, thirtysomething blonde wearing oversized sunglasses who was watching one of the TV screens in a knee-length turquoise and green dress from behind a waist-high wall that skirted a bar just beyond the betting trenches occupied by the gamblers.

She was engrossed in watching the TV screen she had selected out of the scores of screens that were broadcasting live events. Following the direction of her gaze, he realized she was watching a fashion show being broadcast live.

"Is that the Max Reed fashion show?" he asked her.

She turned toward him. "Why, yes, it is."

Supermodels were strutting down the runway in front of the TV cameras as rap music blasted in the background. Clad in dresses for the most part either black or silver, the models were entering the runway from the open mouth of a giant skull with the letters T-E-D perched on its cranium.

“Is that what it looks like?” he said, eyeballing the skull.

“It’s a giant replica of the serial killer Ted Bundy’s skull.”

“Kinda sick if you ask me.”

“Believe me, Max Reed will make millions off his TED fall fashion line.”

The camera zoomed in on members of the audience sitting in the front-row seats that bordered the runway as they ogled the haughty models strutting their stuff with their high cheekbones and creamy complexions. A lot of the models wore black sheer bodysuits. Others wore halter tops and bandeaus. On their feet they wore stilettos and white patent leather go-go boots that clomped down the runway.

The camera focused on three members in the audience. Brody recognized all of them. Rafe Calabrese was sitting next to the supermodel Brigitte Jadot and Max Reed’s personal assistant Preston Wells.

Taken aback, Brody stared at the trio, trying to wrap his head around the significance of his discovery.

“Isn’t that the mobster Rafe Calabrese?” he said.

The dress-clad woman beside him fiddled with her hoop earring, watching the TV screen.

“Haven’t you heard?” she said. “Calabrese and Brigitte Jadot are an item. It’s in all the tabloids.”

“Really? I thought she was seeing Max Reed.”

“I think that was before she met Calabrese.”

“He doesn’t seem the type to go to fashion shows.”

“If his girlfriend wants to go, I’m sure he’s happy to take her.”

“Of course.”

“Is she into serial killer fashion?”

“Everybody is, if Max Reed designed it.”

“Why is Preston Wells with them?”

“Who?”

"Preston Wells. The guy sitting on the other side of Brigitte."

The woman shook her head. "Don't know him."

"He's Max Reed's right-hand man."

"I don't know anything about him," she said, as if Wells was a nobody.

Interesting, decided Brody. Calabrese knew both Jadot and Wells. Could Calabrese have had Reed blown up because he was jealous the guy was Jadot's ex-boyfriend? Or maybe Jadot was still seeing Max when he died.

"Is that show live?" said Brody.

"Yep. It's at the convention center."

"I'd like to go and check it out. Is it open to the public?"

"Sure—if you got fifty thousand dollars on you."

Brody jacked up his eyebrows. "For a fashion show?"

"A front-row seat near the runway is going for fifty thousand bucks. It's not just about seeing the show. It's about being seen at the show. This is the House of Max Reed we're talking about."

"Is he *that* good?"

"He's *that* famous and *that* rich. It doesn't matter how good you are in the fashion business. It matters if your fashions sell." She pointed at the TV screen. "You see those two sitting in the first row?"

"Yeah."

"They're the honchos at Dior and Gucci. And look at that guy a couple seats away"—she pointed at the TV screen—"he's from YSL."

"I thought they hated Reed's guts. Why would they go to one of his shows?"

"You know what they say. Keep your friends close, your enemies closer. If Dior and Gucci see something they like, they'll probably steal it and make it part of their fall lineups."

"How do you know so much about this?"

"I've done gigs at Max Reed as a model. I've worked at Dior and Gucci, too. Freelancing."

"I want to talk to Preston Wells. How do I get into the show to see him?"

Really he wanted to talk to Calabrese, but he didn't want to tell a stranger. After all, Calabrese was a well-known mobster. She might remember him if he told her he wanted to talk to a mafioso. Brody didn't want her to remember him.

"Maybe you can catch him when the show's over and he leaves," she said.

"Do you know when it ends?"

"It should be soon." She glanced at her wristwatch. "Maybe a half hour or so."

When a model strutted down the televised runway in a black nightgown with an ax buried in her skull, Brody decided it was time to leave.

"Is that an ax sticking out of her head?" he said.

"They don't call Reed 'The Vulgarian' for nothing. The model is supposed to be one of Ted Bundy's victims. The ax is a movie prop, of course." She searched Brody's face. "Are you into fashion?"

"I'm on a job," he said.

The woman returned to watching the fashion show.

Brody idled away from the sportsbook and made his way to Caesar's convention center.

Chapter 23

Brody found himself at the back of the convention center. He wandered toward a room where he heard women talking. He cracked the door and peeked inside.

A brunette and a redhead model were sitting in front of a vanity, bare-chested, fixing their makeup in the mirror.

"One of my friends told me about a girl she knows whose mouth got stuck open," said the redhead. "She couldn't close it."

"How awful," said the brunette, applying eyeshade as she stared into the mirror. "How'd she do that?"

"She was doing oral with her boyfriend, and her mouth got stuck open."

"How'd that happen?"

"I guess he's big or something. She couldn't close her mouth."

"How could she eat?"

"She couldn't. She had to go to the doctor."

"How could she tell anyone what was wrong with her?"

"She had to text people. The doctor said her jaw was dislocated. He had to reattach it."

"That's what she gets for biting off more than she can chew," said a bony six-foot-tall peroxide blonde sitting a couple seats away staring in the mirror and wiping off her makeup.

"Shut up, you anorexic skank," said the redhead, picked up her hairbrush from the vanity, and flung it at the blonde. "Everybody knows you gave blowjobs to an entire football team."

The hairbrush hit the blonde in her hair and stuck there.

"Shit," she said, yanking the brush out of her hair and hurling it back at the redhead, missing her by a foot.

"Excuse me, ladies," said Brody, opening the door. "Do you know where I can find Rafe Calabrese?"

The redhead saw Brody in the mirror and screamed.

Brody closed the door and split.

A security guard spotted him and sprinted toward him.

"I'm lost," said Brody.

The security guard launched himself at Brody, tackled him, and floored him.

"No pervs allowed back here," said the guard, straddling Brody's chest and pinning him to the floor.

"I'm lost," said Brody. "I'm trying to find Rafe Calabrese."

"Sure. And I'm Mother Teresa."

"It's true."

"Then what were you doing in the models' dressing room?"

"I thought they might know where I can find him."

"Tell you what. I'll take you to him. And you're gonna regret you ever asked."

The guard hauled Brody to his feet.

In his early thirties, with watery eyes, the guard was spoiling for a fight, looking forward to beating up on a guy that was bigger than him.

Brody was going to fight back, but decided against it, figuring the guard would take him to Calabrese, which was what he wanted. Brody wasn't sure how else he could meet Calabrese. In the end, this might be the best way.

The guard produced a plastic zip tie.

"You don't need that," said Brody. "I'm not gonna resist."

The guard sniggered. He secured the zip tie around Brody's wrists behind his back. He grabbed Brody's arm and marched him down the hall away from the dressing room.

This wasn't how Brody had planned to meet Calabrese. Brody wasn't going to have any leverage over Calabrese with his wrists bound behind his back. Brody figured he was going to need leverage to get Calabrese to spill the beans about why he hired Brody to kill Max Reed.

Brody wondered if Sal had told Calabrese Brody knew it was Calabrese that had set him up to take the fall for killing

Max Reed. If Calabrese did know, Brody figured Calabrese could have already put out a contract on him.

Chapter 24

The audience at the convention center was starting to file out as the guard ushered Brody toward Calabrese, Brigitte Jadot, Preston Wells, and cronies of Calabrese, who were standing near their chairs, preparing to leave.

Fortysomething, wearing a black blazer that was snug around his paunch, Calabrese eyed the guard with humorless black eyes.

"Boss, I caught this perv breaking into the models' dressing room," the guard told Calabrese.

"Why bring him to me?" said Calabrese, annoyed.

"He said he's looking for you."

"For what?"

"We should talk in private," Brody told Calabrese.

"Why do I want to talk to you?" said Calabrese.

"What I have to say would make your guests feel uncomfortable. You get my drift?"

"You telling me what to do?"

"Just giving you advice."

"Shove your advice."

"You two can talk here," said Preston Wells. "I have to leave, anyway."

He made to leave.

"Me, too," said Brigitte.

"Stay where you are," said Calabrese. "Don't let this clown spoil our party."

"We have work to do on fall's fashion lineup," said Wells.

"Who takes over Max Reed Enterprises with Reed dead?" said Brody.

"I do. That's why I need to get back to work. The job needs my full attention. You see those guys over there?" Wells nodded at two men and a woman milling nearby. "They're from Prada, YSL, and Tom Ford. They'd do anything to see our TED line fall flat on its face. They're over there figuring out ways to sabotage it. That's why I need to get back to work. We gotta fight those guys off every minute of the day. Look at them. Plotting to sink our line. You know what they want?"

"No."

"They want to see me fail, to see the TED line fail, to see Max Reed Enterprises fail. Schadenfreude is what it's all about with those hyenas."

"Then why did you invite them?"

"It's the nature of the business. They invite our company to their fashion shows, too. It's important they be seen here by the media. It validates our brand."

"You must know a lot of movers and shakers."

"You bet I do. Getting rich is the key to opening doors in America."

"You sound like Max," said Brigitte.

"I'm not as bloodthirsty as him. He was like a shark prowling through the water searching for more prey."

"His personality must have rubbed off on you."

"I could do worse. He was a narcissistic heel, but he was a great businessman and had good contacts."

"And you know Rafe Calabrese," said Brody.

"I know a lot of people. What's the point of your questions? Who are you?"

"I'm a private detective."

Calabrese exchanged looks with the security guard.

Brody decided not to reveal his name, since it could jeopardize his health. He didn't think Calabrese knew him by sight, or he would be dead by now.

"What are you nosing around here for?" said Calabrese.

"I'm investigating Max Reed's murder."

"Then waste somebody else's time. It took place in Beverly Hills, not Vegas."

"The evidence leads me here."

"What evidence? There's no evidence. You got nothing."

"This is what I came to talk to you about."

"Then talk."

"If you insist. You owe me money."

Calabrese spat out a laugh. "I never saw you before. You're full of shit."

"I delivered a package for you."

"You're living in cloud-cuckoo-land." Calabrese turned to his guard. "Kick this loser outa here."

"My pleasure, boss," said the guard, snagged one of Brody's bound arms, and marched him away.

"I don't ever want to see that guy again."

"You haven't heard the last of me," Brody told Calabrese.

"Shut up," said the guard, and launched a fist into Brody's jaw.

Brody's head jerked back. He winced in pain.

The guard shoved him. Brody stumbled forward, all but losing his balance.

The guard caught up to him and jabbed his knuckles into Brody's kidney. Grimacing, Brody groaned.

The guard guided Brody through the emptying convention center into a large hallway, opened a side door that gave onto a deserted alley, and shoved Brody outside. Brody slewed around to confront him, but he had no means to defend himself with his wrists bound behind his back.

The guard connected with a haymaker to Brody's jaw that sent Brody reeling. Brody fell onto the asphalt on his stomach and rolled onto his back so he could keep the guard in view.

The guard kicked Brody in the slats three times. Brody squirmed in agony.

"Stay away from Mr. Calabrese," said the guard. "Or you're gonna end up dead."

The guard stalked toward Brody, grabbed his head with two hands, and, sneering, smashed the back of Brody's skull against the asphalt, two times. Dazed, Brody shook his head, his eyes unfocused. He thought he might black out any second.

The guard rolled him onto his stomach, released the zip tie from Brody's wrists, and retreated into the hallway. Brody rolled onto his back to keep his face off the asphalt.

He blinked his eyes, trying to focus them, the sun throbbing above him. His ribs burned. He didn't know if any of them were fractured. His head woozy, he sat up, feeling pain in his side. He wondered if he had a concussion. The back of his skull could be cracked for all he knew.

He struggled to his feet, continuing to have difficulty focusing his eyes.

He lurched toward the door, which became two doors and three doors that kept moving. He reached toward one of the moving doorknobs, but it wasn't there.

If he could just keep his balance, he was sure he could latch onto one of the elusive doorknobs.

He withdrew his hand. Maybe it wasn't such a good idea to go back into the resort in his condition. The guard could be waiting for him on the other side of the door, ready to coldcock him.

Brody backed away from the door and shambled down the alley to the traffic-jammed Las Vegas Boulevard. The entrance to the alley was coming into focus. He could make out cars and buses trundling along the boulevard that ran perpendicular to the alley.

Maybe he was going to be OK.

Maybe he was going to throw up.

He emptied the contents of his stomach on the side of the alley. The nauseating acrid smell made him want to throw up again.

Concussion?

He didn't have time for a concussion. He had a job to do, a murder to solve—if he didn't want to go to jail for it. Calabrese owed him money. And an explanation.

Hunched over, Brody kept trudging toward the noisy boulevard, wondering how he was going to get close to Calabrese, who didn't want to talk to him and kept himself surrounded with guards and Mafia soldiers.

Chapter 25

Brody reached Las Vegas Boulevard and started to feel better. Maybe he just needed fresh air.

He could see clearly now. Nothing was swimming around like before, except for thermals rising from the overheated traffic on the tarmac. A twentysomething girl wearing a sequined G-string, a gilt halter top, and a crown of feathers sprouting from the top of her head strutted by him with a smile.

"Want a picture, dear?" she said, smiling, her full lips glistening vermilion in the sun.

He shook his head no and found his way back to Caesar's casino.

He had to figure out some way to meet Calabrese without being intercepted by Calabrese's goons.

Brody wandered through the scads of slot machines and ended up at the sportsbook again.

He spotted Wells watching the TV screens broadcasting sports games.

"Where can I find Calabrese?" said Brody.

Wells turned to look at Brody in surprise. "You again."

"Is he here at the sportsbook," said Brody, scoping out the other spectators.

"No. He's with Brigitte. They said something about Joe's Steak House." Wells returned his gaze to one of the TV screens. "Can you believe it?"

"What?" said Brody, following Wells's gaze.

Wells wasn't watching football or basketball. He was watching a TV screen with a blood-mottled shirt on it.

"I said, 'Can you believe it?'" said Wells. "Max Reed's shirt on eBay is going for $20,000 and climbing."

"Why are they showing it on TV here?"

"The gamblers are betting on how high the bidding will go. The one who guesses closest to the final bid wins the pot."

"That's ridiculous. And sick. The guy just got killed, and they're already auctioning off his clothes."

"Max would be laughing his fool head off if he was here now. He always thought the worst of people, and they're proving him right on eBay," said Wells with a crooked smile.

"Who is auctioning that shirt?"

Wells produced his smartphone and checked the shirt's listing on eBay. "Georgina Spelvin."

"That's a fake name used by actors when they want to hide their real names."

"How did someone get their hands on that shirt? That's what I want to know."

"Especially if it's evidence in a murder investigation."

"People will sell anything if the price is right. That's what Max always used to say. Don't get me wrong. I never liked him. He *was* a bastard, but he was rarely wrong. All the more reason to hate him."

"Hate him enough to kill him?" said Brody.

"Looks that way."

Brody searched Wells's face.

"You mean me?" said Wells in shock. "You think *I* did it? Ha!"

"You said you hated him."

"Everyone hated him. Not just me."

"Did he associate with Calabrese?"

"I'm sure he bumped into him several times. Calabrese attends fashion shows with Brigitte."

"Did Reed have financial problems?"

Wells laughed. "He had too much money. *That* was his financial problem—if you want to call it that. Most people would welcome a problem like that."

"He never had to borrow money?"

Wells did a double take. "You mean, from Calabrese? Is that what you're getting at?" he said, squinting at Brody. "I can't see Max borrowing money from Calabrese."

"They were on good terms?"

"What's your definition of 'good terms'? I'm sure they bumped into each other at parties. I don't know of anything more than that."

"Wasn't Brigitte Max's girlfriend before she took up with Calabrese?"

"So? What's your point?"

"Maybe there was animosity between Max and Calabrese because of that."

"Are you implying Calabrese had something to do with Max's murder?"

"Well?" Brody paused. "Who do you think killed Max?"

"I have no idea. He had a slew of enemies, though. I do know that. Mostly in the fashion world. Where there's envy, there's hate."

Brody mulled it over. "Do you know if Max gambled."

"He liked coming to Vegas. I don't remember seeing him gamble. He spent every waking hour promoting himself. Even when he put on a show in Vegas."

"What about you? Do you like to gamble?"

"I play the slots."

"Do you ever win?"

Wells shook his head. "Nobody wins in Vegas. Gambling losses pay for the palatial casinos that line the strip."

"Do you have gambling debts?"

"Why is that any of your business?" said Wells, confronting Brody.

"Just wondering."

"Maybe it's time for you to leave."

"What about Reed's vacations? Did he vacation here in Vegas?"

"The guy rarely took vacations. It was all about work with him. Constant self-promotion. Constantly telling the world how great he was."

"How'd he do that?"

"On social media. Gimmicky stuff, like he'd show pictures of himself flying in his private jet on Instagram with the caption about how high he was above everybody else in fashion. His ego was titanic. He had to constantly feed it any way he could. On Facebook, Instagram, Twitter, whatever."

"He must've taken some time off."

"I'm here to tell you he didn't. Even his 'vacations'"—Wells made air quotes—"were more about self-promotion than about vacationing. On his vacations to exotic locations, the Greek Isles or whatever, he and his girlfriends wore his fashions like his sunglasses and bathing suits—and, of course, their pictures ended up on Instagram and Facebook."

"Nobody can go 24/7 without taking a rest. They'd burn out."

"He even showed pictures of himself on Instagram sleeping in his brand of pajamas. He promoted himself even as he slept."

"No," said Brody in disbelief.

"You think I'm exaggerating, but I'm not. The guy was a workaholic, and then some. Working every angle he could to milk every drop of publicity for himself and his brand." Wells's eyes widened as they took in the TV screen showing Reed's blood-splattered shirt. "Look at that. It's now going for thirty grand. Unbelievable."

"Why did Calabrese hate him? You don't hate someone just because they're a workaholic."

"What gave you the idea Calabrese hated Max?" said Wells, facing Brody.

"I have my reasons," said Brody, wincing at the pain in his lower ribs.

"Are you all right?"

"Something I ate."

"Everybody hated Max," said Wells, as if to himself.

A couple of broken ribs never stopped anybody, decided Brody. And they might not be broken, maybe only bruised. Cold comfort. Nothing changed the fact they hurt like a bastard.

"I gotta get back to work," said Wells. "The show can't run itself."

He left the sportsbook, glancing fitfully over his shoulder at the TV screen showing Max Reed's shirt on eBay, as football and basketball games played on the surrounding screens, with gamblers' eyes glued to all of them.

The bid on eBay for Reed's blood-splattered shirt flashed up to fifty thousand dollars.

Chapter 26

"Can you believe somebody putting Max's shirt on eBay for auction?" said a woman's voice over Brody's shoulder.

He turned around to see a thirtyish Hispanic woman with shoulder-length brunette hair standing behind him watching Reed's shirt being auctioned on TV. She had heart-shaped lips and large brown eyes highlighted with eyeshadow and mascara.

"Did you know him?" said Brody.

"Unfortunately."

"Were you at the fashion show in the convention center?"

"Yeah. I'm a makeup artist for the models."

"How interesting. I'm a PI. I'm trying to find out why someone would murder Max Reed."

"That's easy. Because they hated him."

"Does that include you?"

"He gave me a hard time. He was into body shaming. If you weren't a perfectly shaped model, he dissed you. Not just me. All of the women who worked for him."

"You could always quit."

She heaved a sigh. "He paid well. Very well. A lot of people will put up with anything if the price is right."

"And what is your name?"

"Debbie Hernandez. Look at that. Somebody's just bid 75K on Max's bloody shirt. What kind of sicko wants a bloodstained shirt so bad they'll pony up 75K?"

"Do you have any idea who put the shirt on eBay?"

"None. You ask a lot of questions."

"I'm trying to find out who killed Max and why."

"I hate to admit this, but the world is a better place without Max Reed in it."

"A lot of people share your opinion." Brody paused a beat. "Do you know if there was bad blood between Max and Rafe Calabrese?"

"I didn't even know they knew each other. You should talk to the models about Max."

"Why?"

"He would invite them to parties at his mansion with tables of cocaine and all sorts of drugs near the pool. They say some bad stuff went on at those parties."

"What kind of bad stuff?"

Debbie lowered her voice. "They shot torture porn movies of models when they were on drugs. Some of the movies were pretty sick, I hear."

"You weren't there?"

Debbie shook her head no. "He only invited models and big shots to his bashes. Another reason to hate him."

"Did they sell these movies?"

"I don't know what they did with them. I only know I overheard models in the dressing room talking about these sleazy parties. Girls getting their brains fucked out on film. Pardon my French."

"Did you ever see one of these movies?"

"I wouldn't watch one if someone offered it to me for free," she said, pulling a face. "I'm not into BDSM."

"Did any of the models ever file charges against him?"

"Not that I know of. They were too afraid of him and all his power."

"If they were drugged and forced to perform in these films, they could press charges against him."

"Maybe one of them decided to take the law into her own hands when she sent Max a bomb."

"Did any of the models mysteriously vanish?"

"What do you mean?" said Debbie, rucking her forehead with bafflement.

"Did any of them act in snuff films?"

"What are snuff films?"

"Actors are killed on film. For real. They're not acting."

"Do they do sick stuff like that?"

Brody nodded yes, face grim. "There's a black-market audience for those types of movies, and money to be made on them."

"I wouldn't put anything past Max Reed. It makes you wonder how a guy so sick could become so filthy rich."

"Money has nothing to do with morality. The drug cartel kingpins prove that every day."

Debbie shrugged. "What can you do?"

"Could Calabrese have had anything to do with these torture pornos the models were forced to take part in?"

"I don't recall his name being mentioned. The models were recruited at Max's mansion in Beverly Hills. I remember hearing one of the models say that much."

"I'm thinking Calabrese and the Mafia could be involved in the distribution of these pornos. The Mafia is known for making and distributing porn. They were the ones that made *Deep Throat*."

"I have no idea," said Debbie, looking anxious. "I need to get back to work."

"Wait a second. Could I have your phone number, in case I want to contact you about this?"

She shrugged and gave it to him. "No cops, though. I'm not talking to any cops about this. I'll deny everything. I don't want to lose my job," she added, looking scared.

"I don't work for the cops. I'm not talking to them."

"Keep my name out of this. I don't want them coming after me."

"Them? Who is 'them?'

Looking suspiciously around her to see if anyone was watching them, Debbie lowered her voice.

"Nobody is allowed to say anything bad about the company," she said. "They'd can me in a New York minute if they heard what I just told you about those films."

"Who are 'they'?"

"Spies. Everyone spies on everyone at Reed's. They get promotions if they can expose someone badmouthing the company or Max Reed."

She looked genuinely terrified, decided Brody.

"Do you know where I can find Calabrese?" he said.

"Brigitte and him are eating at Joe's Steak House on the first floor."

Debbie took one last look at Reed's shirt on TV, shook her head in disbelief, and bustled away.

Brody didn't have any evidence connecting Calabrese to Max Reed, other than they had the same girlfriend at different times. Brody had a lot of possible motives for Calabrese to murder Reed, but no evidence supporting any of them. Maybe Reed had a degenerate gambling habit and borrowed money from Calabrese that he never paid back. Maybe Reed and Calabrese produced torture pornos together using Reed's models as actors. Maybe this, maybe that. Nothing but maybes.

He headed for Joe's Steak House.

Chapter 27

Calabrese was sitting at a table on the indoor patio of the steak house across from Brigitte Jadot when he noticed Brody standing behind a large fluted marble column watching him. Brody ducked behind the column when he caught sight of Calabrese eyeballing him.

"That son of a bitch is stalking me," said Calabrese.

"Who?" said Brigitte, putting down her glass of Sancerre and swinging around in her chair to look in the same direction as Calabrese.

"That PI."

"He has no life," she said, facing Calabrese and lifting her wine glass again.

"He won't have any when Vito gets through with him."

"What?"

Calabrese motioned to Vito, a heavyset guy in his thirties wearing a navy blue blazer and black slacks, his loud button-down shirt open at the neck, chatting with the black-suited, smiling maître d'. Vito broke away from the maître d' and approached Calabrese.

"What's up, boss?"

"There's a peeping Tom over there spying on us, Vito. Bring him over here."

"No problem," said Vito, cracked the knuckles on his massive hand, collected two mobsters at another table, and headed out of the patio.

Brody watched them approach him.

"The boss wants to talk to you," said Vito.

"It's about time," said Brody.

"There's no reason to get snarky," said Vito, and buried his fist in Brody's solar plexus.

Gasping, Brody doubled over, his ribs acting up on him again as a result of the impact's blow.

The two goons with Vito snagged Brody's arms and hauled him toward the steak house to meet Calabrese.

Menu in hand, the maître d' looked concerned as Vito and his goons dragged Brody onto the patio.

"You got something to say to me, Peeping Tom?" said Calabrese.

"Where's the rest of the money you owe me?" said Brody, straightening up.

"I don't owe you jack shit."

"I delivered your package for you."

"You're nuts. Package? What package?"

"You know what I'm talking about."

"I know you're nuts. You're delusional."

"What did you want Max Reed killed for?"

"You're talking bullshit."

"You hired Sal Andrasi to hire me to deliver your bomb to Max Reed."

Calabrese stared at Brody. "I don't do shit like that. The Gambinos do that kind of crap. You know what they call me?"

Brody stared back at Calabrese.

"They call me 'The Saint,'" said Calabrese. "You wanna know why? Because I never been convicted of anything in my entire life. Not even a ticket for jaywalking. You heard of John Gotti? They called him the Teflon Don because the feebs could never convict him of anything. But Gotti did time. Sammy the Bull ratted him out. I never did time. Not once. I never been inside the joint. I'm cleaner than Caesar's wife."

"It doesn't mean you're innocent. It just means they haven't caught you yet."

Calabrese grabbed Brody's ear and slammed Brody's face into the bowl of fried calamari set in front of him.

"Do you have something to say?" said Calabrese, lifting Brody's face out of the calamari.

"Why did you try to whack me out in Reed's office?" said Brody, sauce running down his cheeks.

Brody hoped Calabrese was having fun. The guy would live to regret this, decided Brody, bridling his smoldering anger.

Calabrese guffawed. “If I wanted you whacked out, you’d be dead. I never set foot in that guy’s office.”

“I want the rest of the money you owe me.”

Calabrese shoved Brody’s head away from him in disgust. “Get away from me. You got it all mixed up. I don’t owe nobody money. They owe me. I own everybody in this town.”

“You owe me a quarter of a million bucks. I’m not leaving here without it.”

“You clown,” said Calabrese, laughing. “You’ll leave here whenever I say you’ll leave.”

“I want my money. And I want you to confess on TV that you’re the one that blew up Max Reed.”

“Do you think I care what you want? You’re a nobody. A bottom feeder. And you’re spoiling my appetite. Get outa here.”

“Not before you pay me my money.”

“Get this bum outa here, Vito. Take him to the warehouse and tell him what’s what.”

“Get him,” Vito told his two cohorts. “Pat him down.”

One of the goons found Brody’s SIG P365 and disarmed him.

“Figures,” said Calabrese, picking up on the SIG.

The two goons latched onto Brody’s arms and dragged him off the patio. Brody tried to break free, but his ribs continued to burn, limiting his movements.

“The creep gave me gas,” said Calabrese, getting to his feet, massaging his stomach.

“I didn’t have my dessert yet,” said Brigitte, remaining in her seat.

“That’s all right, dear,” said Calabrese, smiling. “Take your time. Meet me later tonight at my penthouse. I’ll send a limo for you.”

Calabrese and Vito headed out of Joe’s.

Chapter 28

One of the goons pulled a piece out of his blazer, flashed it in front of Brody's face, and put it back. Brody got the idea.

"Get moving," said the goon pushing thirty, who had slicked back black hair and a pockmarked complexion.

His shorter pal, thickset with a barrel chest, led the way toward Caesar's exit.

When they left the air-conditioned resort, the Vegas heat overpowered them.

"I'm gonna enjoy putting the wood to this bum, Ralph," said the thickset goon, his face starting to sweat in the dry heat.

"He'll wish he never laid eyes on us, Paulie," said Ralph, snickering.

"Why did Calabrese want Max Reed dead?" said Brody.

"Who gave you permission to talk?" said Ralph, squeezed Brody's arm, and drew his pistol.

"You're not gonna shoot me in broad daylight."

"Wanna bet your life on it?"

Chattering pedestrians approached them on the sidewalk. Ralph hid his piece.

In the distance Brody could see the valet entrance to Caesar's Palace, where a white stretch limo pulled up and disgorged its occupants. He picked up on Calabrese strutting out of the casino making for his black Caddy, which was parked near the entrance.

"There's the boss," said Paulie.

"Why doesn't he let you ride with him?" said Brody.

"Shut your mouth."

"The only car you're gonna be riding is a hearse," said Ralph.

Calabrese opened his Caddy's door, climbed into the driver's seat, and pulled the door shut.

Ten seconds later the Caddy exploded.

The Caddy jumped a foot in the air, belching flames and clouds of black smoke that billowed over the other cars arriving and leaving the U-shaped passenger loading area. Several women near the casino entrance screamed as they watched flames engulf the Caddy.

"Jesus," said Paulie.

He sprinted toward the burning car over three hundred feet away.

Others near the entrance tried to rescue Calabrese from the flaming wreckage. Holding their hands in front of their faces, they retreated, driven back by the overwhelming heat. Every square inch of the Caddy was awash with hungry flames devouring it.

When Paulie reached the Caddy, his face sweaty, he made a beeline for the driver's-side door and in desperation tried to open it. He thought he could make out Calabrese's charred face through the driver's-side window, his head bowed forward in his seat, but it was difficult to see because of the smoke swirling in the car's interior and the jagged flames lashing the headliner.

Paulie howled in pain as he touched the Caddy's white-hot steel door handle. He jerked his burnt hand away, shaking it, grimacing. The Caddy's flames leaping into the sky, he backed away, coughing on the smoke.

"Where's the fire department?" he cried.

Two casino security guards ran through the plate-glass doors at the entrance, carrying fire extinguishers. They commenced spraying the burning car with little effect.

"We need firemen," said Paulie.

"They're coming," said one of the security guards, continuing to spray the Caddy.

"Get the boss out. He's in the driver's seat."

The guards circled the blazing car to focus their attention on the driver's side. They trained the fire extinguishers on the door.

Paulie dashed to the driver's-side window and with his elbow tried repeatedly to bash in the glass. However, the glass was bulletproof to protect Calabrese from an ambush and didn't break.

His face blackened with soot, one of his arms blown off leaving only a stump, barely able to move, Calabrese turned his head toward Paulie and begged for help, smoke unfurling around his haggard face.

Feeling lightheaded from breathing smoke, Paulie started to back away from the Caddy.

The Caddy exploded again, as the fuel tank burst. The force of the blast hurled Paulie and the security guards sprawling on their backs on the blacktop.

Ralph's eyes bugged out at the second explosion.

A fire engine's siren keened down Las Vegas Boulevard.

Brody used the distractions to plant his fist in Ralph's jaw, sending Ralph windmilling backwards. Ralph's spine slammed the sidewalk. Brody kicked Ralph in the temple, knocking him senseless, withdrew his confiscated SIG from Ralph's waistband, and wedged it inside his own.

Brody sprinted full-tilt away from the burning Caddy, hoping he would soon be out of Paulie's eyesight before Paulie knew what was going on. Paulie was still preoccupied with Calabrese's flaming deathbed.

Wincing from his sore ribs, sweating in the afternoon desert heat, Brody kept running till he crossed the boulevard to the Margaritaville Restaurant.

He slowed down and caught his breath.

The sidewalk was chock-a-block with showgirls and cowboys clad in G-stings and little else interspersed with sightseeing vacationers. Brody merged into the lot of them, hoping to disappear in the mob of humanity.

He didn't see Paulie or Ralph following him. Maybe they didn't care about him now since Calabrese, who had issued them their orders to take care of him, had just been ousted as capo.

Brody figured Calabrese had been killed in the car bombing. He didn't see how Calabrese could have survived. The Caddy's bulletproof glass and steel couldn't keep out the voracious flames that leapt through the blast's gaping hole in the chassis.

Brody was in a quandary. How could he find out why Calabrese used him to whack out Max Reed? Did the answer die with Calabrese?

But who had blown up Calabrese? And why? Did it have anything to do with Reed's murder? Or was it the usual mob warfare that flared up in Vegas now and then? Probably another gangland rub out. The Mafia were always busy whacking each other out, saving the cops the trouble of busting them.

Brody figured his sojourn in Vegas was coming to an end.

The only lead he had was the possible implication of Max Reed in the shooting of torture porn snuff films, according to Debbie Hernandez, if indeed the films existed. The films could link Reed to the Mafia and to Calabrese. Calabrese and Reed could have had a falling-out over the films, giving Calabrese motive to blow Reed to smithereens.

Brody needed to look into the films. These types of films appealed to unsavory elements in society who might try to whack out an enemy with a bomb.

He needed a mole to burrow its way into the underground filmmaking market—an actress, or a woman pretending to be an actress.

He decided to get in touch with a fellow private detective he had worked with before. Tess Hardwick.

Chapter 29

Brody entered Margaritaville, sat at a wooden table on the patio overlooking the boulevard, and ordered a tropical fruit margarita from a twentyish waitress whose arms were covered in tattoos. A white life preserver hung on the wall that skirted the patio. He kept sneaking glances toward Caesar's Palace to see if Paulie or Ralph was headed his way.

Jimmy Buffett music sounded through the restaurant's loudspeakers.

Brody took a pull on his margarita, produced his cell, and called Tess.

"Hello. Tess Hardwick here. I am open for business."

"Good," said Brody. "I need your help."

"Who is this?"

"Scott Brody."

"Ah. The iconic lone wolf himself. And you're asking me for help?" she said with disbelief.

Boisterous customers were chatting around him. Brody didn't think any of them could hear him on the phone. If they could, they showed no interest.

"I'm investigating a murder that could involve torture porn snuff films," said Brody. "And I need someone to infiltrate that racket."

"Why don't you infiltrate it yourself?"

"I need someone to get inside by posing as an actress. Those rackets don't go around recruiting men. They recruit women. They tend to hire models from what I hear of them."

"Say I agree, what do you want me to find out after I'm recruited?"

"I want to find out if Max Reed's murder had anything to do with the making of these films."

"Reed, the fashion mogul?"

"That's him."

"He died in an explosion the last I heard."

"It was no accident. It was C-4. I'm trying to find out who did him."

"Where are you? I hear a lot of voices talking."

"I'm in Vegas at Margaritaville."

"You want me to infiltrate in Vegas?"

"No. Hollywood. Or the Valley. Wherever they shoot snuff films. Most pornos are shot in the Valley these days, I hear. I wouldn't discount Hollywood, though."

"Would I be working for your client, whoever hired you to find Reed's killer?"

"You'd be working for me. The cops think I took out Reed."

Silence.

"And did you?" she said.

Brody rolled his eyes. "What do you think?"

"All I know about you is, you're unpleasant to work with. The Tyler Keogh case if you remember."

"Because you kept getting in my way in that case. This time we'll be working together."

"A leopard can't change his spots. You'll be difficult to work with, as before."

"I'm not asking you to be my friend. I'm asking you to help me with a case, and I'll pay your usual rates."

Tess paused.

"I'll think about it," she said at length.

"I'm not gonna kid you. This case will be dangerous. Snuff filmmakers are murderers. They may claim they're artists, but they're committing cold-blooded murder to create their art."

"You want me to pretend to be an actor?"

"They're constantly in search of new talent. The big problem with their business is they can't use the same actress more than once."

"You want me to play a lamb going to slaughter."

A drunken middle-aged overweight blonde started laughing her head off at a nearby table, sloshing her turquoise drink with a paper umbrella on the wooden tabletop.

"It's not funny," said Tess.

"That wasn't me," said Brody. "I'm not gonna sugarcoat this. You'll be setting yourself up to be wasted."

"I don't see how these snuff films tie in with Reed's murder."

Brody lowered his voice. "Rafe Calabrese had Reed whacked. I'm trying to discover his motive. It could have to do with black-market films. Otherwise, I don't see why he would want Reed wasted."

"So how do we contact these degenerate filmmakers so I can audition for them?" she said.

"We need to talk to Reed's models to find out if they know anything about the films. Maybe some of them have been approached to star in them."

"Want my help for that?"

"Good idea. The models are probably more likely to open up to another woman than to me about something like that."

Brody tensed when he made out Ralph at the end of the block on the other side of the boulevard striding down the sidewalk along with a mob of pedestrians milling toward Margaritaville, his head bobbing among them swiveling to and fro surveilling the strip in search of Brody.

"Damn," muttered Brody.

"What's wrong?" said Tess.

"I gotta run," he said, put away his cell, tossed a twenty on the tabletop, and ducked out of the restaurant.

Chapter 30

Clad in a pinstripe suit, Megan Reed was sitting in her office on the floor directly beneath Max Reed's ruined penthouse office at Max Reed Enterprises perusing a document on her desktop.

Edvard Munch's "Scream" hung on the wall behind her. In front of her desk sat her lawyer Burton T. Hall, Esq., middle-aged with a prominent nose and wearing a bespoke navy blue suit with a powder blue pocket square. He patted his belly contentedly as though he had just eaten.

"Are you sure this is gonna hold up in court?" said Megan.

"Positive," said Hall, adjusting his glasses. "It's ironclad."

"You as my lawyer guarantee it?"

"I do."

"Will Wells fight it? If he can't win, what's the point?"

"He doesn't want to lose control of Max Reed Enterprises. Of course, he's gonna fight it—even if he's doomed to lose."

Megan looked up from the document and gazed at him. "Would you be willing to bet your life on it?"

The way she was looking at Hall unnerved him. He shifted in his seat. Not that he had anything to fear. He knew Max's will would hold up in court. It was just that her eyes . . . They were probing him like knives.

"Of course," he said. "I've reread the will several times. He appoints you as his successor to his business. It's lucky you found the will."

"I don't believe in luck. I'm a determined woman."

"I don't doubt that."

"What right did Preston Wells have to assume control after Dad's death?"

"Wells was second-in-command. He thought that made him boss with Max gone."

"He must not know about the will."

"Why would he? It wasn't public knowledge that Max had drawn up a will specifying who would assume control of his company."

"It's about to become public knowledge."

"Indeed."

"I want control ASAP."

"Understood."

Megan sat back in her chair, thinking. "Why didn't Wells consult me before taking control of the business?"

"He must have thought he didn't have to. Just because you are Max's only child doesn't mean you automatically take control when Max died."

"Dad's will says otherwise."

"Exactly. But Wells didn't know about the will. If Max hadn't left a will, Wells could have taken over the business because he was second-in-command."

"Will the board of directors challenge my succession?"

"There's nothing they can do about it. If they try, we sue, and you will win thanks to your father's will. You have nothing to worry about. The company is yours. This is what your father wanted. Wells doesn't have a leg to stand on."

"Will he fight me?"

"Not if he knows what's good for him." Hall paused. "On the other hand, the taste of power can do strange things to a man. And Wells has tasted power. He has run the company since Max died."

"Then he *will* fight me?"

"Tooth and nail, I suspect. He didn't get to be second-in-command without being ambitious."

Megan considered this. "Then I'll have to fire him."

"I don't know if you have to go that far. Other workers might object, thinking their jobs are on the line, too."

"If he fights me, I have to fire him. I see no other choice. The company can't have two bosses. It's either me or him. And it's not gonna be him."

"If he doesn't accept you as his boss, he's not gonna leave the company. He'll sue you."

"That's where you and the will come in. Show it to him, and he'll back down."

"If he knows what's good for him. But he might choose to contest the will. He could declare it fake. After all, why would a forty-year-old in good health write a will?"

Megan tensed in her seat. "You've read it."

"Several times."

"Well, is it authentic or not?"

"Rest assured, it is. I know Max's handwriting." Hall stroked his chin. "I don't know why he never told me about this will, though."

"Dad never told everyone everything. He was secretive. You know that."

"I do, indeed." Hall snatched the will from the desktop and perused it. "This reads like a boilerplate will. I could have written a much better one for him. I don't know why he didn't use me to write his will."

"Boilerplate? Does that mean it won't hold up in court?" said Megan, biting her lower lip.

"As long as it has his signature on it, it will withstand any legal challenge," said Hall, and tossed the will onto the desktop, full of confidence.

Megan set her hands on the desktop, palms down. "It's time I declare myself the owner of Max Reed Enterprises."

"You'll need to address the entire organization."

"A lot of them are flying back from Vegas right now, including Wells, after we had a fashion show there. I left Vegas early on the company jet. Wells was the de facto CEO, but Dad didn't like using titles around here so he dispensed with them. Dad was the owner, and that's all anyone needed to know, according to him. What he said overruled everybody else."

"He ran a tight ship," said Hall.

"Wells doesn't know how to run a company. He did what Dad ordered him to do. He is unable to make a decision by himself. We'll go bankrupt with him in charge."

"He seems to be enjoying the job."

"Who wouldn't enjoy being the boss of the richest fashion company in the world?" said Megan, her eyes gleaming.

"He knows trade secrets. Maybe it wouldn't be a good idea to fire him."

"If he decides to fight me, he's out on his ear."

"Very well."

"You can go now. I need to make an appointment with my analyst."

Nodding, Hall got up and made for the office door, briefcase in hand.

"Are you sure all the papers are in order?" said Megan.

Hall smiled at her. "Everything is taken care of. All the i's are dotted and the t's crossed. If it goes to court, we win."

"That's all I wanted to know. Bye."

Chapter 31

Brody took a chance and returned to Caesar's Palace. He wanted to talk to Brigitte Jadot to see if she knew anything about the torture porn snuff films Debbie Hernandez had told him about.

He knew some of Calabrese's knuckle-draggers might be lurking in the casino, but he was gambling they might not expect him to return to Caesar's. What was more likely was, the goons weren't even at Caesar's now because the cops would be swarming all over the joint searching for Calabrese's killer.

Brody avoided the cops when he entered Caesar's. The Vegas cops might know he was wanted for Max Reed's murder in Beverly Hills. He figured they were too busy investigating Calabrese's murder to pay much attention to anyone else, including him.

Brody sat at a slot machine, withdrew his cell phone from his trouser pocket, and called Debbie Hernandez.

"Hello?" she said, suspiciously.

"This is Scott Brody. We were talking earlier."

"What do you want? Did you know a car bomb blew up Rafe Calabrese?" she said, her voice taut with anxiety.

"I saw it."

"We're packing up and leaving Vegas. Half our entourage has already flown back to LA. I want to make sure I catch our flight. I can't talk now—"

"Could you tell me where Brigitte Jadot is? I want to talk to her."

"She's very upset."

"I understand, but I need to ask her a few questions about those pornos."

"Don't under any circumstances tell her I was the one that told you about them."

"Of course not. I told you before, I'm not telling anyone I talked to you. I'm not mentioning your name."

"The last I saw her she was at Joe's Steak House drinking."

"Can you tell me any of the names of the models that did the pornos you were talking about?"

Debbie terminated the call.

Brody shrugged, put away his cell, cut through the slots area, and made his way to Joe's. He kept seeing uniformed cops strutting through the casino, several of them with German Shepherds on leashes. He tried to stay out of their sight and, when he made them, to blend inconspicuously into the crowds of vacationers.

He cast around Joe's patio for Brigitte Jadot. He didn't see her at any of the tables.

Debbie had said Brigitte was drinking. Maybe she was at the bar, or maybe she had already left, decided Brody.

He told the maître d' who was standing at the patio entrance that he wanted to sit at the bar inside. In a black suit, his posture erect, the maître d' in his late thirties escorted Brody to the bar and handed him a menu.

Brody spotted Brigitte sitting by herself at the end of the bar, her face twisted with grief. She was nursing a glass of Sancerre. A half-full glass of red wine stood on the bar at the seat beside her. He approached her.

"I'm sorry for your loss," he said.

She looked up at him with bloodshot eyes. "Do I know you?"

"I'm a PI from LA. I heard about Rafe Calabrese."

"What's scary is I could have been in the car with him," she said, her face ashen. "It was pure luck I wasn't."

Brody sat one seat away from her. He didn't want to crowd her.

"Who do you think did it?" he said.

She rubbed her forehead. "I don't want to think about it. First Max, and now Rafe. They're both gone. Just like that. I can't believe it. Two bigger-than-life men gone in a matter of days."

"Do you feel up to answering questions about Reed?"

She took a pull on her Sancerre. Her face was wet from the tears she had shed for Calabrese. She wiped moisture from her cheeks with her hand.

"I can't understand," she said, as if to herself. "Why me?"

"I'm trying to find out why someone would waste Max Reed. You're one of the company's favorite models and Reed's ex-girlfriend."

"What are you driving at?"

"Did you ever hear of any of the models being approached to do torture pornos?"

"Torture pornos?"

"You know, BDSM. The real thing. It wasn't about acting. The torture and pain were real. Some of the films were snuff films, I hear."

"Models at Max Reed Enterprises?"

"Yeah."

"I never heard of such a thing."

"Nobody ever approached you to be in a movie?"

"Not *that* kind of movie."

A hand jerked Brody's shoulder from behind.

"Who asked you to come over here?" said Preston Wells, seething, his face red from drinking. "Can't you see she's upset?"

"I'm trying to find out who killed Max Reed. I need a motive."

"That's your problem. Now bug off."

Brody stood up. He was several inches taller than Wells and many pounds heavier, all muscle. He could have shut Wells up in a few seconds with a well-placed fist. However, Brody didn't want to make a scene that might attract the cops that kept roaming past the restaurant. He got it that Wells was trying to act protective of Brigitte. Maybe he had a thing for her with Calabrese out of the picture.

"I'm not macking on her," said Brody.

"She doesn't want to answer any of your questions."

"Maybe *you* can help me."

"I don't want to help you. I want you to leave."

"Did you like Max Reed?"

"Nobody liked Max Reed. He was a world-class shite. He treated everyone like dirt. Nobody was ever good enough for him. He was always bragging about all the money he had."

"Do you know anything about torture pornos being filmed at Max Reed's parties in Beverly Hills?" said Brody.

"What the fuck," spluttered Wells. "Who told you that?"

"I'm not naming names."

"Whoever it is better have a good lawyer. I'm gonna sue their ass off. Whatever else people say about Max, he did give great parties. I went to all of them."

"Do you know about anyone shooting snuff films at the parties starring fashion models?"

"Why you . . ."

Wells took a swing at Brody's jaw. Brody parried the blow and shoved Wells backward. The tipsy Wells staggered and fell against a table, knocking it over, spraying the floor with hurtling utensils and glasses as he sprawled on his back.

Brody saw the bartender shoot him a dirty look. Thinking about reaching for the baseball bat behind the counter, no doubt, decided Brody.

He figured it was time to leave.

He strode away.

"That's right," slurred Wells after him, trying to stand up with difficulty. "Run, you coward, run."

The bartender made to go after Brody, but decided against it and remained behind the counter.

Brody figured it was time to head back to LA.

Chapter 32

From her apartment in the Hollywood hills, Tess Hardwick called fashion models that she had gleaned from various sources had modeled for Max Reed Enterprises, trying to find out if they had attended any of Reed's parties and if any of their model friends had disappeared after attending the parties. To get them to open up about their experiences, Tess pretended to be a reporter researching a story for *Vanity Fair*.

Some of the models refused to be interviewed. Others, eager for publicity in a national magazine, agreed to talk.

Livia Mulholland, a statuesque twenty-eight-year-old brunette with stunning electric green eyes, agreed to meet Tess for an interview at Jon and Vinny's in Brentwood. They split a margherita pizza and ordered wine in the beige-paneled Italian restaurant, which had a beige and white motif.

"Do you agree to be tape-recorded?" said Tess, wearing jeans and a shocking pink tank top.

"No. You didn't say anything about taping."

Tess sipped her pinot noir and pulled a notebook and a ballpoint pen out of her pocketbook.

"You said over the phone that you went to several of Max Reed's parties at his mansion," she said.

"I did," said Livia, wearing a yellow halter top and café au lait pants, a glass of sparkling pinot noir/chardonnay in front of her.

Her posture erect, she had shoulder-length hair and bangs. She wore lilac fingernail polish on her long, tapered fingers.

"Did they serve drugs like cocaine and Molly there?" asked Tess.

Tapping her fingers on the tabletop, Livia demurred, but only for a moment. "Maybe. That wouldn't be out of the ordinary. Most of the parties around here have drugs. It's de rigueur nowadays. It's not like you're forced to take them, though."

"Did anyone ask you to star in a torture porno while you were at one of the parties?"

"What?" said Livia, taken aback.

"BDSM. How about snuff films?"

"Why would anyone agree to do a snuff film?"

"The filmmakers wouldn't ask you straight out to do a snuff film, because they would get no takers. How about an adult movie? Did anyone ask you to star in one?"

"Maybe they did. Is that a crime?"

"Not at all."

"A lot of famous people, including filmmakers, go to Max Reed's blowouts."

Tess crossed her legs under the table. "Let's go back to my original question. Did anyone ask you to star in a torture porn movie?"

"No." Livia paused a beat. "Someone did ask me to be in an adult movie, however."

"Did you agree?"

"No. I didn't think it was right for my image. Once you're in one of those, it's impossible to transition away from them. They're the kiss of death in the movie business. They did offer me a lot of money, but no way."

"Do you know if any of your friends were asked to be in torture pornos?"

Livia thought about it. "One of my friends—well, she wasn't really a friend, more like an acquaintance—she mentioned something about a torture porno."

Tess pricked up her ears. "What did she say?"

"She said a filmmaker approached her to be in one at a party Max threw."

"And?"

"I don't know."

"What do you mean, you don't know?"

"I never saw her again."

Tess registered surprise. "Did she say she agreed to be in the torture porno?"

"She didn't say. All I know is, I never saw her again after she brought up the subject."

"Why not?"

Livia shook her head in puzzlement. "All I can tell you is, I never saw her at any parties after that."

"What's her name?" said Tess, pen in hand.

"Meryl Hennessey."

Tess wrote the name on her pad.

Chapter 33

"Did Meryl get out of the modeling business?" said Tess.

"I haven't seen her in any fashion ads," said Livia.

"Did she tell you she was thinking about quitting the business?"

"No. It's a rough business, though. If you don't have the look they want, you're dead in the water. I can see why she would quit."

"I want to talk to her. Do you know where she lives?"

Livia shook her head no. "I have her phone number, though."

She dug her cell phone out of her purse, scrolled through her contacts, and found Hennessey's phone number. She gave the number to Tess.

"Have you called her recently?" said Tess.

"I never called her. I met her at two parties and never saw her again."

"Doesn't that strike you as strange?"

"Not if she quit modeling. I wouldn't recommend modeling. In many cases success is dumb luck and who you know. There's a lot of animosity in this business. It's dog eat dog. Even if you manage to have a career, it's short-lived. The older you get, the less gigs you get. Your face and your body droop, the fashion houses drop you. I know it's a horrible thing to say, but it is what it is. To be frank, you meet a lot of asshole men in this racket." Livia noticed Tess writing furiously on her pad. "I'll deny that last statement if you quote me. It could end my career if I got quoted saying that—even if it *is* true. Speaking the truth in this business can, and does, end careers."

"You don't believe in the Me Too Movement?"

"I do up to a point. But if you make waves in this town, nobody's gonna hire you. All those women who named names in the Me Too Movement don't work in the business anymore.

They sued, made huge out-of-court settlements, and changed careers. It's about knowing which side your bread is buttered on. I want to keep modeling."

"How old is Meryl Hennessey?"

"I think she said she was eighteen, but she looked much younger. She had a naïve quality about her that certain men like. I wouldn't be surprised if she was fifteen."

"If she was under eighteen, would it be legal for her to do fashion modeling?"

Livia nodded yes. "Fashion models can be as young as sixteen. The fashion houses like them young."

"She couldn't act in a porno flick unless she was at least eighteen. I know that much."

"I don't do porn and never will. The young girls, they come to Hollywood from all over the country starry-eyed and dreaming they can make it in the movies. They try for a couple of years and then reality sets in. They can't get work as actors. They're not gonna be movie stars. They're not gonna be anything. They're gonna be broke and living in a tent on the street like the homeless.

"They meet a glib porn producer wearing Ray-Bans who drives up in a fluorescent orange Lamborghini, pretends he's their friend, talks jive, and says he can make them into stars. They're desperate to make it in the movies after years of rejection and poverty. He wines and dines them, takes them to parties, offers them coke and Ecstasy. He tells them pornos are respectable nowadays. Everyone watches them online. There's nothing to be ashamed of. People admire porn queens. People desire them. People fall in love with them. They might even win an AVN award as best actress in a porno in Vegas—"

"AVN award?"

"Otherwise known as the Oscars of porn. AVN is the trade magazine *Adult Video News*."

"You seem to know quite a bit about this."

"Honey, I've been approached to appear in pornos, adult movies, whatever you want to call them. Virtually every fashion model has at one time or another, more so when they're young and starting out. The sleazy porn producers are always on the lookout for young girls to star in their smut with their tight tummies and budding breasts."

"I guess you said no to them."

"I was able to land jobs in fashion modeling. I made enough to get by." Livia took a pull on her pinot noir/chardonnay. "But I understand how you can see the allure of adult videos when you're young and naïve and don't know anything about the reality of Hollywood and the tooth-and-nail competition you're up against, especially if you're under sixteen and still trying to find your way in life."

"And some of those girls you're talking about are runaways."

"I know. It's sad." Livia glanced at her wristwatch. "We need to wrap this up. I have to do a meeting."

"Do you know where Hennessey's from? California or somewhere else?"

"Iowa, I think she said."

"Did she say she was a runaway?"

"She said she didn't get along with her parents. Read into that what you want."

"Do you know if she ever starred in any pornos?"

"I wouldn't know. I don't watch them."

"Would an adult video store know?"

"They might," said Livia, gathering her turquoise Prada pocketbook to leave. "I want to see that article you write about me before it goes to press."

"Of course," said Tess, knowing there would be no article.

Watching Livia leave, Tess decided it was time to pay a visit to a porn store to examine the casts in the films in search of Meryl Hennessey—after she finished her pizza.

In between bites she used her iPhone to google Meryl Hennessey actress.

She found several Meryl Hennesseys, but none of them were listed as actresses. Tess kept scrolling down, continuing her search. She stopped when she found Meryl Hennessey aka

Meryl Anne Monroe. That was all it said. The listing didn't give her occupation or anything else. There was a picture of a young blonde with green eyes who looked fifteen years old or even younger.

Tess decided she would look for a film with Meryl Anne Monroe starring in it.

Before Tess polished off her pizza she used her cell phone to call the number Livia had given her for Hennessey.

"The number you have dialed is no longer in service," came the response.

Chapter 34

Tess drove her white Mustang to an adult video rental store on Hollywood Boulevard near Western Avenue. The shop looked tacky enough and big enough to stock plenty of BDSM pornos. There weren't as many adult video shops as there used to be, because of the proliferation of porn on the Internet, much of it free.

She was lucky to grab a parking space on Hollywood Boulevard, happening to arrive as a beat-up Dodge left a metered space along the curb.

She wasn't looking forward to going inside, but she had a job to do. She inserted quarters into the parking meter and strode toward the shop.

She entered the shop and looked for the video section. Half the store was filled with sex toys, the other half with racks of adult videos and skin magazines.

Some grimy middle-aged men that were roaming the aisles inspecting new releases ogled her. She ignored them. At least they weren't dressed in raincoats, she decided. One of the men reeked of garlic.

She picked up on a BDSM section in the video aisles, angled toward it, and scoped out the titles and casts. Not her cup of tea, but she didn't let on, keeping her face passive. Leather and naked flesh on the DVD covers.

A middle-aged guy wearing a Dodgers baseball cap backwards sidled up to her, appreciating her selection of titles with a leer. Ignoring him Tess read the names of the cast. She didn't see Meryl Hennessey or Meryl Anne Monroe listed.

"That's a good one," said the man.

Tess put the DVD back on the rack. She felt like the guy was crowding her.

"Do you mind?" she said.

"Aren't you an actress?" he said, grabbing his crotch.

"No."

"You look familiar."

"You don't."

"Do you want to look at my handcuffs in my apartment?" he said with a lecherous grin.

"No. I just ate."

He looked bewildered, trying to figure out if she was talking dirty to him.

"Do you like tight leather crotch wear?" he said, his breath laced with booze.

"No. I'm a vegan."

Leaving him speechless, Tess walked away and inspected other titles. She had no luck finding any BDSM pornos that starred Meryl Anne Monroe.

She idled over to the clerk, a twentyish guy with tattoos on his arms and neck, sporting a purple Mohawk, sitting behind the cash register. His rheumy blue eyes roamed up from the book he was reading behind the cash register and checked her out. The name tag on his shirt said Phil.

"Do you know a lot about movies, Phil?" she said, trying to read the title of the book he was reading. It was a paperback about the films of Stanley Kubrick.

"You'd be surprised. I would be a film director by now, if the idiots in the business had any sense to hire me."

"You know how it goes. They only hire their friends and relatives."

"Don't I know it. It's a locked shop."

"Maybe you can help me," she said. "Do you have any movies in stock with Meryl Hennessey in them?"

"Never heard of her."

"How about Meryl Anne Monroe?"

He gave her a funny look, half-suspicious, half-curious.

"Is that supposed to be a joke?" he said.

"No joke. That's her stage name. Young-looking blonde with green eyes."

He searched her face, as if wondering whether he should talk to her.

"What's it to you?" he said.

"I want to rent her movies."

"She made only one, if she's the girl I'm thinking she is."

"Why only one?"

"Beats me. How bad do you want to see it?"

Phil popped a stick of cinnamon gum into his mouth and crumpled the gum wrapper.

"I really want to see it," said Tess.

"I know things," said Phil, winking.

"I bet you do. You look like you know what's what."

"Her film is a collector's item."

"How can I rent it?"

"You can't. You can only see it if you're invited to see it."

"I don't get it."

Phil made sure none of the customers were listening to him. He leaned closer to Tess and whispered to her.

"You need to go to a website on the dark web and put in a bid to watch it. If they accept your bid, they will invite you to a site where they'll run the film for you."

"Why's it so complicated? Can't they make multiple copies of the film and rent them out?"

"I'm just telling you what I know. What I told you is the only way you're gonna get to watch that film."

"What's the name of the website on the dark web?"

"Google the name of the film, and maybe the website will show up in the results."

"What's the name of the film?"

"What's in it for me?"

Tess didn't know if Phil was on the level or not. She opened her purse and flashed a twenty-dollar bill. He didn't look impressed. She flashed two of them. He turned up his nose. She flashed three.

"I'll tell you the name of the film for a hundred," he said.

"If this is a scam, I know where to find you," said Tess, dug out five twenties from her wallet, and handed them to him.

"*The Love Life of Meryl Anne Monroe.*"

"That's the only film she ever made?"

"The one and only," said Phil, looking smug.

"Do you happen to know where I can find her?"

"I have no idea where any actresses live," said Phil, counting the twenties she had given him.

"Why did she make only one movie?"

"How do I know? I never met her. I know nothing about her."

"Have you seen her movie?"

"No."

"Why not?"

"I have no desire to see every porno flick that comes out."

"But if this one is as rare as you say it is with only one copy in existence, why wouldn't you want to see it?"

"I don't think you understand," he said, chewed his gum, and regarded her.

"Enlighten me."

"We don't sell that kind of movie here. No video store does, that I know of."

"Yes, you do. You have plenty of BDSM movies here," said Tess, gesturing with her arm at the rows of videos behind her.

"You can't buy *that* movie. Only a select few are allowed to see it, and they have to sign an NDA stating they'll never say anything about the movie after they've seen it."

"What's so hot about it?" said Tess, her interest piqued.

"I've only heard rumors about it. I told you, I've never seen it."

"What kind of rumors?"

Phil repositioned his body in his seat. "It's one of the most shocking movies ever made, is what I've heard."

"You would think scads of people would line up to see it, if that's true."

"They do. You're not the only one who has asked me about it."

"Then why doesn't the producer print more copies of it?"

"There's only one copy, and the producer has complete control over who views it."

"Who's the producer?"

"I have no idea. I've heard—"

"Heard what?"

Phil lowered his voice. "That the only two credits on the film are those for Meryl Anne Monroe and her costar Moab."

"Moab? Who's Moab?"

"He's an actor that does torture porn."

"How can I get in touch with him?"

"Why? Do you want to be tortured?" said the clerk, chuckling.

"I want to ask him some questions."

"Do I look like a casting director? I don't know how you contact any actors."

"Don't they ever visit your store to promote their new releases?"

"I heard he retired."

"What about the producer and director of the movie? Aren't they listed in the credits?"

"No."

"Isn't that unheard-of?"

"Nothing about that film is normal. In fact, I suggest you forget about it and rent another movie. Give me an idea of what turns you on, and I'll point you to a movie. Big dicks? Big boobs? What tickles your fancy?"

"Hard-to-find movies like *The Love Life of Meryl Anne Monroe* turn me on."

"That's unfortunate. I can't help you. We don't carry it and never will. Next," he said, eyeballing the customer in the backwards Dodgers cap standing behind Tess leering at her backside.

"Haven't we met before?" Dodgers Cap asked her, grinning.

Tess decided it was time to leave.

Chapter 35

Tess returned to her Mustang, produced her cell phone, and called Brody.

"I may be onto something," she said.

"Go on."

"I talked to the model Livia Mulholland, who attended several of Max Reed's drug-fueled parties."

"And?"

"I'm getting to that. She says she met a very young model from Iowa named Meryl Hennessey, who said a filmmaker approached her at one of Reed's parties to act in a torture porn film."

"Very young? Like how young?"

"Livia thinks she was fifteen."

"Did she accept the filmmaker's offer?"

"This is where there's a problem. Livia says she never saw Hennessey again."

"Did Hennessey accept the part in the porn flick?"

"Livia doesn't know. She only knows Hennessey has disappeared."

"Interesting. But maybe she decided to leave Hollywood and go back home to Iowa and Auntie Em."

"That was Kansas."

"You get my drift."

"I thought that might be possible until I did research and found out she starred in a porno flick called *The Love Life of Meryl Anne Monroe.*"

"Cute. Who thought that one up?"

"Somebody with no imagination, in other words, a pornographer."

"Then she must have accepted the job offer from the filmmaker she met at Reed's bash."

"Looks that way."

"The question is, was it a snuff film? What's the film about?"

"That's the problem?"

"Hunh?"

"Hardly anybody has seen the film. There's only one copy in existence, and you can't see it unless you go to a website on the dark web and ask to see it. If the owner of the movie agrees, he'll invite you to watch it."

Tess flicked down her Mustang's sun shade to block the sun that was now shining spang into her eyes.

"You may be onto something," said Brody. "This movie sounds suspicious. Why is there only one copy? How can they make money off one copy?"

"I'm gonna check with the producer to see if I can watch the movie."

"Don't go without me. It could be dangerous on your own."

"Where are you?"

"I'm driving on the 15 on my way to LA from Vegas."

Tess fetched a long sigh. "If I get a lead, I'm gonna follow it, whether you're here or not. I have a gut feeling Meryl Hennessey's life is in danger."

"Your life could be in danger if you go on your own. Another hour or so won't make any difference."

"You can't be sure of that."

"I'm thinking of *your* safety, Tess. If these guys are shooting snuff films, they aren't people you want to tangle with alone—"

"We're talking about a fifteen-year-old kid, Brody."

"I know. And I want to help her as bad as you do. Just wait for me—"

"Her life could be in danger at this very moment."

"I know you like to go off half-cocked. All I'm saying is, wait for me before you go. Then we'll—"

Tess terminated the call.

Chapter 36

Tess drove back to her apartment in West Hollywood, sat in front of her laptop on her desk near her window, awoke the laptop from Sleep mode, and used her Tor browser and a VPN to search the dark web for *The Love Life of Meryl Anne Monroe.*

She found one entry that had the exact wording of the title in it. A synopsis of the movie followed.

The controversial exploration of the love life of a beautiful woman who is doomed by her beauty and for having too much love to give. Banned in the US, it stars the breathtaking Meryl Anne Monroe in her final film. This is the only extant copy of the film that pushed the envelope for erotic movies worldwide and made Meryl Anne Monroe an overnight sensation.

A phone number was given at the end of the synopsis.

Tess called the number on her cell phone.

"Hello," said a monotonic male voice.

Tess figured the guy might be using an electronic voice distorter.

"I'm interested in renting *The Love Life of Meryl Anne Monroe*," said Tess, doing her best to sound young and naïve.

"What makes you think it's for rent?"

"Your listing on the dark web."

"It doesn't say it's for rent."

"Then I'd like to buy it. How much is it?"

"It's not for sale."

"Then how can I see it?"

"Viewing it is by invitation only."

"How do I get an invitation?"

"We decide who is invited."

"I want to see the movie."

"Why?"

"I—I like erotic films."

"This is one of the most erotic and shocking films ever made."

"Great. I want to rent it."

"We don't rent it out. You have to come to the venue of the screening to see it."

"Fine. How much does it cost to see the screening?"

"A hundred thousand dollars."

"What?" said Tess, taken aback.

"You heard me. Do you still want to see the movie?"

"More than ever."

"Do you have the cash?"

"No."

"Then you're wasting my time," said the man, sounding like he was about to hang up.

"Wait a minute. I lied to you about why I want to see the movie."

"I'm listening."

Tess concocted her story on the fly. "I want to see the movie because I've heard rumors about how great it is. I know it made Meryl Anne Monroe an overnight celebrity."

That nobody's ever heard of, she thought.

"Get to the point," he said.

"I want to audition to be in a movie like this."

There was a pause on the other end of the line.

"Go on," said the man.

"I also want to meet Meryl Anne Monroe and ask acting tips from her."

"Impossible."

"Why?"

"She retired from showbiz. Like Greta Garbo, she became a recluse."

"Greta who?"

"Never mind."

"All right," said Tess, hastily. "I don't need to meet her, but I *do* want to audition to star in an erotic movie like this."

"What's your filmography?"

"What?"

"Have you done any erotic films before?"

"This would be my first. I'm new to California, and I'm trying to break into Hollywood."

"Did someone put you up to this?" said the man, suspicion in his voice.

"No way. I found you on my own on the dark web."

"How old are you?"

"Fifteen," she said, hoping she sounded that age.

"You *do* realize this is an adult film?"

"I do."

"Shoot me a photo of yourself in an e-mail and I'll see if you're right for the part."

He gave her an e-mail address.

Tess knew this guy was running an illegitimate business now, because he should have warned her that the law prevented actresses under the age of eighteen from performing in pornos. Instead he solicited her photo.

He hung up.

Tess searched through her pictures in her phone's photo app. She tried to find one of her when she was younger. She didn't think she had one of her at fifteen.

She saw one of her taken before she went to a Halloween party when she was in her late teens. She looked younger because she was wearing her hair in pigtails.

She figured the pornographer would like it because she was wearing a flamingo pink string bikini. In LA you could get away with wearing a skimpy costume like that on Halloween because the weather was frequently hot around that time of the year when the Santa Anas liked to kick in and heat up the city with sweeping offshore desert breezes that careened and howled through the canyons like banshees for Halloween.

Pushing thirty she had kept her youthful toned figure by working out in the gym. Right now it didn't matter how old she looked because the pornographer couldn't see her. What mattered was the photo she e-mailed him. She figured this photo would open doors.

She attached a JPEG of the photo to an e-mail and shot the e-mail to the pornographer.

It didn't take long for him to get back to her.

She answered her cell phone.

"We happen to be shooting a film that would be a perfect vehicle for you," he said. "It will launch your career like you wouldn't believe."

"Sounds wonderful," she said, trying to sound enthused.

"What is your name?"

Tess decided she shouldn't give him her real name. "Uh, Shari Landers. Omigod, I'm so excited."

He told her to meet him at an address on Lankershim Boulevard in the Valley in an hour and hung up.

Chapter 37

Brody was driving his rental west on the I-15 through the Mojave Desert toward LA, soaked with sweat thanks to his AC that was on the fritz, when he felt his cell phone vibrate in his trouser pocket.

He grabbed the plastic liter bottle of water that lay on the passenger seat, tossed down water, and pulled over to the shoulder, his tires crackling on the sand.

Parking his rental on the shoulder, he fished out his cell phone, and took the call.

"Brody, I contacted the producer of Meryl Hennessey's porno," said Tess.

With his hand Brody wiped away sweat that was beading on his forehead.

"Will he let you see the film?" said Brody.

"Not unless—"

"What about Hennessey. Does he know where she is?"

"He says she retired from acting."

"We need her address, so we can ask her whether her film is torture porn."

"I'm gonna meet with the producer."

"What? I thought you said he refused to show you the film."

"You didn't let me finish my sentence."

"Did you find the website?"

"I did."

"Did the owner invite you to watch the film?"

"If I have a hundred grand for the ticket."

Brody whistled. "It must be some kind of movie, if he can get that kind of dough for admission."

"That's why I figure it's a snuff film. What kind of legit movie could command that kind of price?"

"Agreed."

"Listen. I managed to wangle an audition for one of his films."

"No," said Brody, not believing his ears. "No way. You have no idea what you're getting into. You might be auditioning for a snuff film, Tess. We can't be sure Meryl Hennessey is still alive. Just because this porno producer says she's retired doesn't mean squat."

"When you hired me, you suggested I pretend to be a model and audition for a porno."

"I wasn't sure it was a snuff film when I said that," said Brody, regretting the suggestion.

"It's the only way I could get to see him. I need to meet him to see if I can watch that film of Hennessey to see if it's a snuff film."

"Don't meet him till I get there."

"I'm meeting him in less than an hour."

Brody gripped his phone tighter. "Wait for me. You can't meet this guy without backup."

"When are you getting back here?"

Brody glanced at his wristwatch. "Another hour and a half at least. I'm still in the desert."

"Forget it. If I miss the appointment, there's no guarantee I'll be able to get another one."

"You need backup. We're talking about a snuff film producer. These guys kill actors in their movies."

"I know. I'm taking my piece."

"He could have a whole film crew there waiting for you with guns. You need backup. Wait for me. I'll try to get back to LA faster."

"You'll never make it in time. I gotta run. This may be the only chance we get to meet this smut dealer and see if he's killing off models. Hell, he might be the one who wasted Max Reed."

"That's the problem. That's why you can't go alone—"

"I need to get a move on it."

"At least tell the cops where you're going—"

Tess terminated the call.

"Tess," said Brody into a dead line. "Tess?"

Gritting his teeth he flung his cell phone onto the passenger seat, fired the rental's engine, and pulled onto the interstate. He floored the gas and got the rental up to ninety miles an hour.

He had to reach her in time.

It was his fault she was walking into danger. He was the one that had hired her to investigate the snuff film. If something happened to her, he would never forgive himself.

He didn't even like her in the first place. She kept getting in his way when he was conducting his last investigation. Why did he have to drag her into this? Because he needed her to talk to the models, since they clammed up when he was around. They were more likely to open up to another woman.

Now her death would be on his hands if she infiltrated the snuff film ring and paid for it with her life.

He heard a siren behind him. He glanced at the rearview mirror and spotted a highway patrol cruiser bearing down fast on him, the light bar flashing red and blue.

"Hell," muttered Brody.

He debated whether to try to outstrip the cop. He didn't like his chances. Even if he managed to pull away from the cop, the guy would call for reinforcements. Then they'd haul him off to the slam for resisting arrest.

The worst he could get for speeding was a ticket.

He took his foot off the gas and pulled onto the shoulder.

More time lost, he decided, disconsolate.

He entertained the idea of calling Lt. Macready and telling him Tess was on her way to meet an armed and dangerous smut film producer. Then he realized with a slump of his shoulders she hadn't told him the producer's address.

Parking the rental he snagged his cell phone and called Tess. The phone kept ringing.

"Answer," he said, desperate for her to pick up.

"Speeding *and* texting at the same time, huh, sir?" said the CHP officer striding up to Brody's driver's-side window in his butternut uniform, stone-faced, mirrored aviators shielding his eyes. “I hope it was worth it,” he said, pulling out his ticket pad.

Chapter 38

Preston Wells was flying with Brigitte Jadot on one of Max Reed's private jets, a Gulfstream G650, from Vegas to LA. Being the new boss had its perks, decided Wells, flying in style and comfort. Still, he was resentful.

"He treated me like a dog the entire time I worked for him," he told Brigitte, who was sitting next to him nursing a Chablis.

"He wasn't the easiest person to get along with," she said, and glanced out the window at the carpet of fleecy clouds floating underneath them.

Wells looked at her. "That's putting it mildly."

"He was rich and successful. He earned the right to be a bastard."

"Is that how you see it?"

"He had a good side beyond his 24/7 self-promotion and boorish behavior."

Wells shook his head. "I never saw it. And I worked for him for ten years. That is, I had to suck up to him for ten years. I swore I was gonna quit every day."

"But you kept coming back."

"He paid well. A lot of the time I hated myself for continuing to work for him, though. I resented his humiliating me. I felt like a cringing worm. A *gusano*, the Mexicans call it."

"It's over now. You should be happy."

"I'm telling you, I hated the guy. It's such a relief not having him around. I've always been a better fashion designer than him. That's why he had to keep me under his thumb, so I couldn't go off on my own and compete with him. I don't know how many more years of truckling to him I could have taken."

Brigitte sipped her Chablis. "He's gone now. You don't have to worry about him."

"Right. I'm the boss. And I'm gonna stay the boss for a long time."

Brigitte's eyes teared up. "I miss Max . . . and Rafe. I think my love life is jinxed."

Wells heaved a noisy sigh, not knowing what to say. He didn't like Brigitte's choice of men, but he liked Brigitte. He wasn't naïve enough to think he was the only one who had the same feelings. But now that Calabrese and Max were out of the way, he was feeling much better about his chances with Brigitte.

He knew she would require time to mourn her losses. He would have to wait, to endure. He was good at enduring. He had endured ten years of Max's humiliations and had risen to the top of the corporate ladder.

Megan Reed's face appeared on the TV screen mounted on the bulkhead in front of his passenger seat.

"Hello, Preston," she said.

"Hello, Megan."

"I never got a chance to congratulate you on becoming the head of Max Reed Enterprises."

"Thank you."

"You misunderstand. I'm not calling to congratulate you."

"I don't get it," said Wells, bewildered.

"I'm calling to tell you you took over the company illegally. You jumped the gun. You have no right to take the reins of power."

"What are you talking about?" spluttered Wells.

"I'm taking over Max Reed Enterprises as my father's only issue."

"I was his vice president. You have no right."

Megan smiled. "His will says otherwise. He appointed me sole heir of the company. According to the law, it's *my* company now. And I'm assuming control as of this minute."

White-faced, Wells stared at her image on the TV screen.

"Impossible," he said. "Max didn't leave a will. He was in his forties. Why would he make a will in his forties?"

"Nevertheless, he did. You're out, and I'm in."

"I don't accept this," said Wells, eyes popping, a vein bulging in his forehead. "There is no will."

"My lawyer Burt Hall says otherwise. He has a copy of the will, signed by my father."

Wells bolted to his feet. "Bullshit."

"Don't fight me on this, Preston. It will end badly for you."

"I'm the boss. I don't recognize your authority," said Wells, balling his fists at his sides.

"You aren't the boss. And you'll never be the boss. You're out. If you challenge my authority, I'll see you in court," said Megan, her face stern.

"You bet I'll challenge your authority. You think some fake will is gonna get rid of me? You and your lawyers forged the will. Do you think I'm stupid? I'll do everything in my power to oppose you. I didn't endure ten years of Max Reed's insults for nothing."

Megan smiled. "Toodle-oo, Preston. You're history."

Megan's face disappeared from the screen.

"I didn't even know she wanted the damn job," said Wells. "She never showed any interest in running the company. Max and me made all the business decisions."

"She spends all her time at her analyst," said Brigitte.

Wells did a double take. "Analyst? She has an analyst?"

"Didn't you know? No big deal. Half the models in town do."

Wells chewed it over. "We may be able to use it against her. I'm gonna use every weapon I can to thwart her. I can tell you that much. This is *my* company and I'm not giving it up without a fight to the death."

If Megan wanted an internecine war, he was going to give it to her hook, line, and sinker, decided Wells.

"I can't believe she cares about the company," said Brigitte. "She did some modeling on the catwalks, but she showed little interest in the job."

"I guess she's good at dissembling. She had everybody fooled." Wells paused a beat. The same could be said of him, he realized. People actually thought he liked Max, because he sucked up to him. Nothing could be further from the truth. Wells had to admit he was a great actor. You had to be a great actor to succeed in life. "She's gonna find out she picked the wrong guy to wage war with."

Chapter 39

Checking to see there were no cops on the interstate, Brody produced his cell phone and, using a burner app, called Detective Macready while he drove his rental toward LA, relieved his phony driver's license with a fake name on it had fooled the CHP officer who had pulled him over earlier.

"Macready here."

"This is Brody. I'm willing to trade information with you."

"What could you possibly have that I want? The only thing I want is to bust you for the murder of Max Reed."

"Has the FBI's TEDAC determined what type of bomb killed Bambi Patterson?"

"Why should I tell you? You're a murder suspect. Anyway, you ought to know the type of bomb, since you're the one that blew Patterson up."

"It wasn't me. I'll tell you who did it, if you trade information with me and drop the warrant for my arrest."

"Not gonna happen."

"You need to hear what I have to say," said Brody, checking his rearview mirror for the presence of cops behind him on the interstate.

"Turn yourself in. Stop trying to cut a deal with me. I don't cut deals with murder suspects."

"You don't want to know who blew up Max Reed?"

"I already know. I'm talking to him."

"I didn't know I was carrying a bomb in the bowling bag when I took it to Max Reed's office. Rafe Calabrese used me. He's the one that sent the bomb to Reed."

"How convenient."

"What?"

"Isn't it convenient that Calabrese is dead and can't refute a word you say?"

"What type of bomb wasted Bambi?"

Macready paused, debating whether to tell him. "All right. I'll play along. According to TEDAC, it was C-4. The same thing you used on Max Reed."

"Calabrese whacked Reed."

"Why?"

Brody was sweating thanks to his rental's AC cutting out again. In frustration Brody hammered one of the AC vents with his fist, trying to get the AC to come back on.

"I didn't get a chance to ask him." said Brody.

"Like I said, how convenient he died before you could ask."

"It might've had something to do with a snuff film."

"You expect me to believe this?"

"Meryl Hennessey starred in the film, and she's gone missing."

"Who the hell is Meryl Hennessey?"

"She was a model who went to one of Max Reed's parties, met a porn producer there, and agreed to star in his film."

"So?"

"I believe it was a snuff film."

"What proof do you have?"

"She vanished without a trace."

"That proves nothing, and you, a PI, know it."

"What if I can get you a copy of the film?"

"If the film is of her getting killed and she is, indeed, missing, I'll investigate it. Where can I get a copy of the film?"

"You can't. There's only one copy. The producer carefully screens anyone who wants to view the movie and charges a hundred grand for the privilege. If he says yes, you are invited to a secret location to watch the movie."

"Why all the rigmarole? What kind of nincompoop would pony up a hundred K to see a movie?"

"You'd be surprised."

Macready thought about it. "There *are* some sick degenerates out there."

"If it *is* a snuff film, he wouldn't want a cop to see it. He would take off if you told him you were coming to see it."

"In other words, you got zilch. Forget all the bullshit and turn yourself in. My only question for you is, why did you blow up Reed and Patterson?"

"I have no motive, because I didn't do it."

"Reed's private security CCTV recorded you delivering the bomb."

"I told you, I had no idea I was carrying a bomb," said Brody, tired of repeating himself. "I was set up."

"By Calabrese?"

"Right."

"And he was in a car bombing in Vegas, so he can't deny it. Like I said before, how convenient. Maybe *you* were the one that blew *him* up, too, so he couldn't testify against you."

"I had nothing to do with Calabrese's death."

"Where were you when it happened?"

"At Caesar's Palace."

"Which is exactly where Calabrese was murdered."

"I wasn't the only one there."

"By a bomb. The same MO you used to take out Max Reed."

"Calabrese took out Max Reed."

"The best advice I can give you is to turn yourself in," said Macready, sounding weary. "Maybe the judge will go easier on you if you surrender."

Brody cut his eyes to the rearview mirror and picked up on a squad car behind him.

Brody terminated his call, hoping the cop hadn't seen him talking on his cell phone while driving, which was illegal in California. He also reduced his speed, which was ten miles above the speed limit. He checked his wristwatch and felt uneasy. He was never going to get to LA in time to reach Tess before she left for her audition.

If she aced the audition, they would snuff her in front of a movie camera. They might even snuff her during her audition.

He hammered his steering wheel with the bottom of his fist in frustration, overcome by a feeling of helplessness.

After the cop passed him without incident, Brody breathed easier and texted Tess.

At least tell me where you are going.

After a few minutes she texted him an address on Lankershim Boulevard.

He would head straight there when he reached LA.

Chapter 40

Tess drove her Mustang to the address on Lankershim where the porn producer had told her to go. It turned out to be a brick warehouse, which loomed in front of her, deserted and foreboding.

She had no idea what she was getting into. Was this guy really a maker of snuff films or just pornos? If it turned out to be pornos, there was no reason to believe they had killed Meryl Hennessey. In any case, Tess was carrying her piece in her purse.

The Valley was hot, and she had the Mustang's AC on.

Wearing jeans and a grey T instead of a dress, she pulled into a parking space at a parking meter on the curb, killed the Mustang's engine, set her parking brake, got out, and strode to the warehouse in search of its entrance.

The grimy, tinted windows were shut, reinforced with wire mesh behind the glass panes to prevent break-ins. It could have been a prison. But she couldn't imagine the city building a prison here on this segment of the boulevard what with a plethora of mom-and-pop stores like flower shops, bakeries, art-frame stores, and restaurants lining the sidewalks.

Maybe warehouses were good places to shoot movies, she decided.

She was having second thoughts about having come here alone. On the other hand, Brody might not get back to LA for several hours. It wasn't in her nature to wait. She had to be active. If this producer was shooting snuff films, more girls' lives could be at stake beside Hennessey's.

She found the entrance no more inviting than the rest of the building. She climbed the cement steps to the large wooden door, whose teal paint was peeling.

Her armpits were sweating as she approached.

She didn't see a doorbell. She knocked on the door.

Nobody answered.

She knocked harder.

No response.

She dug her cell phone out of her purse and called the porn producer.

"Hello," he said.

"I'm here."

"The door's not locked."

She put away her phone and tried the doorknob. It gave. The door squeaked open. She walked onto a cement floor. The air was cool and musty inside the warehouse. She couldn't make out much, since there were no lights on and the windows were tinted, preventing sunlight from entering.

Tess guessed the porn producer didn't believe in natural lighting.

She found herself in a capacious room with a cathedral ceiling. No furniture anywhere. She crossed the floor and heard her footsteps echo off the walls, accentuating her apprehension and sense of solitude.

"Hello," she said.

Her echo answered.

She didn't see anybody.

"I came to audition for your movie," she said.

No answer.

"Let's get the show on the road," she said, surveying her surroundings, casting around for the porn producer.

Silence.

"Say something or I'm leaving," she said.

A spotlight flared in front of her and shone directly into her eyes, blinding her. Squinting, she shielded her eyes with her hand.

"Where's Shari Landers?" said the pornographer's voice over a loudspeaker.

"I'm Shari Landers."

"You're fifteen in a pig's eye."

"I *am* fifteen and I want this part."

"Liar. I smell cop."

"I'm no cop. I'm an actress. I came here all the way from Norfolk, Nebraska, to be in the movies."

"If you're a cop, you're legally required to tell me you're a cop."

"That's only if I'm posing as a hooker."

"And how the hell do you know that—unless you're a cop?"

"I'm not a cop."

"You're not right for the part. You're too old. That photo you e-mailed me was fake."

"It was not. It was a photo of me."

"Twenty years ago, maybe. Good-bye. Don't call us. We'll call you."

"You didn't even let me audition," said Tess, searching the room for the pornographer, who was nowhere to be seen.

He must have been watching her from a CCTV camera in another room, she decided.

"I told you, you're too old for the part," he said. "You came here under false pretenses."

"I want to talk to Meryl Hennessey."

"Who?"

"Meryl Hennessey. Where is she?"

"How should I know?"

"She was in one of your movies."

"She made one movie with me and left town."

"Where'd she go?"

"I don't know, and I don't care. She's just another actress wannabe who couldn't cut the mustard."

"Let me see the movie she was in."

"Why?"

"Because I can't find a copy of it anywhere."

"There's only one copy in existence."

"I want Meryl Hennessey's autograph."

The pornographer laughed. "Go back to Nebraska."

"Her mother said she came here to Hollywood, and she hasn't seen her since."

"So she ran away from home. So what? Teens do it all the time."

"Come out of your hiding place and talk to me face to face. Or are you afraid?"

The pornographer laughed again. "Trying to bait me, huh? Nice try."

Tess got the impression the pornographer was preparing to leave. "Did you know the fashion designer Max Reed?"

"I went to some of his parties. So?"

"Did you shoot movies for him?"

"I have my own company. What's it to you?"

"Why did you go to his parties?"

"Are you kidding? Everybody wants to go to a Max Reed bash. Scads of good-looking girls there."

"You went there to recruit actresses for your movies?"

"What's with all these questions? You sound like a cop."

"I'm trying to find Meryl Hennessey."

"Get outa here."

A door creaked open. In the lamplit doorway Tess saw the imposing profile of a large, snarling Doberman Pinscher, its jagged teeth exposed, saliva dripping from its mouth.

Shit.

She thought about reaching for her piece in her pocketbook, but she had a thing about killing dogs. She wasn't sure she could bring herself to blow away a dog, even one that was bent on mauling her to death.

The Doberman barked and bolted toward her.

She sprinted toward the front door where she had entered.

Without looking behind her she could feel the dog gaining ground on her. She could hear his paws clicking on the cement as he tore across the floor in pursuit.

She was glad she had worn her jogging shoes and jeans. She needed to reach the front door. Ten more feet—

She felt the Doberman bite her right heel, sinking its teeth into her shoe leather.

Screaming, she jerked her foot forward, trying to break free from the dog. She crashed into the front door, twisted around to face the Doberman, and tried to wrest her foot from his jaws. She balled her fist and hammered him on the nose as hard as she could.

Wincing and whimpering, he let go of her foot. She took advantage of her freedom to fling open the door, spring onto the porch, and shut the door behind her, gasping for breath.

The pornographer might be approaching the door this very minute to open it and sic the Doberman on her, she decided.

She couldn't dally.

She flew down the concrete steps, down the sidewalk, and back to her car, disregarding the pain in her mauled foot. Sliding into the driver's seat, shutting the Mustang's door behind her, she could breathe easier. The Doberman couldn't get her here.

Her cell phone chimed in her purse. She took the call.

"I was impressed with the way you ran," said the pornographer. "You move like a jungle cat. I might have a part for you in my next movie *Cougars on the Make*."

"Asshole," she said, and hung up as he broke into laughter.

Chapter 41

"That was the mayor," said Burt Hall, putting away his cell phone in Megan's office.

He removed his glasses and polished their lenses with a handkerchief he withdrew from his jacket's breast pocket.

"What did he want?" said Megan, sitting behind her office desk that was chockablock with glossy magazines packed with Max Reed fashion ads.

"He says he's gonna cancel Max Reed's permit to shoot ads at crime scenes unless he is provided with more girls."

"You're coming at me from left field," said Megan, bemused.

"You didn't know about the arrangement?"

"What arrangement?"

Hall held his spectacles up to the light, inspected the lenses, exhaled warm breath on them, and polished them some more.

"Max had an arrangement with the LA mayor so he could shoot ads of his models wearing his fashions at active investigations of crime scenes," he said, replacing his spectacles on his nose.

"And?"

"In exchange for the permit, Max provided models for the mayor to sleep with."

Megan took a moment to absorb this.

"The models are OK with this 'arrangement'?" she said, making air quotes.

"Oh, sure. Some of them moonlight as call girls. They like big bucks, and the mayor pays them well. No problem there. They're not gonna talk. Everybody's happy. Why should anyone talk?"

"And Dad agreed?"

"Why wouldn't he? He wanted those fashion shots at crime scenes. They sell his product. You scratch my back, I scratch yours. The way of the world. Max had access to beautiful women. The mayor knew this and took advantage of it."

"Where does the mayor get money to pay for call girls?"

Hall shrugged. "I don't want to speculate, but there's a rumor he's looting his campaign funds for that very purpose."

Megan walled her eyes. "Are you sure we want to get involved with this?"

"Do you want Max Reed Enterprises to keep coining money?"

"OK. So what's your advice?"

"Do you want to keep shooting ads at murder scenes like your father?"

"Of course. Business as usual. If it ain't broken, don't fix it. He used violence in his ads, but the ads were meta."

"Then we provide the mayor with more hooker—I mean, models."

"And this is legal?"

"Not exactly. But as long as everybody's happy, who's gonna report the violation to the cops?"

Megan studied her lilac-enameled nails. "I want the company to continue being prosperous. Dad's ads were eye-catching, and they sold clothes. Give the mayor what he wants."

"Max was the one who contacted the models. That would be your job now."

Megan looked at him. "Do you know the name of the models involved with the mayor?"

"I do."

"Then you talk to them."

"I can't be involved with that. They took their marching orders directly from Max. They work for him, not for me. I'm an attorney."

Megan heaved a sigh. "All right. Give me their names."

"I got the impression from my talk on the phone with the mayor that he wants new blood." Hall paused. "And he likes them young," he added with a wink.

Megan didn't want to delve further into the meaning of Hall's wink. She told herself not to read anything into it. After all, nineteen-year-olds were considered young. What grown women did with their bodies was up to them, not her. She wasn't going to back out of this job simply because of the mayor's arrangement with her father.

Her father was tough, and she was going to fill his big shoes. In fact, she planned on expanding the company, making it bigger and better than ever. There was room to grow, as she saw it. Plenty of room.

"My father was a savvy businessman, and I am all of that," she said. "And then some."

"No doubt," said Hall. "No doubt."

Chapter 42

Arriving in LA Brody pulled his rental over on Wilshire Boulevard at a parking meter, dug his cell phone out of his trouser pocket, and called Tess.

She didn't answer. Not a good sign.

He let it ring.

He figured she had gone to the pornographer without him, since he had arrived in LA later than he had expected thanks to traffic congestion on the freeway.

His body tense, he was getting ready to hang up when she answered.

Relieved, he said, "Where are you?"

"What took you so long?"

"Don't ask."

"I'm at the hospital."

Brody's heart skipped a beat, his palms sweaty. "Christ. Why didn't you wait for me? I asked you to wait for me."

"You hired me to do a job. And I'm doing it. If you don't like it, fire me."

"Forget it. The point is, are you OK?"

"I'm fine."

"You didn't go to meet the pornographer?"

"I did go. And I met him, in a manner of speaking."

"What's that supposed to mean?"

The driver of a Mercedes blasted his horn as he barreled past Brody's parked rental. Brody winced at the distraction.

"I spoke to him at his 'studio,' I guess you could call it, on Lankershim," she said. "But I never saw his face."

"Was he wearing a mask?"

"He never showed himself. He was watching me on CCTV in another room."

"Did you find out anything about Meryl Hennessey?"

"Not much. He said they did one movie together and she vanished."

"Is the *Love Life of Meryl Anne Monroe* a snuff film?"

"He didn't let me see it."

"What about your audition?"

"He said I was too old for the part."

"Because you're over sixteen, I bet."

"We got no evidence against this guy whatsoever. Though, he did admit he attended several of Max Reed's parties so he could meet models."

"There's nothing illegal about that."

"Like I said, we got zilch."

"Didn't you try to meet this guy face to face when you were at his studio?"

"That's why I'm at the hospital."

Brody felt like kicking himself. He was the one that had got her into this. "What the hell did he do to you?"

"He sicced a Doberman on me. It bit my heel. I'm here getting a tetanus shot."

Brody felt better. He thought the pornographer had beat her or shot her.

"Do you think this guy just does smut films or snuff films as well?" he said.

"I think he's dirty as hell. But he might just be doing smut films of underage girls."

"That doesn't explain Meryl Hennessey's disappearance after she starred in his movie."

"He's hiding something. Why didn't he agree to see me in person?"

Brody was having the same thoughts. "Do you have any idea what his name is?"

"No. I haven't been able to find any credits for that movie on the Internet. The only thing I found was it starred Meryl Hennessey and Moab. No writer. No director."

"Moab?" said Brody, puzzled. "Is that a guy's name?"

"I guess."

"What was the name of the guy you went to see on Lankershim?"

"He didn't give me a name. I called a phone number listed on the movie's website for *The Love Life of Meryl Anne Monroe* on the dark web. Nobody's name was listed with the number."

"Maybe the pornographer's name is Moab."

"I don't think so."

"Why not?"

"Moab is Meryl's costar. The cashier at the video store I talked to said Moab is a porn actor."

"Maybe he produced the movie as well. Actors frequently help produce their movies."

"I doubt it. Porn actors get their jobs because of only one thing. And it's not the size of their wallets. Moab's no producer."

"Is he a well-known actor in the business?"

"I know nothing about porn."

"Of course."

"The cashier heard of him. That's all I can tell you about him."

"Maybe we can get some answers out of Moab about his film with Meryl Hennessey. Or did he disappear after he starred in the movie, too?"

"I haven't looked for him—yet. I'll send my hospital bill to you."

"You ought to sue the producer for the dog bite."

"Whose name do I put on the lawsuit?"

"Good point."

"I'll live."

"These porn makers could be dangerous. Half of them are laundering drug cartel money through the production of their films. We should work together on this—"

She hung up.

Not that he liked working with partners. It had never worked out for him. Which was why he had gone solo with his business. Maybe they were better off working on their own. She could take care of herself. And so could he.

He still had to clear his name of Reed's murder. The only way he could do so was to find out why Calabrese had done it. The porn film might be the way to connect Calabrese and Reed. It could have led to bad blood and a murder plot.

Brody wondered if Sal Andrasi knew anything about Calabrese's involvement in the porn racket. Andrasi, as a soldier in the Mafia, might be involved as well, come to think of it. Andrasi might be his best bet as the one who could shed light on the matter.

Chapter 43

Brody called Andrasi.

"This is Brody. We gotta meet."

"I'm gonna make you dead meat. That's the only meet you're gonna get."

"I met with Rafe Calabrese in Vegas. He refused to talk. He said he didn't hire you to send me with a bomb to Reed's."

"So why'd you whack him with a car bomb?"

"I had nothing to do with that."

"Then who did?"

Brody thought about it. "Maybe you did."

"Me? You gotta be kidding."

"Maybe you didn't want me to ask Calabrese questions about Reed's murder because Calabrese had nothing to do with it."

"It was him. He ordered the hit."

"I need answers."

Andrasi's tone became amiable. "All right. Come down to my office and we'll talk over some coffee."

"Fat chance. You got mechanics there waiting to blow me away. We meet at Tom's Pool Hall."

"Why do I want to do this?"

"Because if you don't, I'll tell the cops you hired me to blow up Max Reed. I'll meet you there in forty minutes."

Brody terminated the call. His stomach growled. He realized he was starving. He hadn't eaten since he had driven out of Vegas. Trying to make time and catch up with Tess, he hadn't stopped to eat lunch. It was past dinner time.

He stopped at a Habit fast-food joint and ordered a double charbroiled burger with French fries and a Coke.

Feeling better after he ate, he drove his rental to Tom's Pool Hall in Inglewood, a stone's throw from the Forum, not far from the Hustler Casino and the defunct Hollywood Park

Racetrack. It was getting dark, and the circular Forum dominated the skyline with its glowing purple columns.

He parked in the pool hall's parking lot.

The pool hall was jumping, as he figured it would be. With all the customers jamming the place Brody figured Andrasi wouldn't try a hit on the premises. Not that Brody was going to let down his guard. He wasn't going to be foolish enough to ever trust a wiseguy that wanted him dead. He figured Andrasi's goons would be with him—either visible or lying in wait close by.

Brody strode toward the pool hall, listening to the clacking pool balls as he entered the smoke-filled joint. Half the customers were black. Brody figured they would be since this was Inglewood. He also figured Andrasi wouldn't whack anybody surrounded by brothers lest he trigger a war with the gangsta Bloods and Crips.

Brody rented a table, racked it for nine ball, selected a cue from a wall rack, and started shooting pool as he waited for Andrasi. Most of the other players had brought their own cues. Brody chalked his cue and played several games. On his fifth game he ran the table and pocketed the nine ball. He checked his wristwatch. Andrasi was already twenty minutes late. Brody wondered if the guy would show.

Brody decided he would wait another half hour. He shot more pool.

Maybe Andrasi would jump him when he returned to his rental in the lot. Andrasi's goons could be waiting to bushwhack Brody outside even now.

Racking the balls for another game, Brody spotted Andrasi out of the corner of his eye strutting through the door, scoping out the joint, spotting Brody, and angling toward him. Brody didn't see anybody with him. Andrasi's goons could have entered earlier by themselves or they could be waiting outside in the parking lot.

Andrasi was wearing a purple and yellow Lakers jacket and Air Jordans trying to blend in with the brothers. Brody picked up on a couple of the brothers, a tall skinny guy and a short guy with peroxide hair, pool cues in hand, at another pool table giggling as they laid eyes on Andrasi.

"You should invest in a new Rolex," said Brody. "You're almost an hour late."

"You're wasting my time with bullshit."

"What's Calabrese's connection with Max Reed?"

Andrasi retrieved a cue stick from the wall rack.

"Who cares?" said Andrasi.

"Then why did Calabrese want Reed dead?"

"I dunno."

"Are you and Calabrese in the porn distribution racket?"

"And what's wrong with that?"

"Nothing—unless the actors are underage."

"There's nothing illegal in the stuff we handle. It's strictly legit. There's nothing more natural than naked men and women fucking. If that's illegal, the human race is caput."

Brody missed the six ball in the side pocket.

Andrasi dropped the six in the corner pocket.

"What about Max Reed?" said Brody. "Was he in on it, too? Was he providing you with his fashion models for actors?"

"What would be wrong with that?" said Andrasi, lining up his next shot.

"A whole lot if the models were under eighteen," said Brody, chalking his cue and blowing on it.

"We aren't in the business of shooting illegal films."

Andrasi shot the seven ball. It jawed in the corner pocket.

"This table's tilted," he said.

He threw his cue on the tabletop with disgust. Leaning over he inspected the pool table's leg nearest him. He got down on his haunches and removed a matchbook shim from under the bottom of the leg.

"I told you," he said, flinging the matchbook on the green felt table.

"Do you know Meryl Hennessey?" said Brody.

"No."

"What about Moab?"

"Moab? What the fuck is that? The white whale?"

"He's a porn actor."

Andrasi raised his bushy eyebrows with indifference.

"You should be thanking me I let you live this long," he said.

"What about snuff films? Are you guys into snuff films?"

"I oughta sue you."

"Were you in cahoots with Max Reed cornering the porn market? Did his fashion clients like underage girls? Snuff films. Did they like snuff films?"

Shaking his head Andrasi stalked toward the front door.

Brody tossed his cue on the pool table and followed him. "Why get rid of Reed?"

Andrasi kept walking and exited the pool parlor.

Brody reached the doorway and cast about for him. Brody didn't see him. His skin crawled. He got the feeling somebody was staring at him. Feeling exposed in the lighted doorway, he ran for cover behind a van in the parking lot.

Gunshots rang out. Two bullets ripped into the van's side.

Brody withdrew his SIG P365 from his ankle holster and peeked around the van seeking the source of the gun reports. A bullet sang past his forehead. Ducking behind the van he returned fire. He heard more shots coming from behind him. Wheeling around he spotted two gangbangers at the pool hall's entrance firing their pieces at the gun flashes of Andrasi's goons in the parking lot.

A gangland war was erupting between the local gangbangers and the Mafia.

Seizing his chance to escape, Brody charged to his rental, clambered into the driver's seat, shut the door behind him, fired the engine, and tore out of the parking lot as the Mafia goons exchanged fire with the gangbangers. Under the barrage of gangbangers' fire Andrasi and his soldiers withdrew, having no taste for a turf war.

Gangbangers piled into their white Caddy in the parking lot and gave chase, firing at the withdrawing Mafia cars all the while.

Brody hung a right in his rental and checked his rearview mirror.

He didn't see any of Andrasi's speeding cars chasing him in the night. Their drivers were traveling in a different direction, intent on evading the gangbangers chasing them in a Caddy firing out their windows at them.

Chapter 44

Tess returned to the Hollywood adult video shop in her Mustang.

She saw Phil with his purple Mohawk manning the cash register again. A guy like that was hard to miss, she decided. She limped toward him on her dog-bit foot.

"I'm back," she said.

"Happy customers always return," said Phil. "In the market to buy hot new vids?"

She smelled the acrid scent of patchouli. She couldn't tell if it was coming from Phil or from one of his customers cruising the adult video lanes.

"I couldn't find the actress Meryl Hennessey," she said.

"I'm not surprised. I bet she quit the business. I haven't seen her in any recent films."

"The producer wouldn't help me find her."

"Wouldn't or couldn't?"

"He wasn't cooperative."

Phil nodded. "People are close-mouthed in the porn business. Everybody knows everybody else, and if you don't run with their crowd, they don't want you around."

"The real reason I wanted to find Meryl Hennessey was to ask her to star in a new movie I'm producing."

"You don't say."

"She has a real following among porn connoisseurs."

"I don't see how. Hardly anyone has seen the one movie she ever made."

"Word gets around—especially when it comes to rare adult videos that are hard to find anywhere."

"Hard to believe. You're the only one that ever asked me about Hennessey and her movies."

"What about Moab?"

"I don't understand."

"Can you lead me in his direction? I'd like to offer him a part in my movie."

Phil acted defensive. "Why do you think I'd know where to find him? I'm a cashier in a video store."

"I think you know more than you let on," said Tess, in an attempt to flatter him. "Maybe porn actors come to your store to promote their latest releases. Am I right?"

Phil watched a middle-aged balding guy in a grey suit and powder blue tie perusing the videos in the Threesome aisle.

"Like I said, the porn business is an insular community," said Phil. "They're wary of strangers."

"I want Moab to star in my movie," said Tess. "He has great potential as an actor."

"'Star,' did you say?"

"That's right. Doesn't he want to be a star?"

"Why would I want to put you in touch with him?"

Tess dug into her purse, withdrew a Ben Franklin from her wallet, and flashed it in front of him.

Phil reached across the glass counter and snagged the hundred.

"I might be able to help you," he said, pocketing the bill.

"How can I reach him?"

"How many movies have you shot? Maybe I know your work. What's your name, or do you use a pseudonym?"

"This will be my first film. There's money to be made in this business. Sex sells."

"I'll see if I can get in touch with him."

"Do you have his phone number?"

"Uh—give me your number, and I'll see if he's interested. He'll call you, if he is."

Tess told him her first name and number. "Tell him I want to audition him for the part ASAP."

She halted out of the store.

She had just slid into her Mustang's driver's seat, wincing at the pain in her foot, when her cell phone chimed. That was fast, she decided. She withdrew her cell phone from her purse and took the call.

"Is this Tess?" said a male voice.

"Speaking."

"I hear you're hiring talent."

"Is this Moab?"

"In the flesh. And I'm ready for action. Are you familiar with my work?"

"Uh-huh. You're right for the part. Your character is a sadist who likes wearing black leather."

"BDSM?"

"Yeah."

"Right up my alley. Lots of black leather and bullwhips. I'm your guy."

"I figured."

"The more pain the merrier," said Moab, laughing.

"You sound perfect for the part," said Tess with a cringe.

"And I don't need a fluffer." Another laugh.

"Great," said Tess, shaking her head in bafflement.

"What kind of a paycheck are we talking about?"

"I'm prepared to offer you a hundred grand," she said, pulling a number out of thin air.

She had no idea how much porn stars made, especially male ones. She doubted they commanded the million-dollar paychecks of Hollywood movie stars. It made no difference. She wasn't going to pay him. She just wanted answers about Meryl Hennessey.

"OK," he said. "I'll audition. Where?"

"In my car."

"Say what? In your car, did you say?"

"Right. I'm parked in a white Mustang on Hollywood Boulevard near Western."

"I never auditioned in a car."

"There's an important scene in the script that takes place in a car. We want realism in this scene."

"I dunno. What's your last name?"

She made up a name. "Lane. Tess Lane."

"I never heard of you. How many films have you produced?" he said, suspicious.

"This is my first one."

"Amateur hour, huh?" he said, turned off.

"You don't have to be Stanley Kubrick to direct a porno. This ain't *Lolita*. It's all about the money, and I got some."

He laughed. "You got a point."

"You need to be able to perform at a moment's notice. Are you the brute I'm looking for?"

"Uh . . ."

"Does that mean you're not interested? I got actors begging to be in this movie."

"Uh . . . OK. When?"

"Now."

"Now? Fuck now. Gimme some time."

"How long will it take you to get here?"

"Where are you?"

"I'm right outside Phil's video store."

Moab hung fire. "Eh . . . twenty minutes."

"Fine."

Tess hung up.

Chapter 45

Tess watched a middle-aged guy with a shock of snow-white hair and a matching walrus mustache cruise by in a red Ferrari, the top down, his elbow leaning on the windowsill, hand gripping the steel lintel of the windshield. He gave her a questioning look. *Are you available?*

She ignored him.

She called Brody on her cell.

"I made contact with Moab," she said.

"Moby?"

"Moab. He's Meryl Hennessey's costar in her smut flick."

"Oh, yeah. You mentioned him."

"He would know if they shot a snuff film."

"Are you sure this is a good idea? If he thinks you know he did a snuff film, he could be dangerous."

"I got my Glock."

"I'd feel better if I went with you."

"I wouldn't."

"Where are you meeting him?"

The sound of knocking on her passenger's-side window gave her a turn. Startled, she looked through the window to see a hulking figure standing in blue jeans in the dark on the sidewalk peering through the glass at her. He pointed at the lock on the door.

"Gotta go," she told Brody, and killed their phone connection.

"What do you want?" she asked the guy at her window.

"I'm Moab."

She unlocked the door.

The guy standing beside her car opened the door and got in. All of six three with a heavy build and thick bones, he sat next to her.

Maybe this wasn't such a good idea, she decided.

She hadn't known what to expect, because she hadn't seen any pictures of him. She should have done her research and checked out some of the porno covers at Phil's to see what Moab looked like. But then again, she realized he was wearing a nylon stocking over his face, disguising his looks, giving him a threatening appearance.

Her pulse raced. Was he here to warn her off by mugging her? Had the porn producer of the snuff film told him she was asking too many questions about *The Love Life of Meryl Anne Monroe*? She had her purse on her lap and could whip out her piece at a moment's notice.

"How am I supposed to audition here?" he said, sounding intimidating.

"How do I know it's really you with that mask on?"

Even with his mask off, she wouldn't recognize him, she had to admit. She didn't know what he looked like.

"Who else would know you want to audition me here?" he said.

She nodded yes.

"Where's the script?" he said. "What are my lines?"

"First, I want to ask you a couple of questions."

"Why?"

"To see if you're right for the part."

"This is beginning to sound like bullshit," he said, shifting his bulk in his seat, bouncing the Mustang.

"I want to ask you about the movie you did with Meryl Hennessey."

"What?" he said with surprise, adjusting the stocking on his head.

"What did it feel like to act with her? That was her first film, I understand."

"What's this got to do with auditioning?"

"I'm trying to find out if you're OK with working with novices like Meryl Hennessey in *The Love Life of Meryl Anne Monroe*."

He didn't answer, searching her face.

"Why do you want to know about *that* movie?" he said.

"Because I'm also trying to find Meryl Hennessey to star in my movie opposite you. You two have good chemistry onscreen."

"How could you even have seen that movie?" he said, his voice menacing. "It's out of circulation."

"Not if you have enough money."

He relaxed somewhat. "Maybe. You must be loaded, then."

"So where can I find Meryl Hennessey?"

He stared through the windshield into the distance. "I have no idea."

Tess whipped her Glock out of her purse and trained the muzzle on his head. "I'm not kidding. Where is she?"

"What the fuck?"

"This is your audition. Play it like a scene in a movie."

He studied her face. He couldn't tell if she was on the level.

"OK," he said, his voice tentative.

"Take off that stocking."

He didn't move.

"Do it for the audition," she said. "I want to see the reactions on your face to see if you can act."

"That would be a first."

"What do you mean?"

"In my other films they don't care about my facial expressions."

"You have to be able to act if you want to star in my film. It's gonna open in mainstream theaters. It's gonna make more money than *Deep Throat*."

"Now you're talkin'."

He yanked off the stocking.

He had brown eyes, bushy black hair, a thick mustache, and a narrow chin. His dry, faintly purple, lips needed Chap Stick.

"Where is Meryl Hennessey?" said Tess.

"Why do you keep harping on her?"

"I want her to star with you."

"Get another starlet. You don't need her."

"I'll make that decision. Just tell me where Meryl is."

"She vanished after the movie. I haven't had any contact with her since we wrapped that film."

"Why would she up and vanish? It makes no sense."

"How do I know? I don't know anything about her. Just because I shot a film with her doesn't mean I know squat about her."

"Maybe you had something to do with her vanishing. Maybe you buried her dead body."

He bridled. "What the hell? It was a movie. It wasn't real."

"Where did you bury her corpse?"

"Who are you? This ain't no audition I ever heard of. I'm getting outa here," he said, reaching to open his door.

"Don't."

"What are you gonna do? Kill me? You'd never get away with it. There are people all around here. Look at the sidewalks."

"Tell me. Did you murder Meryl Hennessey?"

"What? Are you crazy? No."

"You and your producer buddy won't let anyone but rich degenerates see the film because it's a snuff film and you don't want it reported to the cops. You know the degenerate voyeurs who see the movie won't report you because they want to see more of the same."

"You're nuts, lady," said Moab, his eyes wild, taking in her Glock.

"If you turn yourself into the cops, they'll go easier on you."

"Turn myself in for what? For being an actor?"

Tess didn't plan on shooting the guy, but she wanted answers. She was convinced Moab and his shady producer friend had killed Meryl Hennessey and filmed the murder.

"Did you bury the body near the set?" said Tess, taking a guess.

Moab froze in his seat. His stunned look morphed into anger.

"You're the one that needs to be busted by the cops," he said. "I have a good mind to report you for assaulting me."

"Did you know Max Reed?"

"No."

"What about Rafe Calabrese?"

"The Mafia capo that died in a car bombing in Vegas? Why would I know him?"

"Maybe he finances your pornos."

"I don't produce them. I star in them."

"Show me where you buried Hennessey's corpse, and the cops'll go easier on you."

Shaking his head Moab flung open the car door, clambered out of his seat, and stalked away down the sidewalk into the dark, his shoulders hunched, not sure she wouldn't shoot him.

He had seemed to react when she had accused him of burying Hennessey near the set, decided Tess. Hennessey's burial on the set was a shot in the dark on her part, and maybe she was misreading his reaction.

She had no intention of blowing him away. She put away her pistol.

Chapter 46

At her apartment in West Hollywood Tess called Brody on her cell phone.

"I just finished talking with Moab," she said, dropping her purse on her sofa and flicking on her flat panel 4K HDTV.

"I hope you're not in the hospital," he said, concern in his voice.

"I'm in my apartment," she said, kicking off her shoes. "He didn't admit to anything. Which is strange."

"Why's it strange?"

"Because I had a gun pointed at his head the whole time."

"Did he assault you?"

"I didn't give him a chance."

"Why'd you pull the gun on him?"

"Because I wanted him to tell me the truth. I think he's lying."

"About the snuff film he did with Hennessey?"

"He claims it wasn't a snuff film. That Hennessey retired from acting after she made one picture."

"I find that hard to believe."

"Me, too. I think they whacked her, and did it in front of a movie camera so wealthy degenerates could pay beaucoup bucks to watch a BDSM porno with an actual murder committed onscreen. A depraved example of cinema verité."

"The question is, was Calabrese involved?"

"I asked Moab. He said no. He also said he didn't know Max Reed."

"He could be lying." Brody paused. "Do you think Moab is the one that whacked Hennessey?"

"It must've been him. There's no one else listed in the film's cast. Just him and Meryl Hennessey. I bet he tortured and wasted her on film."

"For all we know, there could be more of these snuff films involving models that used to work for Max Reed."

"That would make Moab a mass murderer if he also starred in them."

"If Reed knew he was involving them in snuff films, he's as guilty as the killer."

Tess watched the image of a blood-splattered shirt on the TV news.

"You know the shirt Reed wore when he was blown up?" she said.

"I know. Somebody's selling it on eBay."

"It's selling for $150,000 now, according to the news."

"They were betting on it at the sportsbook at Caesar's Palace, seeing who could come closest to picking the actual sale price."

Tess scratched her head in bemusement. "What does someone want with a bloody shirt? It's not like you can wear it."

"If Max Reed's name is connected to it, it's as good as gold. And that shirt has his actual blood and DNA on it."

Tess pulled a face. "That makes sense then."

Tess's white Persian cat with aquamarine eyes made an appearance and rubbed against her leg, trying to persuade her to get out the cat food. Tess reached down and petted her.

"Where have you been, Lady?" she said. "Sleeping away your life?"

"Did you find out anything else from Moab?"

"I have a hunch Hennessey's body may be buried near the movie set where they shot the picture."

"Why?"

"When I asked Moab if he buried her on the set, he had a strong reaction."

"They could have incinerated her first," said Brody, damping her enthusiasm.

"Which would make ID'ing the ashes difficult, I know. But I still think it's worth a try."

"What's worth a try?"

"Searching the movie set for Hennessey's corpse."

"You would have no idea where to look."

“I wouldn’t need one with a cadaver dog. A friend of mine, Diane, trains cadaver dogs. I could get one from her.”

“Wait a minute. This Moab character and the producer sound dangerous. I’m going with you this time—”

Tess terminated the call and padded to the kitchen to feed Lady.

Chapter 47

Megan watched Preston Wells strut into her office in Beverly Hills. He wore jeans and a white T with a black skull silkscreened on it designed by Max Reed.

"I'm glad you could make time to see me," he said, his voice dripping with sarcasm.

"Can I offer you a drink? Coffee? Water?"

"Let's skip the amenities."

"You said you had something to tell me about the company," she said from behind her desk that had several sketches of new fashions lying on it. "Have a seat."

Wells sat down. "You act like you're the boss."

"This *is* my office."

"This isn't over by a long shot. I'm not backing down."

"I thought you came here to talk about the company, not about yourself."

"I am the company, now that Max is gone."

"His will says otherwise," said Megan, her face smug.

Wells tried to compose himself. "Why didn't you tell me you wanted to be the CEO of the company? I'm sure we could've worked something out. Instead, you go behind my back and tell everyone you're the boss without even telling me what you're planning to do."

"I didn't like the way you took over the company like it was your divine right."

"It was my right. I was his second-in-command."

"My father's will says otherwise."

"Why didn't you tell me you wanted control? I never had any idea you wanted to lead the company."

"Why should I tell you? You had no right to take over. You made your move without making any attempt to contact me."

"You never had any input in Max's business decisions."

"What's that got to do with anything?"

"He used me—and me alone. It was only natural I take over."

"In your opinion."

"It's a fact. You don't know anything about running a business. I was with Max whenever he made a business decision. You never were there. You have no idea what he wanted to accomplish with his brand."

"He wanted to make us the biggest, most profitable fashion house in the world. And he wanted to provoke at the same time. Tear down the old fogeys like Dior and YSL and bring in the new entrepreneurs of fashion—us."

"But you don't know how to do it. You don't know the nuts and bolts of the business like I do. I know every aspect. I worked my way up from the bottom, so I had to learn all aspects. I know the unsexy sides, like the costs of production and of the supply chain—"

"Anyone can do that. I'll hire someone to do it. I know the most important thing. I know Dad's dream, his vision, and his style. Nobody knows it like me."

"Why did you have to go behind my back?" said Wells, irritated, squinting at her in paranoid fashion. "I'm sure we could have worked something out."

"I didn't like the way you assumed you were in charge as soon as Dad died. You didn't consult me. Why should I consult you?"

"I had no reason to consult you. I was the obvious choice to lead," he said, gesturing with his hands.

"*I* was the obvious choice to lead." She paused for effect. "Everyone knows about your problems with substance abuse."

"What?" said Wells, his eyes popping.

"You got problems with nose candy."

"I can't believe you would stoop this low," said Wells, bolting to his feet.

"If you insist on going to court, your drug problem will come out during the trial."

"Dragging my name through the mud isn't gonna work. I'm not backing down. I'm not gonna stand by and let your coup succeed."

"The law says I'm the new boss," she said, jumping to her feet and pounding her desktop with her fist.

"We'll see about that."

"Don't fight me. You'll regret it. I'll fire you. I mean it."

"You can't fire me because I'm in charge. You're the one that's gonna get fired."

"You have no chance of winning against me."

"The other employees will side with me."

"Who cares what they do? They can't decide who's boss."

"The company will collapse under you. Mark my words," said Wells, brandishing his finger at her. "Do the right thing and bow out."

"I *am* doing the right thing. I'm taking over."

Wells stalked to the door, flung it open, and burst out.

Megan plumped herself down on her chair in a huff. The war with Wells had begun, she decided. He had let her know he had no plans to step aside. And neither did she.

Chapter 48

From his motel room in West LA, Brody used the burner app on his cell phone to call LAPD Lt. Macready at the downtown police station.

"Have you decided to drop charges against me for Reed's murder?" said Brody.

"No."

"Then why should I talk to you?"

"It's your dime, not mine."

"If I give you more information about the murder, will you drop the charges?"

"I doubt it. I don't see how you could have any info worth my attention."

"I believe I do."

"What is it?"

"Clues have led me to the belief that Max Reed and Rafe Calabrese might have been involved in the porn racket. They actively recruited fashion models for their pornos."

"Do you have proof?"

"Not yet."

"Then don't waste my time."

"Agree to drop the charges against me and I'll share my info with you when I get it."

"Is this a joke? I don't cut deals with murder suspects, especially one that was photographed carrying a bomb into a building that blew up moments later."

"Calabrese ordered the hit on Max Reed."

"And you took the contract? Is that what you're confessing? I have my tape recorder running, by the way."

"I had no idea I was carrying a bomb. He used me."

"What makes you think Calabrese and Reed were involved in the porno racket?"

"I know a porn producer who recruited fashion models at Reed's parties to be in his films."

"What's illegal about it?"

"One of the models was underage, and she disappeared right after she made the movie."

"You got proof? Is she willing to testify to that?"

"She vanished off the face of the earth. I believe the producer shot a snuff film with her in it."

"What's the name of this porn producer?"

Brody hesitated.

"Well?" demanded Macready.

"We're having trouble finding out his name. It's not listed on the film's credits on the Internet."

"You don't even know the guy's name?"

"We're gonna get it any time now."

"Give me proof," said Macready, his voice rising in anger. "You've given me zilch so far. Not even the guy's name."

"I can tell you the name of the missing actress. Meryl Hennessey."

"And how do you know they killed her during a snuff film?"

"Because she disappeared right after she made it."

"You expect me to take that case to the DA?" said Macready in outrage. "You're wasting my time."

"I'm working on getting evidence."

"Turn yourself in, and I'll be willing to hear you out."

Brody didn't trust Macready. If he turned himself in to Macready, the guy would lock him up so he couldn't clear his name by finding evidence to implicate Calabrese in the murder of Reed.

"I can't do that," said Brody.

"Where the hell are you?"

"I can't tell you."

"We're gonna find you, and I'm gonna throw the book at you for resisting arrest."

Macready hung up, spitting out a curse.

Chapter 49

Shirley Kinsey, Max Reed's twenty-nine-year-old blonde mistress, stepped into the elevator of her condo building in Brentwood to return to her room with no idea she had but a precious few more seconds to go on living.

Who could have guessed she would start out as one of Max Reed's fashion models and end up as his mistress? It had all been so sudden and unbelievable—like a fairy tale. And yet it was true. And then it had ended as suddenly as it had begun with his assassination by C-4. Just like that.

Everybody had to die, of course, but Max had been so young, she decided.

Ever since he had died, she had been depressed and been seeing her psychiatrist. At times she had felt suicidal. She didn't think she would ever get over Max's death. It had been so abrupt and unexpected. He was in the pink the last time she had seen him.

Her psychiatrist had told her she would get over Max's loss in time. Time healed all wounds, was her shrink's mantra. He could not know her time was running out.

Wearing a cerise minidress and matching pumps she stood alone in the elevator waiting for it to rise. The doors remained open as if waiting for more passengers.

Why weren't they closing? she wondered.

Maybe she hadn't pressed her floor's button. She was like that nowadays, always forgetting what she was doing, her mind elsewhere.

She glanced at her floor's button on the annunciator panel in the elevator. The button was lit. Which meant she had pressed it. Then why wasn't the door closing so they could start the trip upward? she wondered.

She reached over to the panel and pressed the button again, hoping the doors would close and they could get moving.

Nothing was happening.

Maybe this elevator was broken, she decided. But her floor's number was lit. Didn't that mean the car was in operation?

Her stomach grumbled. She hadn't eaten all day except for a blueberry yogurt and a glass of orange juice she had had for breakfast. She felt like a dish of scrambled eggs and crispy bacon for lunch today. Her mouth watered at the thought. Throw in an English muffin smeared with marmalade. Yummy.

If this elevator was broken, she would need to get out and enter another one, she decided. It must be one of those days where everything went wrong.

She was about to exit the elevator when the doors started closing.

Finally.

Maybe someone had been holding the elevator button in the lobby, which would have prevented the doors from closing, she decided.

She saw a figure in a black trench coat standing in the lobby wearing a wide-brimmed fedora facing away from her.

She wondered if the person had been pressing the button so her elevator couldn't rise. Whoever it was wasn't pressing the lobby button now. The figure spun around, flipping something in Shirley's direction.

Before the doors closed, an object flew into the elevator from the lobby and skittered across the floor, landing near Shirley's pumps.

She gazed at the object.

It looked like a flesh-colored plastic dildo, similar to the one Max had given her for her birthday. What was it doing—

The ear-splitting explosion in the elevator and her subsequent death prevented her from finishing her thought. Her amputated arm lying in the doorway prevented the elevator doors from closing.

The figure in the trench coat dashed out of the lobby.

Chapter 50

Brody watched the crime scene on the flat-panel TV fixed to the wall across from his bed in his motel room.

Inspector Macready appeared on the screen standing on the sidewalk in front of the Brentwood condo that had sustained damage in the explosion. Yellow crime-scene tape kept rubberneckers away from the area as a redheaded TV reporter in a mint green dress jutted a mic in Macready's face and asked him what had happened.

"There was an explosion in the elevator in the condo," said Macready.

"Why are the police involved?" said the reporter.

"Elevators don't normally blow up. We're treating this as a homicide."

"Somebody died?"

"We've notified her next of kin. Her name is Shirley Kinsey."

"The fashion model?"

"Yes."

"Didn't she used to work for Max Reed?"

"That's what we've learned."

"Do you think her murder is related to Max Reed's?"

"We're not allowed to comment on that at this time."

"Do you think it was the same person that murdered them?"

"I can't comment on an ongoing investigation."

"Are you saying a bomb was used to kill Ms. Kinsey?"

"An explosive device of some sort. The FBI is helping with the investigation."

"The FBI? Why?"

"The bureau's TEDAC is set up for bomb investigations. They have the best equipment in the country."

"But why are they being called in? Isn't this a local murder?"

"Bombings are treated as terrorist attacks until we know otherwise. The FBI always investigates terrorist attacks."

"You suspect terrorists?"

"I can't comment on an ongoing investigation."

Macready turned away from the reporter and left the picture.

Brody awoke his laptop from Sleep mode and googled Shirley Kinsey. A former fashion model for Max Reed, she was now reputed to be one of his not-so-secret lovers. So far, the bomber had killed Reed and two of his lovers, not to mention the two Reed Enterprises office workers that died along with Reed in the bombing. It had to be the same killer, decided Brody. Even the MO was the same. Brody figured the two office workers hadn't been intended targets. They had happened to be in the wrong place at the wrong time—what the military euphemistically called *collateral damage*.

Calabrese was not a suspect in Kinsey's murder, decided Brody. Calabrese was dead and couldn't have taken out Kinsey. It was someone else that had murdered her. Was there another killer beside Calabrese? Was his mob continuing the killings by going after Kinsey? It didn't track. Why would the mob kill Reed *and* his lovers? Somebody else must be involved in the killings.

The mysterious porn producer who filmed the missing Meryl Hennessey? Was he involved in the bombings? Brody couldn't see what the guy's motive would be. Maybe Reed's lovers refused to be in a porno. It could be anything, Brody decided. He needed more information. The porn producer had become Brody's prime suspect in the killings of Reed's lovers.

And Brody still didn't know why Calabrese had blown up Reed.

Was it possible Calabrese hadn't put out a contract on Reed? wondered Brody. Had Sal Andrasi lied to him when he said Calabrese had been the one responsible for sending the bomb to Reed? Was Andrasi the one that had wanted Reed dead?

The TV news cut to a related story.

Max Reed's blood-splattered shirt appeared on the screen. The shirt was now selling on eBay for $500,000, and the bids kept flooding in to the website.

In an accompanying story the female announcer said Reed's fashions were flying off the shelves since his murder, and his Instagram followers were increasing by millions every day.

"It may turn out that in death Max Reed and his fashions will be even more popular than when he was alive," she said.

Chapter 51

When Tess drove to her friend's company to rent a cadaver dog, she also rented a tranquilizer gun.

"Why do you need the gun?" said Diane, the tall, thin, middle-aged owner of the business who had a suntanned, wizened face with her grizzled chestnut hair tied back in a bun.

Wearing jeans and suede coffee cowboy boots she was standing in her dog kennel, gripping the leather leash of her Alsatian cadaver dog Willy.

"I might have to trank a guard dog," said Tess, smelling the odor of wet dog fur.

Maybe Diane had just washed the dogs, she decided.

"Carfentanyl is in the darts, so be very careful when you handle them," said Diane.

They walked to a cabinet, which Diane opened to display several tranquilizer guns that looked like rifles. She handed one to Tess.

"I understand," said Tess, accepting the weapon.

"And don't trank Willy. He's your friend," said Diane, petting Willy's head.

"I know. He's in good hands," said Tess, smiling at Willy. "How accurate is his sense of smell when it comes to cadavers?"

"He can smell human remains even if they're fifteen feet underground. He's *that* good."

"Wow. I had no idea. He's just what the doctor ordered. What about human ashes from cremation?"

Diane nodded yes. "He can smell them."

"Perfect."

"I hope you're not putting Willy in danger," said Diane with concern, eying the trank gun in Tess's hand.

"No. There's just a pesky guard dog that I don't want to have to deal with. That's all."

"All right. Because Willy's not an attack dog. He won't protect you if you're assaulted."

"I can handle myself. I just have to neutralize the guard dog."

"Don't miss. You're only gonna get one shot. You can't reload."

"What's the range of the dart gun?"

"The gun's accurate to thirty feet, but I wouldn't use it over twenty, especially if you've got a dog attacking you—unless you're really skilled with it. And you're not—even though you may be good with a traditional gun. A moving target is always harder to hit."

"I know. I'm good with guns."

"Whatever you do, don't shoot at the dog's head. You might hit him in the eye."

"I'll aim for his chest, if he attacks me."

"I wouldn't recommend his chest. Aim for his shoulder muscle. If you hit the chest, you might pierce the dog's lung and kill him."

"It would be hard to hit the shoulder area if he's charging me."

"You need to trank him before he attacks, so you can hit his shoulder. You want to shoot him from the flank, not the front. There's a scope on that dart gun. It's accurate."

"I dunno. It might be tough to get a flank shot. I think he's gonna smell me before I see him. Then he'll charge."

"He knows you?"

"Let's put it this way. We've met." Tess glanced at her dog-bit foot and winced.

"I see. You can still hit his shoulder from the front. But you'll have a smaller target."

"And a moving target." Tess paused. "How long will he be out from the drug?"

"About an hour. When he comes to, he'll be groggy and have trouble controlling his reflexes. He'll still be feeling the effects of the drug for up to three hours."

"That'll give me plenty of time to finish my search—I hope. Now for the most important question. How long does it take for the trank to work after the dog's been hit? Will he fall to the ground right off the bat?"

"No, he won't. A lot of people think that's true—maybe they saw it in the movies—but they're misinformed. It should take anywhere between three to ten minutes to incapacitate him. You'll have to keep him at bay for that long."

"Wonderful."

"Unless . . ."

"Unless what?"

"Unless you hit the dog in the heart. The drug would go much quicker through his circulatory system to the brain and knock him out faster."

"The heart, huh?" said Tess, becoming despondent.

"A very difficult shot because of the heart's protection by the rib cage."

Tess nodded. She wasn't even sure where a dog's heart was located.

"Is there some way to speed up the process?" she said.

"No. A larger dose won't act any quicker. And it might kill the dog."

"I don't want that."

"Even if you did, I wouldn't give you that large a dose. I love dogs. I love them more than I love people," said Diane, gazing warmly into Willy's brown eyes.

"I don't blame you. Dogs don't murder each other." Tess thought about it. "I'll have to figure out some way to stay away from the guard dog after I trank it."

"If you're outside, I suggest you hide in a tree or on top of a wall or something."

"I'll probably be inside, but I see what you're saying. Get on top of something out of the dog's reach."

Diane petted Willy's head again. "I don't usually loan my dogs to anyone other than law enforcement, but you're a friend and I know you would never mistreat Willy."

"I appreciate it, Diane."

“There’s not a big demand for cadaver dogs. Mostly law enforcement and the military.”

“The police aren’t gonna believe me, if I bring this murder case to their attention. They’re not gonna look into it. I have to provide my own cadaver dog.”

“Why’s that?”

“I don’t have any evidence of a murder. But I’m pretty sure a murder took place on a movie set I visited.” Tess shrugged. “Well, call it a hunch.”

“It sounds like it could be dangerous.”

“Danger goes with my job.”

“Don’t let anyone harm Willy,” said Diane, handing Willy’s leash to Tess.

“They’ll have to get through me to get to him.”

Willy opened his mouth and grinned, slopping out his pink tongue, which curled at the tip. He was looking forward to a good time.

Tess knew better. They were both heading for trouble.

Chapter 52

Brody ordered tamales with Megan Reed at the Farmer's Market. She had agreed to talk to him about her father's murder. She was wearing jeans, a loose cream blouse, and white jogging shoes, all designed by Reed Enterprises. She was a walking advertisement for her company.

"Was your father upset about anything before he died?" said Brody.

"I don't think so." She took a pull on her bottle of lime soda. "I love lime soda. Reminds me of when I was a kid and went to school picnics," she said, licking her lips. "He was annoyed at Preston Wells."

"Oh. Why was that?"

"Wells wanted to take the company in a different direction. Away from its 'tawdry' side, as he termed it."

"The emphasis on blood and violence in Reed's ads?"

"Right. Wells wanted to tone it down. He thought it was turning off customers."

"Did either one of them know Rafe Calabrese?"

"The Mafia guy?"

"Yeah."

"Not that I know of. Why would they know him?"

"I dunno," said Brody, not wanting to tip his hand.

"You said you're a PI. Who are you working for?"

"I don't divulge clients' names."

Which in this case happened to be himself, decided Brody.

"I don't know who would be so interested in my father's death that they would hire a PI," said Megan. "After all, the cops are investigating it."

"They don't always do a good job. And . . ."

"And what?"

"And politics might be involved, which could hamper the investigation. The mayor and your father were pretty close, I hear."

Megan didn't show any interest in pursuing the matter. "I don't know him."

"What about you? Did you know Calabrese?"

"No."

"You never saw him with you father?"

"Never. I don't see what Calabrese has to do with anything. Are you trying to say my company is corrupt?" she said, becoming resentful.

He leaned closer to her. He could smell her subtle perfume, recognizing a faint lavender scent.

"I haven't told this to anyone but the cops," he said. "I have reason to believe Calabrese ordered the death of your father."

"What?" she said, taken aback. "I don't understand. Why would he?"

"That's what I'm trying to figure out."

"You must be mistaken. My dad had nothing to do with the Mafia."

"Did you know your father was arranging for a porn producer to hire his fashion models as actors in adult movies?"

"I don't believe it."

"The porn producer went to your father's parties, met models there, and arranged for them to act in his movies."

"Even if that's true, it doesn't mean my dad knew it was going on. He invites hundreds of people to his parties. They're huge galas."

"Maybe Calabrese was involved in the porn racket with the producer and your father."

"You have no proof. You're making things up. How dare you drag my father's name through the mud?"

"I'm trying to find out what's going on."

"I'll sue you if you go public with any of this slander."

"I don't plan on going public with anything until I know the truth."

"Who is this porn producer you're talking about?"

"I don't know his name. Maybe you can help me with that."

Megan stood up. "Like I said, you're making this up. You don't even know the guy's name? Come on."

"Sit down."

"Why?"

"There's more."

Grudgingly, Megan took her seat. "More speculation, or facts?"

"I have good reason to believe he produces snuff films as well as smut," he said, keeping his voice low.

"What's your definition of 'good reason to believe'?" she said, her tone skeptical.

"One of his actresses disappeared after the producer did a movie with her as his star. I believe he wasted her on film. If we can view that film—"

Megan knocked back her lime soda. "I believe *you* have an overactive imagination."

"Is there any way you can find this producer's name for me by going through your lists of guests to your dad's parties?"

"I don't see what any of this has to do with Dad's murder."

"This producer may be mixed up in it, if he was consorting with Calabrese, who distributes porn."

"Why would a porn producer kill Dad?"

"Calabrese killed your dad—"

Megan searched Brody's face. "Wait a minute. Aren't you the guy the cops want for murdering Dad?"

"I delivered Calabrese's bomb to your father's office, but I had no idea what was in the bowling bag I delivered to him."

Megan stood up. "How do I know you won't try to kill me, too?"

"I was a cat's paw. Calabrese used me to do his dirty work."

“I should turn you into the police,” she said, her body stiff.

Brody stood up, becoming nervous. “I’m your only chance of finding out who really killed your father.”

“You said Calabrese did it.”

“The problem is, I don’t know why. There’s a piece missing from the jigsaw. I can’t ask Calabrese because he’s dead. The porno producer may have the answer. If you could give me a list of your dad’s guests to his last party, it might help me find him.”

She looked like she believed him or wanted to, decided Brody, watching her.

“I guess I could do that,” she said, not sounding eager about it.

“Thanks. Send it to my e-mail.” He gave her his e-mail address. “When was the last party your father gave?”

“A few weeks ago, I think. It’s gonna be a big list. My dad didn’t do anything in half measures, especially parties. He threw humongous parties to impress VIPs and tout his brand.”

“I understand.”

Megan chewed it over. “You know, now that I think about it, there was one guest who looked like he was drooling over all of the fashion models. He was sizing them up like they were pieces of meat.”

“Do you remember his name?”

“I never got his name. I remember him because he was confined to a diamond-studded platinum wheelchair. He reminded me of the dead smut publisher Larry Flynt. He couldn’t get enough of the fashion models, stalking them in his wheelchair like he wanted to devour their flesh.” Megan shivered. “It was creepy.”

“Do you remember what he looked like?”

“How can I forget? He had peroxide blond hair and slimy blue eyes always ogling the models’ figures—and mine, too, by the way. He wore his shirt half unbuttoned, revealing his chest hair and a gold cross he wore around his neck. One of those loud Hawaiian shirts, you know.”

"Good. That's helpful. If only I had some idea of his name . . ."

"I was never introduced to him."

"Did your father talk to him a lot?"

"Not that I saw. One of the fashion models complained to me about him. She didn't like the way he was looking at her. There was nothing I could do. It was Dad's party. And there's no law against a guy giving a woman dirty looks."

"This could be the guy I'm looking for."

"I have a meeting with my lawyer," said Megan, glancing at her wristwatch and gathering her purse. "Preston Wells is trying to take over my company."

"I thought he already took it over."

"He did, but he had no legal right to. Dad's will says I'm in charge."

"Wells can't be too happy about that. He thought he was next in line to take control."

"He's gonna fight me, but I'm gonna win. There's no way he's taking my company from me."

Brody mulled it over. "Do you think he could have had anything to do with your father's death? After all, he thought he was next in line to take over the company."

"I never thought about it. I can't imagine he would do such a thing. But I wouldn't put it past him. Did you see how quickly he took control of the company after Dad's death?"

"Yes."

"Anyway, you said the Mafia guy murdered Dad."

"I know," said Brody, rubbing his forehead. "But I can't find his motive. Something's hinky."

"I really do have to go. I have a feeling this could be a nasty battle brewing between me and Wells. I'm gonna spend every waking minute fighting him," she said, and bustled away.

Brody picked up on a young uniformed cop with a brush cut strutting through the market. He wondered if Megan had called the police. Brody wasn't going to stick around to find out. He left his half-eaten tamale, gulped down his Coke, paid the bill, and bugged out.

Chapter 53

Tess drove Willy to the porn producer's brick warehouse on Lankershim. Willy liked the ride. Sitting in the passenger seat he stuck his head out his open window the whole time, laughing at the wind rushing by his face.

She parked along the curb at a parking meter on the side of the street in front of the warehouse.

Her cell phone chimed in her purse as she stood on the sidewalk holding onto Willy's leash. She set her purse on the hood of the Mustang, fished out her cell phone, and checked the screen to see who was calling.

It was Brody.

He probably was calling to tell her to wait for him.

She didn't accept the call. She didn't want to wait for him to arrive at the warehouse. This was her job, and she didn't need any help.

She popped the Mustang's trunk and withdrew the trank gun. She didn't want to walk on the street carrying the gun in full view, which would have drawn too much attention. She had a jacket in her trunk. She draped the jacket over the gun.

She closed the trunk and eyeballed the brick building. She wondered if she should take Willy to the backyard first to search for a cadaver—if there was a backyard. She couldn't see from the street if there was any land behind the building. She saw no access to the back from the street either.

Her hands were full with the trank gun, her purse, and Willy's leash. She slung her purse strap over her shoulder, leaving her hands free to carry the trank gun and the leash, and approached the front door.

As she had expected, the door was locked.

She placed the trank gun and her jacket on the concrete stoop, withdrew a lock pick gun from her purse, and picked the door's dead bolt.

She slipped inside the warehouse with Willy and closed the door behind her.

She scoped out the dark interior. She didn't see any movement or hear any sound. If the Doberman guard dog was in the warehouse, he wasn't moving.

She let go of Willy's leash.

"Do your thing, Willy," she said.

Willy commenced sniffing around the building, trying to pick up a scent.

Tess wandered around, peeking into rooms. She took out her smart phone, flicked on the flashlight, and, phone in one hand and trank gun in the other, peeked into rooms that bordered the warehouse's perimeter. She heard Willy's nails scuttling across the concrete floor.

She wondered if Willy could smell a body buried beneath concrete. She noticed some of the rooms had hardwood floors, in lieu of the concrete used in the main section of the warehouse.

To bury a corpse beneath concrete would be an arduous chore, she decided. You would have to break the concrete, dig a hole, and then pour new concrete after burying the body. She didn't think the killer would go to that much trouble.

Willy entered one of the rooms, sniffed around the hardwood floor, and commenced making a noise. Tess cut across the warehouse to reach him. He was sniffing the corner of the room, which contained an old sofa and other movie props.

"Is this where they buried her, Willy?" she said.

Willy snuffled around the floor intently, absorbed in his world of scents.

She heard a noise in another part of the warehouse. Her pulse raced.

It sounded like something was rolling along the floor toward her. She stole out of the room and shone her cell's flashlight in the direction of the sound. Before she located the sound, the guard dog bolted toward her.

Her heart in her mouth, she raised her trank gun and trained it on the charging Doberman. The red light on the scope located the snarling dog, baring its teeth. Tess steadied her aim and fired the trank gun at the oncoming beast.

The tranquilizer needle struck the Doberman in full stride and lodged in the shoulder area. The dog yelped when hit and slowed down, wondering what had happened.

She searched the warehouse for a place to hide while the drug knocked the Doberman unconscious. She had to avoid the attacking dog for three to ten minutes, according to Diane, while the drug did its job tranquilizing the animal.

Luckily for her, the Doberman had slowed down when the dart hit him. He was trying to figure out what had happened to him, sniffing and licking the dart stuck in his flesh. Tess doubted he would spend much more time thinking about the dart.

She had to hide before he resumed his attack on her.

Willy emerged from the room and started barking at the Doberman.

Tess took the opportunity to dash toward a six-foot-high stack of pallets piled against the wall on the other side of the warehouse. Diane had told her to seek the high ground. Tess intended to climb the pallets before the Doberman could reach her.

Ignoring Willy's barks the Doberman launched itself at her.

She ran as fast as she could, injured foot and all. Fear was a great motivator. Adrenaline churning through her system, she leapt onto the stack of pallets and scrabbled up them.

The Doberman bounded after her, unfazed by the carfentanyl invading its bloodstream.

Gasping for breath she reached the top of the stack of pallets and jerked her feet out of the way of the Doberman's snapping mouth. She sat on the stack. The dog leapt high enough that its face was gazing directly at her as it tried to bite her face. She pulled back from the creature all the way to the wall behind her. The dog returned to the ground and jumped up again. She pulled her feet away from him and sat in a ball, gripping her bent knees with her arms. The dog's head disappeared then bobbed up again, snapping its jaws and biting the air.

What was taking the drug so long to act? she wondered. Had she missed the animal's shoulder? If so, what did she hit? Did she hit bone instead of muscle?

Willy loped toward the Doberman and barked at him. The Doberman ignored him, bent on sinking its teeth into Tess.

She had lost track of time. She didn't know how long ago she had shot the Doberman. It seemed like it was half an hour ago, but it couldn't have been that long. How could the dog still be conscious after a half hour? Had the hypo needle broken when it hit the dog? What if the carfentanyl hadn't entered the Doberman's bloodstream?

She started when she heard another noise in the warehouse. It was the same sound she had heard earlier. The sound of rolling wheels.

She realized the Doberman wasn't trying to jump onto the pallets anymore.

She edged toward the rim of the stack of pallets and peeked over, apprehensive about the dog jumping up and biting her.

She discerned a figure on the floor twenty-odd feet away from her. The figure rolled toward her.

She could see it was a man sitting in a gleaming motorized wheelchair. She could also see he had a pistol in his hand aimed at her.

Chapter 54

Tess saw the Doberman's body lying on its side on the floor.

"You killed my dog," said the man in the wheelchair. "Give me one good reason I shouldn't kill you."

"He's drugged," said Tess, "not dead."

"And?"

"And what?"

"That's not a good reason I shouldn't kill you."

"How about, murder is against the law?"

"You're trespassing on my property. I have the right to shoot a trespasser."

"Maybe in Florida, but not in California."

"What are you? Some shyster?"

"Who are you? What's your name?"

"Matt Steward. What's yours?"

"Tess Hardwick."

Tess realized she didn't have her piece with her. In her haste to evade the Doberman she had dropped her purse that contained her weapon.

She could see Steward better now.

In his fifties he had rheumy blue eyes and peroxide blond hair. A gold cross on a silver chain depended from his neck.

"Are you the producer who shot the movie *The Love Life of Meryl Anne Monroe*?"

"How would you know anything about that?"

"I—"

"Wait a minute. I recognize you. You're the girl that wanted to be in one of my films. You were here before."

"What of it?"

"You said you were fifteen and your name was Shari Landers. You're fifteen in a pig's eye. And your name's not Shari Landers."

"I used to be fifteen."

"Very funny. Didn't you get the message last time? I don't want to hire you."

"You already got a movie star for your next porno?"

"One man's porno is another man's art."

"So how come you have to hire different movie stars for each of your movies?"

"Because I like finding new talent—if it's any of your business."

"Or is because you shoot snuff films?"

Nonplussed, he stared at her. His right eye twitched. His already-pale complexion turned paler.

"Nobody's shooting snuff films," he said. "I'm gonna sue you for slander if you go around shooting your mouth off about this. Your career in movies will be over. I got a lot of juice in showbiz, and I can destroy actors' careers. You want your career destroyed?"

"I want to know where Meryl Hennessey is."

"Who's Meryl Hennessey?"

"She starred in your porno *The Love Life of Meryl Anne Monroe*."

"I resent your calling my films pornos. I'm exercising my First Amendment rights when I make a film. My films are art, not pornos."

"Shooting pornos with underage models starring in them is illegal."

"Freedom of speech is never illegal in this country. I have the right to freedom of speech."

"Your rights mean nothing if they infringe on others' rights. Infringing on others' rights nullifies your rights."

"That's all I need. Some shyster telling me how to live."

"I'm no shyster."

"You're not an artist either. You know nothing about art."

Tess wondered why the guy's face was so white. She thought he might be wearing makeup, but it was hard to tell in the dimness.

"I didn't come here to discuss art," she said. "I want you to tell me where Meryl Hennessey is."

"She made no impression on me. I don't remember her."

"You killed her for a scene in your porno snuff film, and you don't even remember her?" said Tess, her voice ringing with outrage.

"I don't make snuff films. I don't make pornos. I make adult art films."

"Starring fifteen-year-olds."

"She told me she was eighteen. None of this 'she was fifteen years old' crap you're spewing out," he said, sliding back and forth in agitation on his wheelchair.

"You turned her into a whore and killed her in front of the camera. And you think that's OK?"

"Anything done in the name of art is permissible. This is a free country. We believe in freedom of speech here. It's not Nazi Germany or the USSR. This is America."

"What did you do with her corpse?"

"You're certifiable, lady."

"Your actor Moab is a murderer, too. He's the one that raped Meryl and murdered her in front of your movie camera," said Tess, her voice rising in accusation.

"Everything that occurs in front of my cameras is staged. I don't do documentaries."

"If there's nothing wrong with the movie, why don't you let me watch it?"

"It's out of print," he said in a throwaway tone.

"I've heard otherwise. There's a website on the dark web that says the movie can be viewed for a pile of money. And that website gives your phone number to call."

"Is this your way of trying to land a starring role in one of my films? Breaking and entering and insulting them? You really think I'm gonna let you star in any of them after all the bilge you've been spewing?"

"You really think just because there's demand for your snuff films, there should be supply for them? Demand doesn't justify supply. Killing people onscreen is illegal. You *will* do time for it."

"In your dreams," said Steward, his face smug. "Where there's no corpse, there's no crime. Meryl Hennessey probably upped and went back home to Iowa to her mother—like all the other wannabe movie stars that can't make it in Hollywood."

"I thought you didn't remember her. How'd you know her home state is Iowa?"

"I made it up. It was a lucky guess. She really is from Iowa?" he said in surprise.

"Still pretending you don't know her."

"You know nothing about art. You're no better than a trespassing thug."

"You wear a cross like you're righteous and then you go shoot snuff films. What's that make you?"

"An artist."

"A hypocrite, is the answer. A murderer pretending to be righteous. You're the epitome of hypocrisy. It's sickening."

"If what I'm filming is so awful, why do so many people want to see my films? I'm feeding their appetite. If I don't, somebody else will and rake in all the megabucks."

"Tell that to Meryl Hennessey."

Steward gritted his teeth in anger. "I'm an artist. Artists are accountable only to themselves."

"I didn't come here to argue. How you can defend a snuff film in which you murdered a fifteen-year-old girl is beyond me."

"How can anyone defend anything in this insane world? I'm a cripple. I have tons of money and I can have almost any woman I want, and you know what?"

"You only want underage girls," said Tess in disgust.

"It doesn't matter who I want, I can't have sex with anyone. You understand what I'm saying? It's physically impossible. So am I angry and bitter about it? I have good reason to be. But I'm not gonna sit around and mope. I shoot the kinds of movies I like—and a lot of people like, it turns out."

"What do you want from me? Tears? Applause?"

"You have no idea what I'm going through. I have the urge to be with these beautiful, sexy woman and I can't satisfy it—ever. How would you feel?"

"So you take out all your anger and bitterness on the world, especially on underage beautiful girls."

"The world is a sick joke. No matter what you do, the joke's on you. I make a lot of money and what do I get for my trouble? A wet noodle for a cock."

"I don't care if you got a wet noodle or a string bean. Being screwed in life doesn't give you the right to commit murder to entertain yourself. That's self-righteous bunk."

"Talk about being self-righteous. You give the word *self-righteous* a whole new meaning, the way you go on preaching your sermons. You're the one that's self-righteous, preaching about what I can and can't do for my art. You sanctimonious asshole."

"You know I'm right."

"I entertain a lot of people with my art. You want to know why? Because it's based on reality. All good art is based on reality. Killing a money-hungry prick teaser on film makes my audiences happy. That's what Meryl Hennessey was. My audiences feel satisfied because she deserved it, flaunting her hot body and giving them nothing."

"That doesn't give you the right to kill her. Pretending she's killed in a movie is one thing. Killing her for real in front of the camera is something else entirely."

Steward hawked phlegm and spat on the floor. "You can tell me what it feels like when you star in my next movie spread-eagled naked on a cross waiting for Moab to skin you alive."

"You're forgetting. I'm over fifteen."

"But you're a good-looking asshole. Everyone likes to watch a good-looking asshole get tortured and murdered."

He looked like he was preparing to shoot her.

"You don't have a movie camera here," she said, her pulse racing. "You're not gonna shoot me without a camera present."

Not that she really believed it. She was hoping to convince him to let her live a little longer.

He lowered his pistol. A smile came to his lips.

Chapter 55

"You're right," he said. "Moab's gonna do a number on you in my next film. He'll whip you and beat you and puncture your flesh with sharp utensils—and that's just for the beginning. The pièce de résistance will be a whole new world of pain for you to explore before he blows your brains out."

Tess thought about leaping down upon Steward and overpowering him. Since he was confined to a wheelchair, his movements would be limited. She might have a chance to disarm him before he got off a shot at her. On the other hand, he might get off a shot and kill her as she leapt.

The dim lighting would help her, she decided. It would provide cover for her surprise attack. Adrenaline coursed through her body, as she prepared to leap onto Steward.

"Moab," said Steward.

Tess heard a noise in the darkness and froze. Boots clomped on the concrete floor.

Moab approached through the warehouse's shadows. She couldn't see his face in the darkness, but she figured it must be him.

As he came closer, she saw he was dressed in a black leather outfit that looked like a one-piece bathing suit for women or something a professional WWE wrestler might wear. A black leather zipped-up executioner's hood concealed his head. In one hand he gripped a black bullwhip, in the other a pair of high-tensile steel handcuffs.

"I'm here," said Moab.

"It's time to start shooting another film," said Steward. "We have a new actor called Tess. She's dying to be a movie star," he added with amusement.

"Is he supposed to scare me?" said Tess, trying to sound brave, though she didn't feel it. "He looks like a reject from a carnival sideshow. Like one of those geeks that go around biting off chicken heads and eating them."

Moab bristled.

"The bullwhip's not just for whipping, if you know what I mean," said Steward, laughing, leering at her with black eyes. "You won't have time to tell jokes while he's working on you. You'll be too busy screaming in pain."

Tess's throat felt dry. She glanced at Willy, who was sitting on the floor watching them with curiosity. A guard dog he wasn't, she decided. Diane had been right about that.

"So you have to torture women because you're such a flop in life. Is that it, you impotent loser?" she said.

"Shut up, you foul woman. Your mouth won't be talking trash after Moab's done with you." Steward turned to Moab. "Get the skank down from there, get the camera, and we can start production." Steward stroked his chin in thought. "Maybe we can use the guillotine in this film."

Chapter 56

Megan was in the process of shooting an ad on the bombed-out penthouse floor of Max Reed Enterpriscs in Beverly Hills.

The idea of using the damaged penthouse as a photography set for an ad had come to her in a dream. She knew it was exactly what her dad would have done if he was alive. All the scene was missing was a corpse. Dad always used violence-charged backgrounds in his ads to clash against the beauty of his fashions and highlight it.

Wearing a marabou-fringed black catsuit and a feathery boa around her neck, Brigitte Jadot strutted through the penthouse's charred ruins, oblivious to the destruction that surrounded her, her haughty face undeterred by the bombed-out wreckage.

Johnny Wikowski photographed Brigitte as she struck elegant poses in her catsuit that had the image of a human skeleton silk-screened on its back.

"Shoot her next to that damaged wall, Johnny," said Megan. "If only we had a dead body here," she said, scanning the ruins.

"Anything else?" said Wikowski, shooting pictures of Brigitte.

"Shoot her next to Dad's blown-up desk over there," said Megan.

She scrounged around the rubble strewn all over the floor and found her dad's nameplate that used to sit on his desktop. She retrieved the nameplate from the dusty debris, wiped it off with her hands, blew on it, wiped it on her blouse, and took it over to the desktop, where she set it so Max Reed's name faced the camera lens.

Brigitte struck a pose in front of the half-burned desk.

"The House of Reed lives on," said Megan, looking on, "no matter how many bombs blow up the company's headquarters. The message is clear."

"Max would have strived for authenticity," said Brigitte.

"I know. That's why we should have a dead body, or even a part of one. Is there any way we can get the bodies of the blast victims from the cops so we can pose them here?"

"I doubt it," said Wikowski. "Your dad was always getting into fights with the cops when he shot ads at homicide scenes. The cops never did him any favors."

"I'm afraid you're right," said Megan, her face sullen.

Wells burst onto the set, voicing his displeasure.

"What the hell are you doing shooting here?" he said, confronting Megan. "People were killed here. What you're doing is disgusting. Have you no decency?"

"Who told you you could come here?" said Megan.

"This is my company. I can go anywhere I want in this building."

"Not according to Dad's will. It's my company, and I don't want you interrupting our photo shoot."

"Max died here. How can you possibly use his office in an ad? It's disgraceful. You're desecrating the dead."

"Dad always pushed the envelope in his ads. I know what he wanted. You have no idea about his vision. That's why you can't lead the company. And you don't. You're outa here. You'll lead the company to the brink of ruin. No way are you taking the reins. Good-bye."

"I refuse to let this travesty continue. Stop taking pictures here," said Wells, holding his hands in front of Wikowski's camera lens.

"Get out of here, Preston, or I'll call the cops," said Megan.

"I won't let you trash Max Reed's name."

"We're not trashing it. We're glorifying it. I don't want anybody to forget the day they blew up my dad."

"You're exploiting his death to sell clothes. Our customers will turn against us when they view these hideous ads."

"You never understood Dad—and never will. He wasn't afraid of crossing the arbitrary line between good taste and bad. That's what made him great. That's what made him a visionary genius who sells more fashions than anybody else in the world."

"I will not approve of this disgusting ad."

"Your approval means nothing. You have no power here. I'm not gonna let you shut down production. We're shooting ads here. Get out this minute."

Chapter 57

In his motel room Brody used his laptop to search for a porn producer confined to a wheelchair. The first name that came up was Larry Flynt. He couldn't be the guy that had produced *The Love Life of Meryl Anne Monroe*. He was dead.

Brody searched for another crippled porn producer.

He had to sort through a raft of entries till he arrived at a guy called Matt Steward. Steward had produced only one porno that he got credit for on IMDb, an online database of information dedicated to movies consulted by professionals in the motion picture business. Brody figured the porno wasn't a snuff film. Snuff films wouldn't get listed anywhere. They were underground movies that you needed a special invitation to see in secret.

Steward owned a diamond-encrusted platinum wheelchair. Indeed, he owned a mansion in Bel Air. He wasn't hurting for money, even though he had only one movie listed to his credit. Which made Brody wonder how Steward had accumulated his fortune.

Steward must have been the porn producer Megan had met at one of Max Reed's parties. Brody figured it was Steward that had filmed *The Love Life of Meryl Anne Monroe*, which Tess had told him about. Steward must have been the guy she had encountered when she tried to audition for a part in a porno.

If Brody could find a connection between Steward and Rafe Calabrese, he could connect Max Reed to Calabrese, which might lead to a motive for Calabrese to murder Reed.

Googling Steward, Brody found out Steward had been crippled in a car accident ten years ago. Steward had been drunk and speeding on Mulholland Drive at the time of the accident. The woman with him in his car had died in the collision. She had starred in several porn pictures, including the one credited to Steward on IMDb.

Steward's career hit the skids. He stopped producing and directing pornos—at least, the kind that got recorded in IMDb, which didn't acknowledge snuff films. Even if he wasn't making pornos anymore, he could still be making snuff films and recruiting fashion models at Max Reed's extravagant parties to act in them.

If Steward was shooting snuff films, he had to be considered armed and dangerous.

Brody wondered where Tess was. He needed to tell her about Steward and warn her not to approach the guy alone.

Brody produced his cell phone and called her.

He heard four rings before the call went to voicemail.

He left a message for her to get in touch with him ASAP.

He wondered where she was. Why wasn't she answering her phone? She had mentioned something to him about getting a cadaver dog to check out Steward's studio. Could she have gone there on her own without even telling him? He got the impression Steward wasn't somebody to fool around with. Anyone shooting snuff films was a murderer. Whether the producer fired the bullet or not, he was the one responsible for whatever went on before the camera lens.

He tried to remember the name of Tess's friend who trained cadaver dogs. Donna? Something like that. Something that started with a *D*. Debbie? Dinah? Daisy? Diane? Was that it? Diane?

He googled cadaver dog trainers in LA County whose first name was Diane.

There wasn't a huge list to pick from. There wasn't a big demand for cadaver dog trainers. He found a trainer named Diane Salerno located in the Valley.

He called her number.

She didn't answer.

He left a message on her voicemail to call him back at his number.

She must have been busy at her job, he decided.

His cell phone chimed. That was quick.

"Hi, Diane," he said. "I want to ask you about Tess—"

"I don't give a fuck about Tess," said a man's gruff voice. "And my name's not Diane. Is this Brody?"

"Who wants to know?" said Brody, warily.

"Dominick."

"I don't know any Dominick."

"I understand you want inside skinny on Rafe Calabrese."

Brody became alert. "Could be."

"I have info you want."

"Spill it."

"No way. I understand this info is a valuable commodity."

"What do you want?"

"I want ten grand in Ben Franklins."

"How do I know what you got is the true gen?"

"There's only one way to find out. Meet me in an hour in the parking lot of Jimmy's Liquor Store that went belly up on Wilshire."

"Does this have to do with Max Reed's murder?"

"I have all the details."

"I can't get ten grand."

"Get it from Megan Reed. She's loaded, and she wants to know what I know."

"Wait a second. Why's she gonna give me ten—"

Dominick terminated the call.

Brody needed to know why Calabrese had offed Max Reed. The goon Dominick must have tumbled to Brody's need and figured Brody would pay for the info. Brody suspected he could be walking into a trap. But Dominick might know something. If he did, Brody had to find out what.

Brody would be packing when he met Dominick.

Chapter 58

Brody drove his rental to Jimmy's Liquor Store. Instead of the cash, he carried a Trader Joe's plastic bag with newspapers stuck in it. Brody didn't have ten grand, and he couldn't get it on such short notice. He didn't need it. He had no intention of paying the goon.

It was getting dark as Brody drove into the liquor store's parking lot, which was surrounded by a rusty chain-link fence whose gate hung open. The deserted store was being prepared for demolition. Several cars were parked in the lot. Over the ocean in the distance the sunset was orange and peach scored with electric streaks of cerise.

Brody had arrived early, hoping to get a jump on Dominick, but the presence of cars in the lot suggested Dominick was already here. Of course, the parked cars in the lot could belong to other people.

Brody scoped out the buckled asphalt parking lot. He didn't see anyone. He got out of his car, clutching the Trader Joe's bag.

He wondered if Dominick was waiting for him inside the unlit liquor store.

Brody was going to check out the store when his cell phone vibrated in his trouser pocket. He took the call.

"This is Diane Salerno. You asked me to return your call."

"Hello," said Brody. "I'm wondering if you've seen Tess Hardwick lately."

"That's what I called you about," said Diane, her voice sounding strained.

"She said she wanted to borrow one of your cadaver dogs."

"I loaned her Willy. That's the problem."

"What?" said Brody, gripping his cell phone tighter.

"She borrowed my dog Willy. Willy just came back here to the kennel alone."

"Why would he do that?" said Brody, eyes intent.

"He wouldn't. I'm afraid something must have happened to Tess."

"How did he find his way all the way back to your kennel?"

"He's a smart dog. I'm just glad he wasn't run over."

"Did Tess tell you where she was going with him?"

"I don't remember. Sorry."

"Never mind. I know where she must have gone."

"I'm worried about her. She would never let Willy come back here on his own."

Brody figured Tess had gone to the producer's studio without telling him. The producer must have caught her trespassing. There was no telling what he would do, or had already done. A guy who created snuff films was capable of doing anything, including murdering a trespasser.

"OK," he said. "I'll see if I can find her."

He pocketed his cell.

Right now he had to deal with Dominick.

Brody thought he saw movement in the dingy store's dark interior. He ducked behind a parked silver sedan in the lot.

He peeked over the sedan's hood into the store. He didn't see any more movement. Maybe a passing headlight had reflected off the grimy picture window creating the illusion of movement he had seen earlier.

He stood up and stole toward the store's entrance, bag in hand. He didn't know if Dominick was inside the store, but there was no sign of him in the parking lot. Brody had to check out the movement he had seen, or thought he had seen, in the store.

He peeked through the plate-glass door. All he could see were rows of empty shelves and the empty aisles between them. The white linoleum floor looked dirty and scuffed from heavy equipment moving across it. The only reason he could see inside was because of the wash of the sodium vapor streetlights on the sidewalk that shone through the windows into the otherwise dark store.

He tried the door handle. It opened.

Maybe the owner had left it open, since the store had nothing in it to steal. Which meant Dominick could be inside waiting to sandbag him, decided Brody.

Chapter 59

"Dominick," said Brody.

Nobody answered.

Brody made his way down the nearest aisle past empty shelves to the back of the store.

"I got the money," he said.

Brody reached the end of the aisle and scoped out the back of the store. He saw a green steel Dumpster half filled with trash the owner had thrown out while vacating his store.

At the front of the store, Dominick appeared wearing a Rams sports jacket. He had a long, thick nose whose tip curved over his lips that were greasy from linguine sauce. His hand held a Glock. His black eyes had the look of a caged wolverine's—wary but ready to attack at a moment's notice.

"Toss the money down here," he said.

"First, tell me about Calabrese and Reed."

"Not going down that way. Look what's in my hand. Now do as I say."

"Why did Calabrese kill Reed?"

"Gimme the dough," said Dominick, raising his voice and training his Glock on Brody.

Heart pounding like mad, Brody had to decide his next move. He couldn't reach his SIG in his ankle holster in time to shoot Dominick before Dominick got off a shot at him. Brody ducked behind the end of the shelf out of Dominick's line of sight.

Dominick fired at Brody. The shot missed.

Brody was on the verge of drawing his pistol when he realized there was another goon, a short guy pushing thirty with prominent, misshapen ears, wearing a grey hoodie that practically reached his knees, standing in the back of the store drawing a bead on him.

Sweating, Brody bolted behind the Dumpster.

Hoodie's shot rang out.

"Say hello to Michael," said Dominick.

Behind the Dumpster, Brody drew his SIG and dropped his plastic bag of newspapers.

"There's no need for this," said Brody. "Tell me what I want to know and I'll pay you."

"Sal wants you out of the picture."

"You wanna pass up an easy ten grand?"

Dominick laughed. "Nobody's passing up anything. I'll get the money when you're dead with a bullet in your brain. And I'll get even more dough when Sal pays me for the contract on you."

Dominick fired a bullet at the Dumpster, which ricocheted into the back of the store.

"The back door's locked in case you're getting any ideas," he said.

Wanting to let them know he was armed, Brody peeked around the Dumpster and fired a round at Michael, winging him. Michael cried out in pain and hid behind a shelf. Brody retreated behind the Dumpster.

"You don't got a chance, Brody," said Dominick. "We got more soldiers coming this way as backup. Throw the money out here."

"Why? You're gonna kill me anyway."

Brody sneaked toward the other end of the Dumpster and cast around for Michael.

"He's behind the Dumpster," Michael called to Dominick.

As Michael poked his head around the end of the shelf, Brody shot him in the eye. Michael collapsed on the floor.

"Which side of it, Michael?" said Dominick, prowling down the aisle in Brody's direction.

No answer.

Brody pushed against the Dumpster and realized he could move it. Whatever junk was in it wasn't heavy. He got an idea. He shoved the Dumpster into the aisle that Dominick was in and trundled it toward him.

Dominick fired three bullets into the Dumpster, hoping they'd penetrate the steel and take out Brody.

"Michael, get him from behind," said Dominick. "He has nowhere to run. I can't see him from here."

Brody peered around the Dumpster, spotted Dominick, and fired. Dominick's knees buckled. Brody didn't want to kill him before he questioned him.

Brody couldn't squeeze past the Dumpster that took up most of the aisle. Brody craned his neck around the Dumpster and scoped out Dominick to make sure he had hit him. He spotted Dominick's limp hand lying on the floor. He retreated from the Dumpster-blocked aisle, walked down the neighboring aisle, and reached the other side of the Dumpster-blocked aisle, where Dominick's body lay sprawled on his back on the linoleum, blood puddling under him.

Brody didn't want him to die without talking first. He wondered if what Dominick had told him about the imminent arrival of Mafia backup was true. If it was, Brody had to make his interrogation quick.

"Start talking," said Brody, gun in hand. "Why did Calabrese want Reed dead?"

Grimacing, Dominick groaned.

"Call an ambulance," he said. "I'm hit."

"Talk first."

"I'm hurt bad."

"Stop wasting your breath and talk," said Brody, brandishing his SIG in Dominick's face. "Why did Calabrese want Reed dead?"

"You idiot. Calabrese was hired . . ." Dominick gasped. "He was . . . hired . . . to take out Reed."

"Someone paid him to do Reed?" said Brody, taken aback.

Dominick nodded yes. "Now call the ambulance. You promised."

"Who hired Calabrese?"

Dominick groaned and started coughing blood. "Call an ambulance, and . . ." Dominick coughed up more blood. "And . . . I'll tell . . . you."

Brody doubted Dominick would live much longer. Brody's slug must have punctured one of Dominick's lungs. The guy would drown in his own blood soon. In any case, Brody didn't want to be here when an ambulance arrived. The cops would pelt him with questions. He had no time for them. Tess's life might be hanging in thc balance at the snuff producer's studio.

Brody pretended to call an ambulance to get Dominick to come clean about Calabrese.

"All right," said Brody. "They'll be here in a few minutes. Now talk."

Dominick's eyes were staring at him, his bloody mouth hanging ajar. The only thing that came out of his mouth was gurgling blood.

"Talk to me," said Brody.

Dominick was done breathing, let alone talking.

Brody cursed. He had to beat it.

If Dominick knew who had hired Calabrese, Dominick's boss Sal must know, too, decided Brody.

Brody bopped to his rental to get out of here to help Tess before the cops arrived at the liquor store. He could already hear sirens keening in the distance. In his mind he could hear their police radios squawking, "Shots fired . . ."

Chapter 60

Tess felt groggy.

They must have drugged her, she decided.

She found herself bound with a rope to a chair naked, her wrists handcuffed behind her, a key light blinding her. She blinked her eyes in the bright beam. The room was dark save for the key light. She could see a Sony 4K 35 mm movie camera set up on a tripod near the light.

Clad in his black leather outfit, Moab approached her in the darkness, and stood beside her, a phone book in his hand.

"Who sent you here?" said Steward sitting behind the movie camera in his wheelchair, his pallid, boyish face barely visible in the darkness.

"Nobody," said Tess.

Moab hammered her on the top of the head with the phone book.

Tess winced in pain, seeing stars.

"Wrong answer," said Steward. "Why are you snooping around here?"

"I'm looking for Meryl Hennesey."

"Why here?"

"Because she vanished after starring in your porno."

"Who hired you to find her?"

"Nobody."

Moab clouted the top of her head with the phone book again.

"Don't bruise her," Steward told Moab. "Don't hit her face. Not yet, anyway."

"I know what I'm doing," said Moab.

"What is your real name?" Steward asked Tess.

"Tess," she answered.

"Tess of the d'Urbervilles. Hardy's protagonist. She was doomed, you know. Like you, I'm afraid."

"You must have some intelligence to know of Thomas Hardy. Why did you become a snuff film producer?"

Steward signaled to Moab, who responded by crashing the phone book down on Tess's head with both hands.

She almost blacked out from that blow, decided Tess, in pain. She shivered in the cold without her clothes on. Dazed, she tried to focus her eyes on Steward.

"Nobody cares about Meryl Hennessey," said Steward. "Why do you suddenly show up out of nowhere looking for her? She was a nobody with no friends and a family that didn't give a damn about her. Why do you? You must be working for someone. Who?"

Tess didn't want to reveal Brody's name. On the other hand, her head was killing her. She didn't want to end up with a concussion, either.

"My client wants to see the movie you made with her," she said.

"Then why send *you* here?"

"Because he's shy."

Moab clobbered her head with the phone book.

Tess threw up. Not much, but enough to soil her chest.

"Clean her up," said Steward, screwing up his face in disgust. "We want her looking beautiful for the camera."

Moab retrieved a towel and wiped Tess's chest off, making a point of feeling her exposed breasts.

"First time you copped a feel?" said Tess. "Hard up for a date, huh?"

"Why you," growled Moab, getting ready to strike her with the back of his gloved hand.

"Don't touch her," said Steward. "I don't want a mark on her when my film starts. The bruises and cuts come later."

"I can't wait to whip her."

"Throw that towel outside," said Steward, sniffing. "I can't stand the smell of puke."

Moab strode to the front door, towel in hand, opened the door, and walked outside, looking for somewhere to dump the towel.

Kids were riding their bicycles on the sidewalk, yelling and having a good time. Their boombox was playing "Stuck in the Middle with You" by Stealers Wheel. They looked up at Moab standing in his leather outfit on the warehouse stoop.

He waved hello at them and started dancing to the music. They stared in awe at him. Continuing his shuffling dance, he looked around for a wastebasket. Not seeing one he tossed the vomit-impregnated towel on the floor, danced backward into the warehouse, and waved good-bye to the kids. He closed the door behind him and returned to Tess.

Tess didn't like her chances. She wondered where Willy had gone. She didn't see him anywhere. Even if he was around, she didn't see how he could help her escape.

She racked her brains trying to figure out her next move. She wondered if she should fake passing out. It might buy her time, if nothing else. But it was just delaying the inevitable. So this was how her life ended—as the star of a torture porn snuff film. If it wasn't so horrific, it would be funny.

She should have waited for Brody to accompany her here, she decided with a sigh.

She had to remain optimistic. Maybe they would release her during some point in the film. Then she could make her move. She would have to bide her time doing nothing until her opportunity arose.

Diane was the only one who knew where she had gone. Tess didn't kid herself into thinking that Diane would come looking for her.

Chapter 61

"I'll give you your motivation in the film," said Steward. "Your name is Kandy Kane."

"How original," said Tess.

"Pussy Galore was already taken."

"Is that supposed to be funny?"

"You're naïve about sex, but eager to find out about it. You're especially interested in BDSM. You are going to find out about it the hard way. You have no idea you're gonna be tortured within an inch of your life."

"You mean, I don't die in the movie?"

"Sorry to disabuse you. 'The end' means the end for you as well as the film."

"Fire the writer."

"How many nails do you want Moab to hammer into your leg before you die"

"None."

"Nine, it is."

"Why do you hate women so much?"

"I don't hate them. Their suffering excites me."

"Just because you can't get it up—"

"Shut up."

"You'll never get away with this."

"I have so far."

Which was admitting his guilt for murdering Meryl Hennessey, decided Tess. And Willy had discovered Meryl's corpse in the other room. Tess was convinced of it.

"You mean Meryl," she said.

"Why do you care about her? Even her own mother didn't give a damn about her. Of course, her mother was a basket case. Did you know she spent most of her life in and out of insane asylums?"

"That doesn't give you the right to kill Meryl."

"She probably would have committed suicide, anyway. With a mother like that . . . That stuff runs in the family, you know. Her alcoholic father ran off a couple years after Meryl was born. Her life was doomed."

"You seem to know an awful lot about her."

"I knew nobody would miss her if she vanished. If your own family doesn't want you, why would anyone else? I did her a favor by making her a movie star. She's immortal on film."

"Immortal? She's dead."

"What about you? Do you think anyone will miss you when you die?"

The question chilled Tess's blood.

"Are you trying to get me to volunteer to star in your sick snuff film?" she said.

"Even your own dog wouldn't miss you. He took off without you."

"You call yourself a film director? You're nothing more than a psychopath with a movie camera."

"You should welcome the chance to become an immortal movie star," said Steward, fidgeting with the camera.

"You're the one who belongs in an insane asylum."

"'Great wits are sure to madness near allied.' Read your Alexander Pope."

"John Dryden, not Pope."

Sometimes her BA in English Literature served her well, decided Tess.

"Shut up," said Steward.

"And he wasn't a murderer like you."

"Shut up, you inconsiderate bitch," said Steward, slamming his arm down on his wheelchair's leather padded armrest.

She had to think of a way out of here. Now that Steward was upset, maybe she could con him into freeing her.

"I need to use the bathroom," she said.

"You're not gonna be alive much longer. Can't you hold it a few more minutes?"

“I have to go now.”

Steward grimaced. “I’m not into golden showers.” He turned to Moab. “Untie her and take her to the bathroom. But don’t take off her handcuffs.”

Chapter 62

Who had hired Calabrese to whack Max Reed, if he could believe Dominick? wondered Brody, as he drove his rental to Steward's porn production studio on Lankershim.

He was in a hurry. He broke the speed limit and ran a few red lights, hoping no cops picked up on him.

He figured Tess's life had to be in danger, since Willy had returned home to Diane without Tess. Could Steward have hired Calabrese to whack Max Reed? Brody couldn't figure out the motive. An argument over who owned the snuff films? Or had someone else hired Calabrese?

Brody wished Dominick hadn't died before he had a chance to tell him who had done the hiring.

Brody turned it over in his mind while he stopped at a red light.

Could the person that had hired Calabrese have been the same person that placed the bomb in Calabrese's car? Brody wondered. It would make sense if Calabrese's client didn't want to be ratted out by the capo. And the killer had used a bomb, the same type of weapon that had killed Max Reed.

The driver of the pickup honked behind him. Brody sped through the green light.

Convinced Tess was in danger, he had to concentrate on saving her.

He caught sight of a squad car off to his right and slowed down. He had no time for cops. He would reach Lankershim soon.

His cell phone vibrated in his trouser pocket. Cursing, he pulled over to the side of the road and parked. He didn't have time for phone calls, but this might be important. It might even be Tess.

He took the call.

"Have you found Tess?" said Diane.

"I'm not at the warehouse yet," he said.

"Willy's acting different."

"Different? What do you mean?"

"He's acting the way he does after he locates a corpse. I'm sure he found a corpse recently. It must have been when he was with Tess."

Whose corpse? wondered Brody with consternation. That was the question. Tess's? Had Steward killed Tess because she was getting too close to something Steward wanted kept secret?

"I have to get moving," said Brody, hung up, and pulled into traffic.

If Tess was already dead, why was he hurrying? wondered Brody. On the other hand, he couldn't be certain she *was* dead. The corpse Willy had found might belong to someone else.

Brody stepped on the gas.

Chapter 63

As Tess entered the bathroom with Moab behind her, she wheeled around and kneed him in the groin. Groaning, he jackknifed and crumpled to the floor, his face turning green.

She dropped to the floor, lay on her back on the linoleum, wriggled her cuffed wrists with difficulty down past her buttocks, up over her feet, and over her bent knees. With her hands in front of her, even though they remained cuffed, she was better able to defend herself.

She stood up and considered Moab writhing on his back on the floor, his eyes shut in pain. She didn't know which pocket he had put the handcuff key in. The leotard, or whatever outfit it was he was wearing, didn't even look like it had pockets. He might have left the key with the camera, for all she knew. She wasn't going to touch him. He could lash out at her if he knew she was close to him. He was much stronger than her, even when he was debilitated by her blow.

She had to get out of here.

Steward could be approaching.

She dashed on her bare feet across the warehouse floor, seeking a place to hide.

"Moab?" said Steward. "Where the hell are you?"

Moab growled in pain as he squirmed on the floor.

"Bring her back here," said Steward. "I want to get the movie rolling."

Tess couldn't find the front door in the dark. She searched for somewhere to hide before Moab recuperated. Then there was Steward's Doberman to worry about. It could sniff her out no matter where she hid. She could only hope the dog would remain unconscious.

It would help if she could find a weapon. She couldn't find much of anything in the dark.

When all else fails, attack, she thought.

It might be her best option. It would only be a matter of time before they found her no matter where she hid, especially after the Doberman resumed consciousness.

She could go after Steward. After all, he was limited by his crippled legs. She had to do it on the double. Moab wouldn't be debilitated much longer, and he would be hopping mad, lusting for vengeance.

She stole through the darkness on her bare feet. Her eyes were becoming accustomed to the dark. She could see the key light that Steward had been shining in her face when she was sitting bound in the chair.

How could she attack him with her hands in cuffs? she wondered, padding toward him. She could see his wheelchair-bound silhouette sitting behind the movie camera. He didn't react to her presence as she snuck toward his back. He had no idea she was there, she decided, lifting her hands as she crept toward him. The handcuffs rattled as she lifted them.

He whipped his head around to see what was behind him.

She looped the handcuff's chain around his neck and gave the chain a hard yank, digging the high-tensile steel links into Steward's throat.

Gasping, he tried to grab the chain with his fingers and pry it off his throat. She pulled the chain with all her strength in order to strangle him.

"Moab," he managed to say, his face flushing. "Ugh. Moab . . . help."

Moab thundered toward her and plowed his fist into her cheekbone, knocking her to the floor. She all but took off Steward's head with the cuffs' chain as she fell.

Feeling the chain slide across his neck, rip open his flesh, and draw blood, Steward yelped, snagged the chain, and pried it away from his throat, ducking his head out of the chain's loop, as Tess toppled to the floor, rendered semiconscious from Moab's blow to her head, taking the handcuffs with her.

She heard a man's voice yelling from another part of the warehouse.

Chapter 64

"Don't touch her," cried the voice.

His face twisted with rage, Moab charged the voice.

Brody shot him in the chest. Moab stumbled and crashed to the floor.

Steward whipped out a pistol from a holster strapped to his wheelchair and trained it on Brody's silhouette.

"He's got a gun," yelled Tess, struggling to keep from blacking out.

Brody picked up on Steward sitting near the key light with a gun in his hand trained on him and fired before Steward could loose a shot.

Steward groaned, dropping his pistol.

"Shit," he howled, grimacing thanks to the bullet wound in his chest.

Brody approached Tess. "Are you OK?"

"Yeah, I'm OK," she said, shaking her head to clear it, still feeling lightheaded from Moab's blow, figuring she was suffering from a concussion. "It'll take more than a couple of two-bit smut dealers to waste me."

"Who are they?"

"They're the clowns that iced Meryl Hennessey. How did you know I was here?"

"Diane called me when her dog Willy returned to her without you."

"I owe my life to that dog."

"Did you find anything here?"

"I think Willy found Meryl's body buried in the other room," said Tess, glancing at the room.

"Did Max Reed know anything about this racket?" Brody asked Steward.

"He helped finance my films," said Steward, wincing from his wound.

"What about Calabrese?"

"What about him? Get me to a hospital. I'm dying."

"Was Calabrese distributing your pornos?"

"Distributing what? What do I have to distribute? I made only one copy. Nobody gets to see it without paying a humongous sum of cash and signing an NDA before watching it."

"To prevent them from telling the cops about watching a murder committed in your snuff film."

"I didn't murder anyone. You'll never get me on a murder charge."

"What about your star Moab?"

"It's a movie. Nobody ever dies in movies."

"Except Meryl Hennessey."

"You're a torturer and a murderer," Tess told Steward.

"I'm an artist," said Steward.

"Isn't that what the Marquis de Sade said?" said Brody.

"Get me to a hospital," said Steward, groaning again, the blood draining from his face.

"Why did Calabrese blow away Max Reed?"

"How the hell do I know? I don't know any Calabrese."

"You're lying."

"Why would I lie?"

"Who hired Calabrese to kill Max Reed?"

"This is bullshit. Call a doctor. You shot me, you fucking psycho."

Maybe the guy was telling the truth, decided Brody. In which case the porn angle wouldn't lead him to Reed's killer.

"Did *you* hire Calabrese to whack out Reed?" said Brody, drawing a bead on Steward's head with his SIG.

"No way are you gonna pin that on me."

"You were jealous of Reed because he got to sleep with his beautiful models, so you had him wasted."

"Look at me. I can't sleep with anyone. I was in a car accident. A spinal injury. Nothing works anymore. Get the picture? Do you think I could care less who anybody sleeps with?"

Then who blew away Max Reed? wondered Brody.

Steward rolled his eyes, like he was on the verge of passing out.

"He may not have killed Reed, but he sure as hell killed Meryl Hennessey," said Tess. "Him and his trained ape Moab. Willy found the body."

"It could be someone else's body," said Brody.

Tess nodded. "There could be scores of bodies buried all over the warehouse, depending on how many snuff films Steward made."

"We have no way of knowing how many he made, since he didn't distribute any of them."

Emitting a death rattle, Steward tilted his head against his shoulder, his body slumping.

"I guess we'll never know," said Tess.

Brody holstered his SIG. "Too bad his movie camera wasn't rolling. He could've been the star of his next snuff film."

He gathered his spent cartridges from the floor to prevent the cops from finding out he was the shooter.

"Who would want to see a movie with *him* in it?" said Tess. "Do you see my clothes anywhere?"

"Why do you need clothes?" said Brody, straightening up after he picked up a cartridge.

"A lot of good you are."

She approached the key light and swung it around the warehouse in search of her clothes.

"I suggest you help me so we can get out of here before the cops come," she said. "Or do you want to spend the night getting the third degree. Aren't you the guy wanted for murdering Max Reed?"

"Point taken." Brody scoped out the warehouse as Tess swung the key light across it. "There's a pile of clothing in that corner over there."

Tess turned off the light.

"Hey, why'd you do that?" said Brody, looking forward to watching a nude Tess retrieve her clothes.

"Nothing's free in this world."

Chapter 65

"We don't have Dad's dead body so we have to improvise," Megan told her cameraman Johnny Wikowski, as Debbie Hernandez applied cosmetics to the foundation on Brigitte Jadot's face.

Megan strutted around her father's blown-up office, rapt in thought.

"Nobody has the dead body," said Wikowski. "Not even the cops."

"Let's put two fake legs with shoes on them behind his desk so they stick out like there's a corpse behind the desk. My dad's corpse."

"I dunno. You may be pushing the envelope too far with that idea."

"You're starting to sound like Wells," said Megan with disdain.

"I'm just sayin'."

"Brigitte is standing in front of the desk as the corpse's two feet, ostensibly my dad's, protrude from behind the desk. She is wearing a sheer bloodred blouse with flared black slacks. She has no idea the legs are behind her. Wait a minute. What if she's wearing a white miniskirt with white vinyl go-go boots? That outfit would look hot with a corpse in the background. And the boots are mottled with red tears to simulate drops of blood, those boots Dad designed before he died." She paused. "Let's go with that. Ditch the black slacks."

"Fine with me," said Brigitte, as Debbie worked on her makeup. "As long as we do it fast. This place gives me the heebie-jeebies."

Wells burst out of the elevator and stormed toward them.

"I'm shutting this obscene production down," he said, full of bluster.

"Not you again," said Megan. "I told you to get the hell out of here."

"I have evidence that will destroy you."

"What evidence? What are you jabbering about?"

"You are unfit to lead this company by reason of insanity."

Megan burst into laughter. "You'll have to do better than that."

"I know you're seeing a psychiatrist. Wait till the media finds out about this. Nobody wants a psycho leading a company. All I do is tell the board of directors your psychiatrist's name and you're out of here."

"Half the town are seeing shrinks. Business as usual. You'll never get rid of me, if that's all you got."

"Your days are numbered, Megan. I'm not gonna give you the chance to turn our company into a horror story that's gonna tank with our customers."

"Nobody understands our customers better than I do. I'm gonna give them what they want."

"Holy moly," said Debbie, looking at her iPhone's screen. "Max Reed's bloody shirt is now worth over a million dollars on eBay."

"That's sick," said Wells.

"It goes to prove that I'm right about what our customers want," said Megan. "They want our fashions to push the envelope. They want to be shocked and awed by our new lines of wear."

"What sicko is selling that shirt, anyway? I can't believe eBay is allowing a blood-soaked shirt to be sold on their website."

"You should see Max Reed's Instagram account," said Debbie. "He's getting a million more customers each day now that he's dead."

"If it was up to me, I'd take that shirt off eBay," said Wells.

"You're an old-fashioned prude," said Megan. "You don't know our customers' taste. I'm never gonna let you take charge. You'll lead us into bankruptcy. Are you descended from peacenik hippies with your love of flower power and your fear of blood and violence?"

"Believe it or not, there's a market for beautiful clothes without blood and violence attached to them."

"Tell that to all the bankrupt fashion companies that weren't in step with their times and ended up litter in the ash heap of history."

Wells grabbed Wikowski's camera and jerked it away from him.

"I'm not letting you shoot any more ads at this site," said Wells. "You're acting like a bunch of bloodthirsty ghouls. You're tarnishing the Max Reed brand."

"Call security," said Megan, livid with fury. "I know more about the brand than you do. My dad's blood runs through my veins. Give that camera back to Johnny."

"I'm in charge, and I'm calling this a wrap. Everybody go home."

"Anybody who goes home now is fired."

Nobody went home.

"Do I need to get a lawyer to shut down this shoot?" said Wells.

"Get all the lawyers you want. They can't shut us down."

Apoplectic, Wells spluttered.

"Get your camera, Johnny," said Megan.

As Johnny approached Wells, Wells hurled the camera onto the floor.

"Where the hell's security?" said Megan. "I'm having you busted for vandalism," she told Wells.

Trembling with rage Wells stalked toward Megan and threw a fist into her face. Megan collapsed on the floor, out cold.

Wikowski grappled with Wells, trying to pin Wells's arms behind his back and subdue him. Wells broke free, bolted to the stairwell, opened the fire door, darted inside, and vanished, still fuming.

Debbie ran over to Megan and hunkered down beside her, seeing if she was all right. Debbie patted Megan's cheeks to rouse her back to consciousness.

"How is she?" said Wikowski.

"Get some cold water," said Debbie.

Wikowski hustled down the hallway to a water dispenser and filled a paper cup with water, as the clear plastic jug bubbled and *glub-glubbed* above it. He returned to Megan and tossed the water into her face.

Megan blinked her eyes, becoming conscious.

"What a coward," said Wikowski. "He hit a woman."

Her face smarting from Wells's blow, Megan sat up.

"Call the cops," she said. "Bust that son of a bitch for assault."

Chapter 66

Brody and Tess sat at a table at an In-N-Out Burger on Lankershim Boulevard in North Hollywood.

"Who's gonna tell the cops Steward's dead?" said Tess, popping a French fry into her mouth.

"I wiped our fingerprints at the warehouse, so you can do the honors." Brody took a bite out of his burger. "An anonymous call, of course, on an untraceable burner phone."

"Don't worry. I won't tell them you did it. After all, you're already wanted for Max Reed's murder."

"Don't remind me. Did you hear about the Shirley Kinsey murder?"

"Is she the one that was blown up in an elevator?"

"Right. The same MO as the Max Reed killing. She was his mistress. Eh, at least one of them."

"Same killer, I'd say."

"So would I. I originally thought Calabrese was responsible for the bombings—"

"But he's dead."

"And these murders of Kinsey and Bambi Patterson were done by the same killer. Patterson and Kinsey were both mistresses of Reed. I'm thinking we're dealing with a crime of passion. A jealous rival, perhaps."

"Another mistress who hasn't been ID'd?"

"Or another lover, in any case. Or a lover wannabe."

"I dunno," said Tess. "Not many women blow up their victims. They usually use knives or poison."

"Good point. Maybe it's a male lover. Isn't Reed rumored to be bisexual?"

"I can't help you. I don't read the tabloids."

"Like I do?"

"You know more about him than I do."

"Research," said Brody, and took a pull on his Coke. "There's a lot of info on him on the Internet." He paused a beat. “Somebody blew up Calabrese, too. It could be the same killer.”

“Why do you say that?”

“Because somebody hired Calabrese to take out Max Reed.”

“And?”

“And the guy who hired Calabrese wouldn’t want him to tell anyone about it, so he whacked Calabrese.”

“How do you know someone hired Calabrese to blow up Reed?”

“An informant in Andrasi’s gang.”

“Oh? And who did the hiring?”

“The informant didn’t live long enough to tell me.”

Tess cleared her throat. “Did you have something to do with the brevity of his life?”

“He tried to blow me away.”

“Let me get this straight. Are you saying the one who wasted Calabrese also wasted Reed and his lovers?”

“It would make sense if the one that hired Calabrese to take out Reed wasted Calabrese, the only one who could finger him in Reed’s death.”

“Who do you think it is?”

“There are plenty of suspects because Reed had plenty of enemies.”

“But if you narrow the short list down to jealous lovers, the list becomes smaller.”

“True. But Reed did have a lot of lovers.” Brody paused in thought. “And what about that shirt?”

“Shirt?”

“Max Reed’s shirt is selling on eBay.” Brody wiped hamburger grease off his fingers and produced his cell phone. “The bidding has increased to over a million bucks with no end in sight.”

“Your point?”

“How did that shirt get on eBay? The person who has it must have been at the crime scene to retrieve it. Not a whole lot of people were allowed at the crime scene after the cops arrived."

"*After* the cops arrived. Somebody could've gotten it before."

"Somebody on the penthouse floor when the bomb blast occurred."

"But who would do such a sick thing?"

"Somebody with a shrewd business sense and no moral qualms. Somebody who puts profit above all else."

"That narrows down the list of suspects," said Tess with a sardonic half-smile.

"The number of Reed's followers on Instagram is also skyrocketing, ever since the bombing," said Brody, inspecting Reed's account on Instagram on his smartphone.

"Because of all the publicity he's getting thanks to his death."

"It's like the best career move he ever made was getting himself killed," said Brody, looking up.

"You don't think *he*'s the one that hired Calabrese to do him?" said Tess, taken aback.

Brody shook his head. "What good are windfall profits, if you're dead?"

"Could the murderer be selling Reed's shirt on eBay?"

"I doubt the murderer was at the scene of the bombing when it took place."

"Are you sure? It would be the perfect cover. A bomb was delivered from somebody who wasn't in the building. Anybody at the bomb site during the blast would be considered innocent."

"I see what you're saying. If the killer was really smart and figured if he was at the bomb site during the blast, nobody would ever suspect him, since everybody, including the cops, knew the bomb was delivered to the building by me, caught on CCTV."

"Then the killer *could* be selling Reed's shirt on eBay."

"He could even have been on the penthouse floor, which would have given him access to the blood-soaked shirt."

"How could he have survived the explosion?"

"Preston Wells survived the explosion, and he was on the penthouse floor when it blew."

"Interesting. And he's involved in a fight to take over the company from Megan Reed."

Brody munched a French fry. "I wish I could take a look at the bombed-out penthouse. The cops are finished inspecting it—"

"You would never get in. You're a wanted man. Security would ID you on the CCTV and call the cops. Let *me* take a look. The cops won't hassle me."

Brody leaned back in his chair, savoring the idea. "That's a thought."

He munched another French fry.

"Don't you put ketchup on those things?" said Tess.

"I don't put ketchup on anything."

Tess shook her head in disbelief. "What do you want me to look for once I get into the penthouse office?"

"Any kind of evidence. I wish I could be more specific. Just snoop around. I'm not optimistic you'll find anything, but who knows?"

"My usual rates will apply."

"Of course. How do you like sitting across from an accused murderer."

"It's no worse than sitting across from my ex-husband."

Brody laughed and polished off his hamburger.

"I don't know whether to take that as a compliment or an insult," he said.

Tess smiled enigmatically.

"We ought to eat out more often," he said.

"We don't even like each other. Or have you forgotten?"

"Other than that, it's pretty much OK."

"Is this your way of getting out of paying for our meal?"

"You mean, it's not gonna work?"

Chapter 67

The next day, Brody used a burner he had purchased at Target to phone Lt. Macready from his motel room. It was a good idea to use as many different burners as possible to conceal his whereabouts from tracking, decided Brody, and he wasn't convinced burner apps were as effective in that regard as burner phones.

"Macready here."

"It's Brody. I got news for you. It wasn't Calabrese that wanted Max Reed dead. Somebody hired Calabrese to take out Reed."

"That doesn't alter the fact that *you* murdered Reed and two other people with your explosive."

"I told you, I had no idea I was delivering a bomb to him."

There was a pause on the line.

"Did you see Reed in his office when you delivered the package to him?" said Macready.

Brody thought the question odd. "I saw him. I delivered the package to him in person. Those were my instructions. Don't deliver the package to anyone other than Reed."

"You're sure he was there in the office?"

"Positive. I saw him." Brody wondered why Macready would ask such a question. "What are you driving at?"

"We're not a hundred percent convinced Reed is dead."

"The papers said he was dead," said Brody, taken aback. "They said you found his DNA at the crime scene."

"That's because we told them that. And it's true we found his blood and DNA at his penthouse office."

"What more do you need to prove he's dead?"

"We couldn't find any of his bones or his limbs or toes or anything. Just blood splatter and a couple gobs of flesh."

"Maybe the bones were disintegrated in the explosion."

"The problem is, bones don't disintegrate that easily. It takes tremendous heat to turn bones to ash. The heat in crematoriums reaches 1800 degrees Fahrenheit I'm told by my forensics department."

"Plastic explosives generate extreme heat and could have turned Reed's bones to ash."

"There should still be some of his bone chunks in the debris. Even crematoriums leave bone chunks that have to be pulverized after cremations. We couldn't find any of his bone chunks."

"Because the fire reduced them to ashes."

"Possible. But there's room for doubt. Especially when you consider that we found body parts of the other two who died in the blast."

"Reed was closer to the blast than the other two, so his body was incinerated."

"Again, possible. But doubts remain without conclusive evidence."

"Then why did you tell the papers Reed was dead?"

"We thought the perp might betray his identity if he believed he had succeeded in killing Reed."

"I thought you said *I* was the perp."

"We believe somebody is pulling your strings, since you have no motive to kill Reed. You were ordered by your boss to blow him away."

"And whose my boss?" said Brody, his voice laced with sarcasm.

"You tell us. We'll cut you slack if you rat him out. Otherwise, you're going down for his crimes."

"Calabrese hired me via Sal Andrasi to deliver a package to Reed. That's all I did."

"Your package killed people in Max Reed's penthouse office."

"It wasn't my package."

"Do you know if Reed is still alive?"

"How could he be? I know he was at the blast site. How could he have escaped the explosion?"

"Then where are his bones?"

"I told you, the blast reduced them to ashes."

"Then you are admitting you murdered Reed."

Brody seethed. "You're twisting my words. I admit Sal Andrasi tricked me into carrying his bomb to Reed's office without telling me it was a bomb."

"How convenient for you."

"If Reed's still alive, why doesn't he reveal himself?"

"Maybe he's scared the killer will try again," said Macready.

"How could his blood and DNA be at the bomb site, if he wasn't killed?"

"Maybe he was wounded, but escaped somehow. The point is, we don't know. We have unanswered questions. We think he *was* killed in the blast, but why can't we find any of his bone chunks?"

"The explosion pulverized the bone chunks like it pulverized everything else. Or maybe it blew them miles away. Somebody might find them a month from now."

"Possible," muttered Macready without conviction.

Brody was sure he had delivered the bomb to Max Reed, and he didn't see how Reed could have escaped the blast. However, he couldn't rule it out.

"It's time to turn yourself in, Brody, and face the music," said Macready.

"I'll turn the killer in when I find out who it is."

Macready laughed. "Like O. J. Simpson looking for the guy who murdered his wife Nicole. What a joke."

"Funny you should mention Simpson, who we all know killed out of jealousy. I believe the killer could be one of Reed's jealous lovers."

"A woman who uses bombs? Hard to believe."

"Not necessarily a woman. Reed was rumored to be bisexual."

"And you want me to believe this person hired Calabrese to hire you to blow up Reed?"

Brody could envision Macready snickering at the other end of the line.

"I know it's complicated," said Brody. "But the perp doesn't want to be found out. They've used as many cutouts as possible to mask their true identity."

"Why use you of all people?"

"Andrasi picked me to do the job for Calabrese. I've done a couple of jobs for Andrasi."

"The mobster? Were they legal?"

"Of course. Once, I investigated his wife to make sure she wasn't cheating on him. So he decided to use me on this job, as well."

"Not a lot of love between you two, huh? Setting you up as the fall guy and all."

"I don't think it was personal. But maybe you're right. Maybe it was. I can't think of why he'd have a hardon for me, though."

"I have a hard time believing anyone who refuses to turn himself in. Turn yourself in, and let's talk."

"I still don't know who hired Calabrese to whack Max Reed. I'm not surrendering to you till I know the perp's name."

"If you're so certain of your innocence, you should turn yourself in. Turning yourself in would help persuade me of your innocence."

Brody didn't believe him. The visual evidence of his delivering the bomb to Reed caught on CCTV was damning.

Brody terminated the call. He had to dump the burner somewhere in case Macready had his men trying to triangulate on its transmission site.

He walked outside his motel room to the street and saw a garbage truck loading trash from a Dumpster. He strode over to the truck and tossed his burner into it with the trash.

Chapter 68

Tess was driving her Mustang to Reed Enterprises when she heard her cell phone chime. She turned into a Bristol Farm's supermarket parking lot, parked, and took the call.

"I found out the cops aren't sure Max Reed is dead," said Brody.

"Interesting. How could he have survived if he was in his office at the time of the explosion?"

"They don't know. Could you search around his penthouse office for evidence that would prove he's dead?"

"I was heading there now to talk to Megan Reed."

"Good. I'm gonna search for blueprints of the building online to see if there's another exit from the office, a fire escape or something, that he used to escape."

"If he escaped, why doesn't he show himself?"

"The cops think he might be scared the killer will try again."

"I thought you said Reed was in the office when it exploded."

"He was. I saw him there soon before the bomb blew."

Tess made a dismissive sound. "I'll poke around—if they let me."

"The cops aren't there anymore. Why wouldn't Megan let you?"

"How could he escape if no one else in his office was able to?"

"Maybe he saw the bomb in the bowling bag before it went off."

"Or . . ."

"Or what?" said Brody.

"Or maybe he knew beforehand that the bomb was in the package and he took off right after you completed your delivery to him."

"How could he know beforehand?"

"I dunno. I'm just throwing out questions. I don't have the answers."

Brody thought about it.

"I just had a wild idea," he said. "What if he sent the bomb to himself?"

"He wanted to blow himself up?" said Tess, incredulous. "Why on earth would he do that?"

"Look at the sales of his fashions. They've skyrocketed since his death. What if he did it as PR?"

"But people died in the explosion," said Tess, her eyes wide.

"I know. He has a history of pushing the envelope in his ads, though, shooting them at crime scenes for shock value."

"Shooting ads at crime scenes is one thing. Killing people is quite another. It would be cold-blooded murder."

"Right. And how could he know he would survive the bomb blast?"

"I can't believe he would commit murder just to sell a few more clothes."

"As I understand it, the fashion business is dog eat dog. The fashion houses are very secretive and will do anything to get a leg up on the competition. Bottega Veneta, Gucci, Versace, Philipp Plein—they all hate each other and want to see each other fail."

"He'd have to be a sociopath to commit murder just to boost the sales of his fashion line."

"We know he wasn't Sir Galahad," said Brody. "His fingers are dirty from lining up models with the smut director Steward to use in his porno snuff films."

Tess thought about turning on her AC. It was getting hot in here. But she didn't like running the AC with the engine off because it would drain the car battery.

"If he sent the bomb to himself, it would mean he also blew up his girlfriends Bambi Patterson and Shirley Kinsey, since their killer used the same MO," she said. "That makes no sense."

"Maybe he thought they were cheating on him."

"Their murders had nothing to do with promoting his fashions?"

"Look, all we can do is speculate. We need evidence. I have a feeling Sal Andrasi might know who hired Calabrese to whack Max Reed. If I could get the guy to talk somehow . . . I'll work on that while you're at Reed's office."

Tess terminated the call and drove out onto the street. On her way to Max Reed Enterprises she drove down Beverly Boulevard and passed Quentin Tarantino's funky New Beverly Cinema in a building constructed in the 1920s that became a movie theater in 1978. Tarantino was fond of boasting the theater showed 35 mm feature films only, never anything digital.

She reminded herself she needed to take time off and go to a movie in the near future.

Chapter 69

Megan was sitting behind her desk in her office facing her lawyer Burton T. Hall, the picture window behind her letting in the sun, which threw beams over her shoulder across the office, reminding her of bars in a jail cell. She felt cooped up. She was in a sour mood.

She didn't mince words, but remained calm as she spoke, despite the rage boiling inside her.

"Wells is gonna try to get me ousted by claiming I'm insane and therefore I can't take over the company," she said.

"Why would he say that?" said Hall.

"He must've heard I was seeing a psychiatrist. But half the town is seeing a shrink. It doesn't mean you're crazy."

"Of course, not," said Hall, pushing his spectacles up his nose with his forefinger.

"Then what's he trying to pull?"

"He's desperate, obviously. As long as Max's will is genuine, and I'm sure it is, he can't oust you. The will says you're the new boss."

"Is there a clause in the company's charter that says a person with psychological problems can't be boss?"

"No. Um, I don't think so. I don't recall ever seeing such a clause. The term 'psychological problems' could refer to anything. It's too broad. They wouldn't use such a term in a charter. He's trying to intimidate you, is all."

"That's what I figured. He'll do anything to take over."

"It looks that way."

"I'm thinking of telling security to throw him off the property, if he tries to come back here."

"You can do what you want. You're the boss."

"Good. I'm getting sick of seeing his face," said Megan, slapping her hands down on her desktop. She regained her equanimity. "On second thought, do you think he would become violent if I had him thrown off the property?"

"That's what you have security for."

"Hmm. Do you think he's the one that killed Dad? So he could take his place at the top?"

"The police say a PI name Scott Brody is their suspect in the murder."

"This Brody could have a partner."

"It's possible," said Hall, nodding in agreement.

"Do you think Wells would try to kill me?"

"I—I—I, uh, don't think so."

"I'm the only one that stands in his way."

"He's trying to scare you into backing down from claiming to be boss."

"I don't scare easy," said Megan, getting up and strutting around the office. "I used to be a marine, you know."

"You? I didn't know."

"I was in the Marine Corps for a year down at Camp Pendleton in San Diego. I wanted to toughen myself up. I love fashion, but all this frilly fashion stuff can make you weak, if you let it get to you."

"I suppose."

"You'd be surprised at how much you can learn in the marines."

"I'll take your word for it."

"Fashion is like war. It's a cutthroat business, despite all the lace and lamé. A lot of people don't realize that. Balenciaga, Louis Vuitton, Hermes, Fendi, Christian Dior . . . The only thing the fashion houses have in common is they want to destroy each other."

"It can be a ruthless business. Down and dirty. That's the truth."

"Speaking of dirt, I wish I had some on Wells. Anything I could use as leverage," she said, standing still, crossing her arms over her chest, deep in thought.

Hall tossed out an idea. "Doesn't he have a drug habit?"

"Everybody does around here. If I went after him for drug use, a lot of company workers might turn against me. I need as many people as possible on my side, if it comes to internecine warfare with Wells."

Hall scratched his earlobe. "Has he been harassing the models?"

Megan's eyes lit up. "Has he?"

"I don't know, but after the Me Too Movement and Harvey Weinstein it would sink his career if he has."

"Good point. I'll have the Black Cube look into it."

Hall smiled from ear to ear. "If Hall has any skeletons in his closet, those Israeli guys will find them. Nobody uncovers dirt like they do."

"I just thought of something. Does Wells own stock in my company?"

"I believe so. But he doesn't have anywhere near enough to force you out and take over."

"Excellent."

"His best bet is to force you out by accusing you of having psychological problems, making you unfit to lead a company."

"You sound like it might work," said Megan, eying him with concern.

Hall shrugged. "Nobody wants a mentally unstable leader at the helm."

The phone on Megan's desktop rang. She put it on speaker.

"There's a Tess Hardwick here asking for permission to examine the penthouse floor," said her secretary.

Megan glanced at Hall.

"If you don't allow her up there, she'll get suspicious and might cause trouble," said Hall, keeping his voice low.

"Who is she?" Megan asked the receptionist.

"She says she's a journalist."

"Sure. Let her have a look."

Megan hung up.

"The cops have already been over the penthouse floor with a fine-tooth comb," she said.

"So, no worries," said Hall.

"She's wasting her time," said Megan, her face impassive.

Chapter 70

Tess walked along the charred, devastated penthouse floor, casting around for clues that would lead her to the murderer. Since much of the roof had been blown off in the explosion, she could see the clear blue sky above. It made her dizzy being able to see the sky from the top floor.

Max Reed had a corner room, but the wall facing Wilshire Boulevard didn't have any windows in it. She wandered through the broken windowpanes and shattered wood scattered in the hall till she reached the wall. When she passed the wall, walking down the corridor, she realized why the office didn't have a window facing Wilshire. There was a stairwell beyond the wall.

She tiptoed around the jagged remains of the office wall that skirted the hallway, reached the stairwell, opened its door, and peered inside. The stairs looked intact.

She returned to the bombed-out office and sifted through the debris. She didn't know what she was looking for. Anything that might tell her more about the murder.

She looked at the wall that bordered the stairwell again. Something bothered her about it. She couldn't put her finger on it. It was just a wall. Why did it bother her?

The wall between the office and the hallway had been obliterated in the explosion so that the hall and the office were separated solely by decimated drywall and the skeletal remains of broken two-by-fours.

Then she realized why the wall on the other side of the office bugged her. It seemed too close. Even taking in the stairwell behind it, the wall should have been farther away from her, she decided. Maybe it was an optical illusion.

She also wondered why the wall was intact. None of it seemed to have been damaged in the explosion. Some cracks in the paint and scorch marks, but otherwise no damage that she could see. Perhaps it didn't receive the full brunt of the blast, since it was on the opposite side of the room where the bomb had exploded.

She crossed the debris-strewn floor to the devastated wall near Reed's equally devastated desk. She stood with her back against the broken wall, produced her iPhone, tapped on the measuring app, and pointed the phone in the direction of the opposing wall, the one still intact. The app measured a length of thirty-six feet between the two walls. She allowed another six inches for the distance between her body and the wall she was standing against. Thirty-six and a half feet.

She called Brody.

"Did you get the blueprint of the Reed building on the Internet yet?" she said.

"I was looking at it before you called," he said. "Let me get on my laptop again and access it."

Tess waited.

"OK," he said. "What do you want to know?"

"What are the dimensions of Max Reed's office?"

"Let's see. Where are you?"

"I'm in his office."

"Hold on. Forty-two and a half feet long and thirty-five feet wide."

"That's odd. I only got thirty-six and a half for the length when I measured it. Are you including the stairwell adjacent to the office in the blueprint?"

"No. The stairwell is eight feet wide."

"That leaves six feet unaccounted for between the office and the stairwell."

"Maybe there's a closet in that area. Do you see a door in that wall?"

"Let me check."

Tess approached the wall in question. She didn't see a doorway. Three six-foot-high metal filing cabinets were lined against the wall. All three had been dented and twisted in the explosion.

"There could be a storage room in that area," said Brody. "Maybe they left it out of the blueprint."

"I don't see a doorframe anywhere."

"Maybe the door's in the hallway."

Tess walked into the hall and examined the six-foot-wide wall between the office and the stairwell. She didn't see a doorway.

"There's no entrance from the hall that I can see," she said.

"Could it be in the stairwell?"

Tess ducked into the stairwell and scrutinized the wall between it and the office.

"I don't see a door here, either," she said.

She returned to the office and inspected the wall again. She couldn't see behind the filing cabinets lined against the wall.

She wondered if the filing cabinets had been lined against the wall before the blast. Or had they been blown there by the bomb blast? In which case, they could be obstructing a door in the wall. It was the only part of the wall she couldn't see.

She stepped next to the nearest bomb-contorted filing cabinet and tried to pull it away from the wall. It was too heavy.

She cast around the office for something she could use as a pry bar.

Wading through the debris she found a broken lamp. She picked it up from the floor. The lampshade and the lightbulb were both smashed. She unscrewed the fluted four-foot-long brass rod from the base of the lamp stand and carried the rod to the filing cabinet.

She inserted the rod between the back of the filing cabinet and the wall and pried the cabinet away from the wall. As she did so, the rod scratched the paint on the wall, revealing steel, not drywall. That would explain why the wall hadn't been damaged in the explosion. Drywall would have been decimated, but not steel.

Why was the wall constructed of steel? she wondered.

After she pried the filing cabinet away from the wall, she was able to get a better grip on the cabinet and shoved it out of her way.

She saw what was left of a fish tank embedded in the wall. The glass had been smashed in the blast, and the water and fish had disappeared, having cascaded into the office, no doubt. She had no interest in finding the carcasses of the fish.

She saw that the back of the fish tank and its sides were constructed of steel, which had withstood the impact of the explosion. The tank measured four feet by three feet, more or less, with a depth of two feet.

She moved closer to the tank to inspect it, crunching glass shards underneath her shoes. Leaning forward, she made out a flange in the steel on the side of the tank near the back.

A noise behind her gave her a turn. She whipped her head around.

Chapter 71

"What are you doing?" said Megan Reed, standing ten feet behind her.

Straightening up, holding her hand on her chest, her heart beating a rataplan, Tess eyed Megan with surprise.

"I'm inspecting the bomb site," said Tess. "You gave me permission."

"I wondered why you were taking so long. There's nothing much to see up here but trash. The police examined every inch and then some. I doubt you could do better than them."

"I like to be thorough. Journalism is all about the details. Be specific when you write, my journalism professor used to tell me. Did you know there was a fish tank here?"

"Yes. So?"

"It's made out of steel."

"Isn't that what they're usually made of?"

"But the entire wall is made of steel. Did you know that?"

"No," said Megan, eyeballing the wall.

"How can you tell?"

Tess pointed to a scratch in the wall that revealed steel beneath the paint.

"What's so odd about that?" said Megan, her expression bland.

"Most builders use drywall."

"I don't know anything about carpentry. Fashion's my expertise."

"A steel wall, a steel fish tank, and a room that's six feet shorter than it says it is on the blueprint."

"I don't understand."

"I don't either," said Tess, twisting her mouth. "Unless . . ."

"Unless what?"

"Unless there's another room behind the steel wall."

Tess crouched down, inspected the metal flange in the fish tank, and pushed it. She heard an electronic buzz, and the rear of the tank swung backward. She saw that the steel in the opening door was three inches thick.

"What the hell?" said Megan.

Tess peered into the darkness beyond the empty fish tank.

"I'm going inside," she said, not knowing what to expect.

She scrabbled through the opening into a dark room. Standing up she flicked on her iPhone's flashlight and inspected the cubicle. The walls were constructed of solid steel. Even the floor and ceiling were steel.

A propane generator stood in one corner. She spotted a lamp standing a foot away from her and flicked it on. Fresh air flowed into the room from a vent in one of the walls that had strips of white cloth fluttering from the grate.

The room was equipped with a small refrigerator and a microwave oven. A cupboard contained dry goods.

There was nothing to indicate any of the food had been eaten. No empty cartons or trash.

"What's in there?" said Megan from the office.

"It's a panic room."

Tess noticed a trapdoor in the floor. She lifted it open. A wooden ladder led into the darkness below. Her pulse accelerating, she climbed down the rungs, wondering where it led. She ended up in a poky, unlit room.

She tapped the flashlight app on her iPhone and lit up the room, which had a door with a dead bolt lock. She unlocked the door and opened it.

It opened into the stairwell.

She closed and locked the door, scaled the ladder, and returned to the panic room.

She scrabbled through the fish tank into Reed's office.

"What does it mean?" said Megan.

"Your father might have escaped the bomb."

"Impossible. He was in the office when the bomb went off."

"He could've fled into the panic room and saved himself from the blast."

"I had no idea it was even there."

"He must not have told anyone."

"You think Dad's alive?" said Megan, astounded.

"It's possible."

"But the cops found his blood and DNA in his office."

"Brody told me they never found any bone matter, though—except for the bone matter of the other victims killed in the blast."

Megan held her hand over her forehead in shock. "How could he get out without being seen?"

"There's a trapdoor that leads to another room below it that has a door to the stairwell."

"I don't believe he's alive," said Megan, rattled.

"All this means is it's possible he's alive. Don't get your hopes up."

"If he's alive, why doesn't he show himself?"

"He could be afraid of another attempt on his life."

"Is there any evidence that he was there in the room?"

"No. He could've just stayed there until the explosion was over then left."

"Or he was never in there in the first place."

Tess nodded yes. "Do you want me to tell the cops about the panic room?"

"No. Why should you?"

"They'd want to know."

"It's their problem they missed it. They had their chance. They blew it."

"Knowing about it now might help their investigation."

"I don't see how. They already know who the killer is. Scott Brody. It's on our CCTV."

"Brody says someone hired him to deliver a package. He didn't know it had a bomb inside."

"How does the existence of this panic room prove who the killer is?"

"It doesn't. But cops like to know everything about a murder, including possible escape routes your father could have used."

"This room doesn't exonerate Brody. He killed two others, besides my father, in the explosion. Brody's a murderer no matter how you look at it."

"We should let the cops know your father might still be alive."

"Why should they care? They're investigating murders, not a disappearance. The existence of this room doesn't prove Dad's alive."

"True. But if he's alive, they'll want to question him, because he might know who sent him the bomb."

"The chances he's alive are slim and none. This room proves nothing."

"I'm not saying otherwise," said Tess, not wanting to raise Megan's hopes only to have them dashed.

"Then what *are* you saying?"

"This room proves your father knew he had enemies and feared for his life."

"You think managing the most successful fashion house in the world is easy? Of course, he had enemies."

Chapter 72

Brody drove his rental to a bowling alley frequented by Sal Andrasi a stone's throw from Andrasi's headquarters in an Italian trattoria.

Andrasi had some explaining to do, decided Brody. He was convinced Andrasi knew the name of the guy that had hired Rafe Calabrese to off Reed.

Wearing a peach and black aloha shirt, Andrasi had the bowling alley to himself. A green bowling ball in his hand, he started his approach shot on his lane, lowered the ball, and rolled it at the standing tenpins. One of his goons clad in a madras shirt was sitting on the orange metal contoured bench behind him watching him with feigned admiration.

"Good shot, boss," the stocky goon said in a whisky-hoarse voice.

Andrasi wound up with a split, as his ball crashed into the pins kicking them helter-skelter, leaving the six, ten, and seven pin standing. The seven pin wobbled, but didn't go down.

Andrasi grimaced. "Not good. The lane must be warped. I threw a perfect strike. Fucking dive."

"Want me to break the goddamn owner's legs for running a gyp joint?"

Andrasi waved him off. "Maybe later."

Brody strode through the lobby toward them.

When the goon picked up on Brody, he pulled a pistol from his shoulder rig and aimed the muzzle at Brody. Brody hurdled an orange metal bench and took cover behind it, as the goon in madras fired at him.

The slug went astray.

Brody withdrew his SIG from his ankle holster from behind the bench, trained the muzzle on the goon's head, and let loose a bullet.

Pink mist blew out of the goon's skull as his brain-splattered occipital bone catapulted into the air behind him rotating like a flying saucer.

The ponytailed, jeans-clad teenage cashier standing behind the bowling-shoe rental counter, bounded over the counter, and scrammed out the front door, not even looking back as he bucketed through the front door into the parking lot.

Andrasi reached into his bowling bag, whipped out a Glock 17, and opened fire on Brody.

Brody kept his head down behind the contoured metal seat he was hiding behind as bullets sang over him. He peeked over the seat back at Andrasi, drew a bead on him, and hit him in the ear, shearing the top of it off. Blood erupted from the wound. Andrasi clutched what remained of his ear, screaming in pain.

Brody shot Andrasi in the arm, forcing Andrasi to drop his Glock.

"We need to talk," said Brody, rising from behind the orange seat and heading toward Andrasi, gun in hand.

"My men'll be here any minute, cocksucker. You're dead."

"That's not what I want to hear."

"I don't care what you *want* to hear. The next thing you're *gonna* hear, and the last thing you're gonna hear, is a slug thudding into your forehead and fracturing your skull."

Brody stood in front of Andrasi, keeping his SIG trained on Andrasi's face.

"Who hired Calabrese to send the bomb to Max Reed?" said Brody.

"How should I know?"

"Spit it out. Who hired him?"

"Bullshit."

Brody cocked his arm and drove his fist into Andrasi's wounded arm. Grimacing, Andrasi howled in agony.

"You shit," he said.

"Tell me," said Brody, getting in Andrasi's face.

"Who knows? Who cares?"

Brody planted another punch on Andrasi's wounded arm, twisting his fist into the bleeding wound.

"Damn you," said Andrasi, gritting his teeth as waves of pain shot through his arm.

"Want me to kneecap you?" said Brody. "You'll be on sticks for the rest of your life."

"Stop it. I'll tell you."

"Talk."

"Calabrese told me it was some woman."

"What woman? I need more than that. Tell me everything."

"Just a woman."

Unhappy with Andrasi's response, Brody snarled, "What woman?"

Andrasi frowned in thought. "Let me think. What did he say her name was? . . . Something with an *M*."

"Go on."

"She was tall, he said, with blue eyes."

"What's her name?" said Brody, losing patience.

He had to beat it before Andrasi's knuckle-draggers showed up. Even though he was the one holding the gun, he broke into a sweat, glancing at the door to make sure Andrasi's soldiers weren't arriving.

Brody drove his fist into Andrasi's wounded arm again, twisting his knuckles into the torn flesh.

"Shit," cried Andrasi.

"Give me her name."

"Mary? No. Mabel? Megan. Yeah's that's it. Megan."

"Megan," said Brody, taken aback. "Megan Reed? That's impossible. She's Max's daughter."

Andrasi took advantage of Brody's confusion and launched a counterattack, trying to snag Brody's SIG. Brody recovered his composure and shot Andrasi in the chest.

Andrasi gasped and crumpled to the floor, sliding his hand down Brody's chest and leg as he fell.

Christ, thought Brody. He had shot the only guy that could clear his name, the only guy that knew who had ordered the hit on Max Reed. On the other hand, if Andrasi lived, he would finger Brody as the one who had shot him. Brody was screwed, whether Andrasi lived or died.

Brody had no time to worry about it. He heard footsteps running through the parking lot. He pelted across the bowling alleys to a back door.

Tess, he thought in alarm. Tess was with Megan at Max Reed Enterprises. He had to warn Tess.

He whipped across the parking lot.

Gunfire broke out. Bullets whistled past him. He ducked and kept running toward his rental, pumping his legs for all he was worth. Half a dozen of Andrasi's soldiers were firing on him from the other end of the parking lot. He jinked to evade a swarm of bullets as he fled, darting between parked vehicles, using them as shields.

Feeling a bullet graze his thigh Brody clambered into his rental and, wincing, fired the engine. He jammed the shifter into drive and peeled out of the parking lot, his tires shrieking, burning rubber, fishtailing onto the boulevard.

Driving, his eyes wild, he produced his cell phone and called Tess.

She didn't answer.

A slug tore apart his side-view mirror, bursting the glass into shivers.

Tess finally answered.

"It's Megan," he blurted. "Megan's the bomber."

Chapter 73

Tess turned to face Megan, who was training a Baretta 92X Centurion semiautomatic on her.

Megan snatched Tess's cell phone from her and hurled it across the office floor.

"I thought you might be a problem," said Megan. "That's why I let you come here to have a look around, so I could take care of you. I had no idea you were gonna find a panic room, though."

"We were beginning to think your father was the bomber, that he staged his own death for the sake of publicity to send his company's stock skyrocketing."

"It wasn't his plan. It was mine. I knew nothing about his panic room. He was supposed to die in the explosion."

"How could you kill your own father?" said Tess in disbelief.

"For money and power," said Megan, matter-of-factly.

"But he loved you."

"Max Reed didn't love anyone. He loved only money and power. I learned from him. I learned to love only money and power. They never betray you. When you love people, they betray you. He never gave me any love. I had to learn to live without it. That was when I learned I didn't need it, that Dad was right all along. You don't need love when you have money and power. Now you know too much and you have to die."

"Brody knows you're the killer. Even if you kill me, he'll tell the cops," said Tess, her pulse racing. "Killing me won't save you."

"You're gonna die in the explosion and fire."

Tess frowned in bafflement, her adrenaline surging. "What explosion?"

"The one I'm gonna set on this floor. One of the few things I learned in the marines was how to set off C-4. I stole some from their armory before I left."

"You'll never pull it off. Brody's coming here with the cops."

"They'll never get in. I've ordered the building locked down. Nobody can leave or enter."

"The whole building will burn if the firemen can't enter it to put out the flames," said Tess, trying to reason with Megan.

"That's the point."

"You'll die with the rest of us. You're committing suicide if you blow up this building while you're inside."

Megan snickered. "You don't know anything. Sales are gonna take off after this is over. The sky's the limit. Max Reed Enterprises will be the talk of the town. We'll be the richest and most famous fashion house in the world."

"And you'll be dead, burned to toast."

Megan chuckled. "A lot you know."

Keeping her Beretta trained on Tess, Megan retreated to the desk, pulled open the top drawer, retrieved a plastic zip tag, and returned to Tess.

"Put your hands behind your back," said Megan.

"What if I don't?"

"I'll shoot you in the heart, and nobody'll ever know you were shot because your body will be burned beyond recognition."

"They'll find the bullet lodged in my heart, and they'll know how I really died."

"From point-blank range? I don't think so. The bullet will burst your heart and pass through your body, leaving no trace."

"They'll find the zip ties around my wrist."

Megan gave her a look. "The zip ties will burn in the fire. I thought you had some brains. I overestimated your intelligence."

"Why are you doing this?"

"I thought you understood," said Megan, eying Tess with disapproval.

"You're acting like a maniac. How can I understand a maniac?"

"I'm doing this for money and power. It's so obvious."

"And they're more important than people's lives."

"How old are you? Haven't you learned anything in your life? It's all about money and power."

"Your father didn't get rich by blowing away people. Why do you have to?"

"He was afraid to take the next step. He traded on sex and violence in his ads, but he wouldn't take it any further. He wouldn't kill anyone to realize his dream of making it in America."

"You'll never get away with it."

"You'll never know, because you'll be dead." Megan prodded Tess's rib with the Beretta's muzzle. "Put your hands behind your back."

Tess complied.

Megan dropped her Beretta, seized Tess's wrists, and wrapped the zip tie around them. Tess struggled to prevent Megan from securing the zip tie, but to no avail.

Megan picked up her Beretta and jabbed the muzzle into the small of Tess's back. "Let's go to the balcony at the end of the hall."

Chapter 74

Brody turned into a Home Depot parking lot and parked his rental. He hoped none of Andrasi's goons had seen his maneuver. He hadn't heard a shot fired at him for the last several blocks. He hoped he had given them the slip.

Brody lifted his burner phone from the passenger seat and called Lt. Macready at LAPD headquarters in downtown LA.

"Macready here."

"I know who wasted Max Reed."

"What'd you do? Look in the mirror, Brody?"

"I'm not joking."

"I'll humor you. Who killed Reed?"

"His daughter Megan."

Macready sucked in his breath. "You expect me to believe a daughter would kill her own father?"

"I know it's hard to believe, but Andrasi just told me the truth. Megan hired Calabrese to waste Max Reed. You've got to arrest her."

"On the word of a mobster? How do you know he's not lying?"

"We don't have time to talk about it. Tess's life may be in danger. She's with Megan now. Megan heard me tell Tess over the phone that Megan took out her father."

"Aren't you the guy that thinks Max Reed might still be alive?"

"Other people died in the bombing, whether Reed's alive or not. Megan is still a murderer. She can't let Tess live and rat her out. You've got to send your men to Max Reed Enterprises to help Tess."

"And you're still the guy that delivered the bomb to Reed."

"Send your men to Max Reed Enterprises now."

Macready heaved a noisy sigh of exasperation. "Why should I believe anything you say? You're the bomber. You left the bomb in Reed's office—"

"We've been all through that. You're wasting time. You can have your men at Reed's building before I'll be able to get there."

"*You're* heading there?" said Macready with interest.

Brody realized why Macready had suddenly become interested. The guy was going to send cops to bust him at Reed's company. Well, if that was the only way to get Macready to send cops there, maybe it was for the best.

"Yeah," said Brody. "But you can get there before me. I might not be in time to save Tess's life."

"I see."

Brody hung up.

He called Tess again.

No answer.

He left a voicemail for her to call him back ASAP at his personal cell number.

He tossed the burner out the window into the parking lot. He fired the rental's engine, reversed out of his parking space, and drove out of the lot, looking around to make sure none of Andrasi's goons were in hot pursuit.

He pulled onto the road. He would have to watch himself when he arrived at Reed's. Cops would be all over the place waiting for him to show. He could only hope some of them would go inside and help Tess.

He realized his mouth was dry. He needed a drink.

He always carried a bottle of water in his Mini. In the rental he had nothing. He would have to do without.

Sweating, he stepped on the gas, hoping he would get to Reed's in time to help Tess, since he couldn't count on the cops to come to her aid.

If seemed like all the cars in front of him were deliberately going slow in order to aggravate him. He hammered his steering wheel with his fist in frustration.

Chapter 75

Macready hung up his handset and looked over his cluttered LAPD office desk at Lt. Ben Chowder, his counterpart at the Beverly Hills PD. Macready was wearing a grey blazer, Chowder a black one.

"It looks like we're gonna bust the perp that killed Max Reed," said Macready.

"How do you know?" said Chowder, brushing his walrus mustache with his fingertips.

"He just called me up and told me where he was going."

"Why would he do such a stupid thing?"

"Because he told me the real killer was at Max Reed Enterprises preparing to harm a friend of his—Tess something. He wants my men to save her."

"The real killer, you said. Who would that be?"

"Megan Reed, according to Brody."

"Pshaw. Kill her own father? No way."

"He says she's the bomber."

"I don't believe it. Have you ever met her?"

"I don't travel in her circles."

"Well, I've met her," bragged Chowder, puffing out his chest. "I met her at several of her father's parties. She's the nicest girl."

"Lucky you," said Macready, feeling resentful. "Why would he invite you to one of his bashes?"

"He used to like hobnobbing with VIPs."

No matter how hard he tried, Macready couldn't see Chowder as a VIP. Chowder was a lieutenant at one of the smallest police departments in the country. How did he rate as a VIP?

"I guess you let him shoot ads at murder scenes in Beverly Hills," said Macready, not without a little spite. "I kept a tight leash on him in LA." He pulled a face. "The mayor had other ideas."

"We don't have many murders in Beverly Hills—unlike LA."

"We have the best police force in the nation," said Macready, bridling.

"I didn't come here to get in a pissing contest with you."

Macready settled down. "I want you to go with me to Reed's, because I'm gonna make the arrest on your turf."

"Fine," said Chowder, brushing imaginary dust off his blazer. "As long as you say you had my help when you brief the press."

"That was my plan. I'll call them now to let them know what's going down. This will be good publicity for both our departments. Something we don't get enough of in the anticop media."

"I'm definitely going with you. I really should make the bust myself."

"You wouldn't even know there was gonna be a bust if it wasn't for me telling you."

"I would've found out," said Chowder, waving Macready off.

"I need to tell the mayor, too. He's been on my case, since Reed died."

"Why does he care so much?"

"Max Reed was friends with the mayor. Provided the mayor with plenty of models for late-night trysts at the mayor's mansion, if you know what I mean."

"Hmm. I didn't know."

Macready wondered whether Chowder was dissembling. It was an open secret about the mayor and his penchant for fashion models. How could Chowder not know?

"Reed provided him with girls in exchange for the mayor's allowing him to film ads at LAPD murder scenes for those sleazoid commercials Reed used to shoot," said Macready.

"I heard rumors," muttered Chowder, his eyes hooded.

"You know the mayor. He never saw a skirt he didn't like. Especially models. They're his favorite piece of ass."

Chowder cleared his throat. "By all means, notify the mayor. Busting Reed's killer should be a major PR event."

"Personally, I never liked Reed. I had a bunch of run-ins with him. He stepped over the line, as far as I'm concerned, when he was shooting ads at homicide scenes. Live by the sword, die by the sword, is what I say. And look how Reed ended up. I tried to get him banned from shooting ads at crime scenes that were under active investigations, but the mayor kept overruling me and siding with Reed, giving him a green light."

"I never had any trouble with Reed."

"Because we have many more violent crimes in LA than you have in Beverly Hills. He wanted to film at particularly violent crime scenes. You're lucky you didn't have to deal with the ghoul."

Chowder gave him a look.

"That's what he was. A friggin' ghoul," said Macready.

"That doesn't give anyone the right to waste him."

"True."

"If Brody sees cops all over the place, won't he fly the coop?" said Chowder, changing the subject.

"He thinks our men are going there to arrest Megan Reed. He has no idea we're setting a trap for him."

"Is he that naïve?"

"He's blinded by his emotions. He's desperate to save his friend Tess."

"He'll be in for a rude awakening. I can't wait to see the look on his face when we bust him."

"It's gonna be epic, worthy of a Hollywood movie."

"Do you think he'll give up and surrender without putting up a fight?"

"He may fight. He's armed and dangerous. He won't surrender unless he sees his situation is hopeless."

"Do I have time to get a shave and a haircut? I want to look good for the cameras."

Macready stood up. "We're leaving now."

Chowder followed suit. "What if Brody's got another bomb with him?"

"If we see he's got another bomb, we shoot to kill. I'm not gonna put any more lives at stake. A bomb could kill scores of innocent bystanders."

"Someone should tell Megan he's coming after her."

"Good point."

Macready dug his cell phone out of his trouser pocket and called Megan.

The call went direct to voicemail.

"Why would he tell you such a cock-and-bull story about Megan being the killer?" said Chowder.

"He's out to save his own skin."

"What kind of proof does he have?"

"He says the mobster Sal Andrasi told him Megan hired the Vegas capo Rafe Calabrese to blow away Max Reed."

"Why would Andrasi tell Brody anything?"

"Beats me."

"And who took out Calabrese with a car bomb?"

"I guess Megan did," said Macready, and guffawed. "Imagine a wealthy, refined girl like Megan Reed using bombs to kill people. It boggles the mind."

"She's the nicest girl. Always well behaved and polite. If I had a daughter, I'd want her to be just like Megan. Do you have any coffee here?"

Macready glanced at a half-full Styrofoam cup of coffee on his desk with distaste. "Don't bother with that slop. We'll stop off at Starbuck's on the way."

They made for the door.

Chapter 76

Megan ushered Tess out to the penthouse balcony that overlooked Wilshire Boulevard. Using a plastic zip tie, she tied Tess's bound wrists to the steel banister handrail at the end of the balcony.

"You're gonna die in the explosion," said Megan.

"What is the point of this?"

"I was gonna shoot you in the heart first and let the fire consume your body, so the cops couldn't tell you were shot, but they might find the bullet in your body and realize you were murdered. I don't want that to happen."

"Why do you have to set off another bomb?" said Tess, trying not to show her mounting terror.

"So everyone will know I died in the explosion. Your buddy Brody is gonna tell the cops I killed Dad, so it's all over for me."

"You'll never get away with it."

"I got plenty of C-4 left. I could take out all of this floor."

"You're OK with committing suicide?"

Megan laughed. "There are worse ways to go. I'm never gonna let the cops get me. Cooped up in a jail for the rest of my life—no way. Not me. I need to set the charges now."

"Why did you kill your own father?"

"I had to. That's how he brought me up. To be strong. To run the business. He was too weak. He fell in love with too many women. He had to be replaced. His lovers destroyed him. Don't you see?"

"I don't understand."

"I killed them, too, for destroying him."

Tess didn't know what Megan was talking about. She must have been talking about Bambi Patterson and Shirley Kinsey, decided Tess.

Megan disappeared down the hall.

Bound to the banister handrail, Tess gazed down at the boulevard below. It was beckoning her. She was terrified of heights. Even though she was cuffed to the banister handrail, she felt like she was going to plummet to the street any second. The cars on the asphalt below looked so tiny. The wind gusted into her face, blowing her hair. She couldn't take her gaping eyes off the street. Petrified, she clung to the banister handrail for dear life, gritting her teeth, her fingers clenched.

She knew it was irrational, but she felt the street pulling her downward, urging her to jump to her death. She told herself to look away, but she couldn't tear her eyes from the street. The icy clutch of fear gripped her heart, sending shivers down her spine.

She kept telling herself she couldn't fall, but it wasn't sinking in. The street kept calling her name.

She wondered if screaming would do any good. She figured she was too high up for anyone to hear her below. Maybe someone on a lower floor would hear her. Then again, the double-paned windows were sealed shut in all of the rooms in order for the air conditioning to work. The high-rise was for all intents and purposes soundproof.

Maybe there was somebody on a lower balcony, she hoped.

Her face sweaty, she cut loose a scream for help.

It got her mind off the street, in any case.

Silence. No reaction to her desperate cry.

No reaction—except for a figure in a black trench coat and a fedora that came running down the hallway toward her.

As the figure came closer, Tess recognized Megan.

"Shut up," said Megan, her face twisted with rage.

"Let me go."

"Stop screaming. It won't do you any good. And it gets on my nerves."

"I'm trying to prevent you from committing suicide. Release me and give yourself up to the cops."

"You think you've figured me out, but you haven't," said Megan with a lopsided smile.

"Serial killers like you almost always end up killing themselves. *You* were the one that killed Reed's mistress and lover. Right?"

"What if you're right?"

"Turn yourself in to the cops and let me go."

"Promise me you'll stop screaming."

"No dice."

Megan sat on a bench skirting a wall in the hall, removed her flats, removed her socks, and balled the socks together. She put her flats back on, returned to Tess, and tried to pry her mouth open.

"What are you doing?" said Tess.

Megan took advantage of Tess's talking to pry open Tess's mouth and shove the balled socks into it to shut her up. Megan withdrew a checkered headband from her purse and slipped it around Tess's mouth to keep her from spitting out the socks.

Megan made her way down the corridor to continue setting plastic explosives around the penthouse floor.

Her eyes bulging with fear, Tess nodded frantically to the pedestrians down on the street, trying to attract their attention for help.

Absorbed in themselves, none of them were paying her any attention. They no doubt couldn't see her terrified eyes all but popping out of their sockets.

She spotted two police cruisers tooling down the boulevard, eighty-five and sixty-three according to the numbers on their rooftops, but had no way to signal them since the cops inside the vehicles weren't looking up at the penthouse floor.

Struggling to free herself from the zip tie binding her wrists, she succeeded in cutting her flesh and drawing blood.

She recalled a movie where the villain had handcuffed the hero's wrist to a pipe and the hero had chopped off his wrist with a hatchet to free himself. She looked around her. There was no hatchet lying near. She didn't know if she could summon the courage to chop off her wrist to save herself anyway.

She saw a man looking up in her direction from the sidewalk across the street. She couldn't make out his face because he was too far away.

She tried to scream, but the gag suppressed it. She twisted her body and nodded vigorously at him, trying to signal him.

He probably thought she was nuts, she decided.

She came up with a plan.

She worked her sneaker off with her other sneaker and kicked the sneaker between two metal balusters out onto the street below, trying to aim it at the guy looking up. She didn't want to hit him, just get his attention.

The sneaker landed in the street, missing a passing white Mercedes G-Wagen by a couple of feet and tumbling onto the pavement, where it was promptly run over by a chalk Lincoln Explorer.

She couldn't tell if the guy looking up at her had seen it. He must have, she decided.

He strode away as if trying not to be seen. Or was she imagining his purpose? Maybe he was late for a meeting and hurrying to be on time.

Damn, she thought.

Well, she had another sneaker. But nobody was looking up at her anymore.

She wondered how much time she had left before Megan blew up the penthouse floor. Maybe if she could talk Megan out of killing herself, she could save her own life as well. On the other hand, how could Megan let her continue to live knowing that Tess knew Megan had murdered her own father? And how could she talk to Megan with the gag in her mouth, anyway?

Where was Megan? wondered Tess, turning away from the street and scoping out the hallway, which was empty. She must be in one of the rooms planting C-4.

Chapter 77

Brody saw a squad car so he ducked into an alley off of Wilshire Boulevard. He had been looking up at the penthouse from the sidewalk watching the woman standing on the balcony. It was too far away for him to make out her face, but she seemed to be in agony of some sort nodding her head up and down and contorting her body as if she was suffering a fit.

And then she had kicked her sneaker off into the traffic below.

Didn't she know she could hurt pedestrians if she hit them with her sneaker falling from such a height? What was wrong with her? he wondered. Maybe she was trying to get attention. Just another lunatic trying to get noticed? Or was she trying to get attention because she was in trouble?

She could have been Tess, he decided. He couldn't be sure without a pair of binocs. He remembered she had said she was going to investigate Max Reed's murder on the penthouse floor. That woman was standing on the penthouse floor.

He decided he should check it out.

He had to be careful around here because he kept seeing black-and-whites patrolling the environs as if the cops were expecting a disturbance.

Ensconced in a knot of pedestrians, attempting to be inconspicuous, he crossed Wilshire Boulevard at the traffic light and reached the high-rise for Max Reed Enterprises. He couldn't enter through the front door. The facial recognition software on the CCTV would pick him up and alert security.

He had to find an alternate entrance.

There must be a back door or a loading dock, he decided.

He circled to the back and picked up on a small loading dock. Since it didn't have any trucks backed up against it at the moment, the dock was unoccupied by workers. He climbed the concrete steps to the dock and looked around. Three empty wooden pallets were stacked against the wall next to a red metal dolly.

He crossed the uninhabited loading dock and entered the building. He still didn't see anyone. He had to find a stairwell before anyone spotted him and the CCTV cameras picked him up.

He couldn't risk taking an elevator to the penthouse. All of the elevators were equipped with CCTV cameras, he recalled from his previous visit.

He cast around for a stairwell. There had to be one in the corner of the building facing Wilshire. He caught sight of a fire door in that area and made a beeline for it, keeping his face averted from the CCTV cameras he could see mounted on the sides of the walls.

The guard at the security desk was scoping out a newcomer who had entered the premises from the boulevard and was angling toward the desk.

Brody stole toward the fire door. Reaching it he elbowed the crash bar and shoved his way into the deserted stairwell. He figured hardly anyone used it, preferring to take the elevator.

He commenced his climb. It was a long grind to the penthouse. He reminded himself Tess was in trouble. Why else would she kick her shoe onto the street from the penthouse balcony? He had to reach her fast. He broke into a run up the stairs, his footfalls echoing through the stairwell. He found himself gasping for breath. He was in shape, but it was a long way up.

He slowed down and halted on the next landing to catch his breath. He wouldn't be of any use to anyone if he reached the penthouse dead on his feet from exhaustion.

Chapter 78

At length Brody made it to the penthouse floor, which was where the stairs ended. He caught his breath, waiting for his heartbeat to level off. He had climbed so many flights he hadn't bothered to count them. What was the point of counting them? No matter how many there were he had to climb all of them. He was better off not knowing.

He pressed his ear to the fire door that led to the penthouse floor's hallway. He didn't hear anything. He knew he was near the balcony where the woman who had kicked the sneaker onto the road was standing.

He nudged open the door and peeked through the crack. He could make out the woman. Since she was facing toward the street, he couldn't see her face. He knew she was in trouble though, because her wrists were bound to each other and to the banister's handrail.

"Psst," he whispered.

She turned around.

It was Tess, her eyes bulging with fear, her mouth gagged.

Peeking down the corridor and not seeing anyone, he stole out of the stairwell to Tess. He ripped the headband off her mouth. She spat out the balled socks.

"Megan's gonna blow up the whole floor," she said.

Brody released the zip tie that bound her wrists. Freed from the zip tie, she wasn't secured to the handrail anymore, either, because the zip ties had been interlocked.

"Where is she?" he said.

"Planting explosives."

"She won't blow it up till she has escaped."

Tess shook her head no. "She said she wants to commit suicide because you know she killed her father and will rat her out to the cops."

In her black trench coat and fedora, Megan emerged from a room at the other end of the hall, spotted Brody, whipped out a pistol from her trench coat pocket, and opened fire.

Brody and Tess ducked into the stairwell.

"Was that Megan?" said Brody. "It looked like a guy."

"That's her," said Tess. "She's losing it."

"Did she tell you why she killed her father?"

"She wants the company for herself," said Tess. "We better beat it. She could set off her bombs any second, especially since she knows I'm free."

Brody withdrew his SIG from his ankle holster. "She can't set off any bombs if I take her out."

"It'll take too long for you to find her and kill her. She could set off the bombs before you find her."

Brody thought about it. But not for long. He figured Tess was right. Not only was Megan a psychotic serial killer, she was suicidal.

He nodded yes.

Sweating, he and Tess charged down the steps, apprehensive that the bombs would start exploding.

"Did Macready make any attempt to contact you?" said Brody.

"I don't know. Megan took my iPhone."

"I told him Megan killed her father and you were in danger. He should be here by now. I saw squad cars on Wilshire."

"Did he believe you?"

"Good question. Maybe he still thinks I'm the one that took out Max Reed."

"By blowing herself up Megan is as good as confessing her guilt."

"I hope that's the way he sees it," said Brody, gulping for breath as he stomped down the steps, clutching the steel handrail to steady himself.

"We need to warn the others she's blowing up the building."

They rested on a landing after descending several flights of steps, their lungs burning, thighs and knees aching.

Brody produced his iPhone, tapped the burner app, and punched out 911.

The dispatcher answered.

“Megan Reed is gonna blow up Reed Enterprises in Beverly Hills,” said Brody. “You need to evacuate the building on the double.”

“Hello. Who is this?”

Brody terminated the call. “Let’s go.”

He and Tess descended the stairs at speed, expecting an imminent explosion to commence rocking the high-rise.

Chapter 79

Megan saw Brody and Tess dash into the stairwell and knew she had little time left to plant all of her bombs and address the crowd. She planted two more bombs. She had equipped each C-4 bomb with a cell phone, electrical wire, a fuse, nine-volt batteries, and a thyristor (a solid-state semiconductor). She would trigger all of the bombs with one call from her burner phone.

She found a bullhorn in a supply room and took it to the balcony.

"I made it to the top of the world, Dad," she announced, as bewildered pedestrians watched her. "Reed Enterprises is the number one fashion house. I finished what you only dreamed, Dad, and could only start but weren't able to finish because you lacked the strength of will. All of you down there, look up at me with wonder and praise. I am the most powerful woman on earth."

She heard alarms going off in the building. Somebody had called in a bomb threat, she decided. Brody and Tess, of course.

"I did it. I did it," she cried into the bullhorn. "I'm the best. Top of the heap. Crème de la crème."

She saw a black-and-white screech to a halt and disgorge uniformed cops. Pedestrians were pointing at her. The cops looked up at her.

It was nearly time, she decided.

One of the cops produced a megaphone.

"Evacuate the premises," he said into it, watching her. "There is a bomb in the building."

More than one.

"This is my building, my company," she said into her bullhorn. "I own it."

"Evacuate the premises. This is an order."

"I'm not going anywhere."

She saw mobs of frightened people scurrying out of the building's entrance onto the sidewalk below, aided by cops, who had halted traffic and were directing the escapees across the street to safety.

Klaxons blared on the floors below as well as on her floor, deafening her.

"Evacuate the building," boomed a voice over the loudspeaker. "This is not a drill. I repeat, this is not a drill. Evacuate the building now."

Cell phone in hand, Megan retreated from the balcony down the hallway. She could feel the cops closing in on her. They were probably heading up to the penthouse even now, using the loudmouth cop below as a distraction so they could sneak up on her and capture her.

She had to act.

It was time.

Chapter 80

Brody and Tess were running down the stairs when they hcard an car-splitting blast rock the building from above. The stairwell swayed as if it would topple any minute. Brody and Tess gripped the handrail on the banister that skirted the steps.

"We can't stay here," said Brody. "The building could collapse."

Adrenaline shooting through them, they bounded down the steps in the oscillating stairwell.

As they neared the ground floor, they saw through the stairwell window debris falling from above onto the sidewalk crushing several fleeing office workers. Screams on the sidewalk rent the air.

Brody reached the next landing and pulled up, grimacing.

"What's wrong?" said Tess.

"My knee. I sprained it or tore something."

Favoring his injured leg Brody led the way as they dashed out of the stairwell onto the ground floor to the loading dock in back. The floor shuddered under their feet.

Their faces flushed, they stormed out onto the loading dock. Concrete debris plummeted from the top of the exploding penthouse onto the parking lot, crashing into cars and the blacktop. Triggered car alarms yelped. Panicked office workers fled through the parking lot, abandoning their cars and running for their lives as contorted steel beams and fragments of glass rained down on them.

A chunk of concrete with rebar sticking out of it crashed three feet away from Brody, shaking the ground. Brody darted in another direction, his knee aching, Tess in tow.

He and Tess sprinted down the sidewalk away from the entrance and the cops that had gathered there to help Reed employees escape the blast. Brody glanced upward.

He saw smoke pluming from the top of the high-rise. All of the explosions had taken place on the penthouse floor. He didn't see any of the other floors damaged, though the entire building had rocked under the force of the blasts.

Sirens screamed as fire engines neared the conflagration. Cops in front of the building warned people to move away from the building to avoid being struck by falling debris. Panicked rubberneckers fled as odd chunks of concrete dropped among them. A slab of concrete the size of a book slammed into a middle-aged brunette's head, dashing out her brains. Her body sprawled limp in an apricot Max Reed pantsuit.

Brody rounded the corner and paused to catch his breath, bending forward, his hands on his thighs.

"Why don't we tell the cops what we know?" said Tess, gasping for breath beside him.

"Later. They'll bust me if they find me here. They probably think I blew up the building."

"We'll tell them the truth. That Megan killed her father."

"I already told Macready. He didn't believe me."

"I'll tell them she confessed to me. And you said Sal Andrasi confessed to you that Megan hired Calabrese to blow away Max Reed."

"I'm not sure Andrasi is still alive."

Tess stared at him. "Why wouldn't he be?"

"I had to shoot him to get him to talk."

"Damn. And Megan died in the explosions," said Tess, gazing upward toward the flaming, smoking Reed Enterprises.

"I'll tell them everything I know later when things die down. Not when these explosions are wreaking havoc. And you can tell them Megan confessed to you. You're the only one living who can confirm my innocence."

"If they believe me."

"They'll have to after they see that Megan committed suicide. Why else would she kill herself if not because she murdered her dad?"

"True."

"Why did she kill him, anyway? Did she tell you?"

"She wanted to take over the company."

"Kill her own father?"

"She thought she could do a better job."

"Did it mean that much to her?"

"The way I see it, there was no love lost between father and daughter. Max was obsessed with his job and with self-promotion and paid little attention to her. She grew up without love and wanted to be like her father. She became an exaggerated version of him. She decided money and power were the only things that mattered, shunning love since she had never had any from him in the first place."

"So she ends up killing him and herself. Grim."

"She bottled up her hatred for her father for as long as she could. Then she exploded with deep-seated rage. Her father bore the brunt of it."

"I saw him around here somewhere," said a man's voice behind Brody. "He was with a girl."

Brody froze. He whipped his neck around in the direction of the voice, but didn't see anyone. He heard footsteps nearing the corner of the block twenty-odd feet away.

He and Tess belted into an alley and hid behind a green metal Dumpster that stood behind the loading dock of a Mexican restaurant.

Two cops in their late twenties strutted down the sidewalk at the front of the alley, scanned the deserted alley, and kept on going.

Chapter 81

Wearing Ray-Bans the shirtless, fortyish man was lying on a yellow nylon lounge chair in ivory bathing trunks next to a turquoise pool soaking up early-afternoon rays on Grand Cayman Island. Beside him on the cement deck, a transistor radio was playing tinny calypso music. Condensation rolling down their sides, a tequila bottle and a half-full margarita glass stood near the radio. Several fan palms arched nearby, their green fronds shuffling in the soft breeze.

Time stood still on the island thousands of miles from the rat race of civilization.

In the distance he could see the aqua Caribbean Ocean barely rippling.

A commercial played on the radio.

"What does it profit a man if he gains the world and loses his soul?" said the announcer in a mellifluous voice, and urged listeners to visit his gospel website.

"I don't know, but I have offshore bank accounts all over the world," said the reclining man, smiling. "And I'm not worried."

He saw a figure in a black trench coat and fedora walking toward him. He thought it odd the person would be wearing a trench coat when there wasn't a cloud in sight and it was eighty degrees in the shade.

As the figure came closer, the man recognized her. It was his daughter Megan.

He jackknifed upright on his lounge chair.

"I heard on the news you had died in an explosion in Beverly Hills," said Max Reed.

"I heard the same about you," said Megan.

"How did you escape?"

"The same way you did. In the panic room."

"The news also said I left a will. There was no will."

"I know. I forged one."

Max Reed considered this and drank his margarita. "How did you find me?"

"I had someone hack the eBay account that was selling your bloody shirt. Your address here in the Caymans was listed for the account."

Max smiled with satisfaction. "That shirt's up to two million bucks already and climbing."

"Is it really your blood on it?"

"Of course, and some of my flesh. When I bolted into the panic room, the bomb blew up, hitting my arm with shrapnel. My blood and DNA splattered the wall. I barely got the door shut in time to keep out the blast."

"I can't believe you survived."

"Lucky I had my secretary open the bowling bag. I was near the fish tank when the bomb went off."

"Not lucky for her."

"My whole life has been a million-to-one shot. No one ever expected me to succeed in fashion either. If I had listened to the naysayers, I would have cut my throat a long time ago. I was a nobody, and against all odds I fought tooth and nail, made a name for myself, and succeeded where most others fail."

"When I found out about the existence of the panic room, I figured you must be the one selling your shirt on eBay."

"The shirt turned out to be a great idea. That bomb turned out to be a great idea, too, though, I hate to admit, it wasn't mine. Sales of my brand are skyrocketing ever since the papers reported me dead. Do the cops know who sent the bomb yet? I doubt it was the guy who delivered it to me. I don't know that guy from Adam."

"He was a stooge." Megan paused. "I was the one who sent you the bomb."

Basking in self-satisfaction, Max did a double take.

"What?" he said, perplexed, as if he hadn't heard her right.

"Your time has come and gone," said Megan, withdrew her silenced Beretta from her trench coat pocket, trained the muzzle on him, squeezed the trigger, and emptied the Beretta's magazine into his chest.

Groaning, Max sprawled on the lounge chair, dropping his margarita glass on the pool deck, his chest splattered with blood.

Pocketing the Beretta, Megan turned and walked away.

Twenty feet from Max's corpse, she halted, wondering if she should retrieve Max's bloody bathing trunks and auction them on eBay.

"What does it profit a man if he gains the world and loses his life?" said the commercial announcer on the radio.

Megan returned to Max's corpse, removed his bathing trunks, stuffed them in her pocket, and left.

ABOUT THE AUTHOR

Award-winning author Bryan Cassiday writes thrillers and horror fiction. His post-apocalyptic horror thriller *Horde* won the "American Fiction Award" for Best Horror Novel 2021. He has written three other Scott Brody thrillers. He lives in Southern California.

Made in the USA
Columbia, SC
16 March 2022

57668112R00163